THE ULTIMATE SELECTION

To,
Dale,
Hope you enjoy the book!
Best wishes.

Acorn Independent Press

ISBN 978-1-908318-53-4

www.acornindependentpress.com

About The Author

With a BA in Prose Fiction Writing and Journalism, S J Wardell openly admits to his love and respect for the written word. His passion for writing had been hidden away, until his literary calling became too strong for him to ignore any longer, bringing to surface the publication of the highly acclaimed novel, *The Ultimate*.

Using a wide range of research techniques, S J Wardell always delivers accuracy within his fiction, with an added raw, gritty reading experience.

Follow S J on Twitter: @sj_wardell

Acknowledgements

To my wife; I thank you immensely for the copious amount of support you have given me; the patience you have afforded me, and for our two beautiful children you have gifted me.

To my publishers; Ali and Leila at Acorn Independent Press, thank you for all your combined hard work; for making sense of the original manuscript, and most importantly, for believing in me and my work.

To Louise; thank you for all your hard work in designing such a fantastic book jacket.

And finally; to you the reader, a very, very big thank you for buying my book – I hope you enjoy it.

Chapter One

The whole idea had popped into Greg's head when he was about nineteen. This was the time that his mother and father had moved back to Ireland with his sister. He was very well settled in his flat and completely independent. This was the first time he had felt alone, but also the first time he had felt truly free.

Greg read an article in a daily tabloid newspaper. A Frenchman had gone on a killing spree and had left the French police in turmoil. The French authorities were hopelessly lost – they had no leads and were totally clueless as to how they were going to catch this murderer-turned-serial-killer.

Greg collected all the online newspaper reports of the incident, in English, and stored them on his laptop in an encrypted file. The file had been password protected with a self-destruct Trojan Worm. From time to time, Greg would reacquaint himself with the details of the case.

The Frenchman had started his reign of terror in his early fifties, when he had come home early from a business trip and caught his wife in bed with another man. The police had been called but he cleverly told them that he had been away on business, which his employer verified, and that he had simply returned home to find the two dead bodies. Somehow the brutal murders awoke a monster inside him. At his trial, he described his hunger for murder as the most addictive, powerful drug he had ever known.

Greg liked the idea of playing a game with the police, a treasure hunt, the kind of game where you could lead them in whatever direction you chose, frustrate them and make them look incompetent.

The Frenchman had only been caught by DNA that he foolishly left at the scene of one of his later crimes. He had slaughtered eight young women, all in their early twenties before being locked up. Greg thought this was either a clumsy mistake, or that he wanted to get caught and put a halt to his newfound addiction. Maybe eight victims had been enough for him, or their faces haunted him in his sleep.

Greg knew that if you take a person's life away from them in a violent manner, the images of that could stay with you forever. You would either have to be very sick or resilient to erase those kinds of images from you memory. Though, if the images that he saw were only images, they could remain locked away in the dark depths of his mind, he could detach and archive them. That would be different. He could handle that, or he believed he could.

Two months earlier, he had decided to test his theory. North London was full of stray dogs abandoned by people who only ever wanted a puppy. He combed the streets until he found a moderately tame dog. After giving it food and making a fuss of it, Greg befriended the animal. Within a short time, the dog started to follow him.

Then he proceeded to lead the dog to a large park known as Barn Hill. It was a massive place, with miles of woodland and fishing pools dotted around. Greg knew the area very well. As a child, he and his friends would spend a lot of lost youthful time there, playing childhood games in the woods or fishing at one of the many pools. One of his memories of the place was the cross-country run endured twice a year as part of the curriculum.

Greg could not harm the animal, as the animal had not done anything wrong. If the dog had attacked him or shown any unprovoked aggression then there might have been a just cause. The innocent are the innocent – the guilty would provide Greg with reason to act.

Greg was totally sane, or was he? He seemed to think he was! Well, the way that he had meticulously planned out his first crime would indicate that he was in control. His plan was not to commit any of the murders. This would be left to others. It should be their choice, he would never force them. He would just make it possible although there would seem to be no alternative for his victims.

His plan was to choose carefully and kidnap the intended victim. He wanted his first victim to be someone with whom he had no links at all, so that there was absolutely no way to trace it back to him. He was undecided whether it would be a male or female, though it had to be someone he could overpower and control with the least amount of physical effort, cleanly and very slick. He wanted to give the people who were being shat on in life a chance to get even and exact their revenge on their tormentors. It would be the ultimate revenge. A revenge that could result in slow long-term suffering or simply, bang your dead! Over in minutes, rather than hours or even days – simple, but only by his choice.

Greg knew that whilst he was out and about, either at work, at the gym or even out socialising, both friends and strangers alike would tell him about their personal relationships. It happens every day in such a crowded dirty city.

Most of his friends were either cheating on their partners and spouses or it was the other way round, they felt they were being cheated on. He also knew people that were being treated like shit by their respective other halves… abusive kind of shit. He knew a number of guys who after a bad day, would drown their sorrows at the local pub and then go home and take it out on their so-called loved ones.

Greg believed that it would have only been a matter of time before that happened to him and Karen. He found himself getting bored… stale, it was not for him; anyway, he liked the idea of no strings and all that. He was far too young and busy and, after all, that was never in his plan.

The beauty of the whole thing was that it gave him the freedom he thought he needed to be as sexually promiscuous as he wished. Sometimes he wanted to dabble a little into his sexual fantasies and other times he just wanted roll on, roll off sex. It did not matter if he was good or not; he did not plan on impressing them. It was selfish sex and that is what one-night-stands were all about. It was getting your pleasure and if they got some pleasure too, well that was a bonus... for them.

That was why many people in long-term relationships had affairs. Though this does not excuse the fact that what they were doing was wrong. And those who mistreated their other halves, well, in Greg's mind, they were the scum of the earth! A taste of their own medicine was what they needed.

Greg felt it would not seem right for him to administer the punishment to the condemned. He believed that it should be the party that had been the recipient of the wrongdoing, the person who the shit had landed on, the person who had been cheated on or beaten, the innocent party. Greg had been meditating on this for weeks, mentally preparing, now all he needed was victim number one. He sat in a pub, beer in hand, thinking about what it would feel like when he overheard a guy shouting his mouth off; boasting about how badly he treated his girlfriend. He was a chubby guy, he could even be considered fat. He was the kind of person that had only ever experienced a workout in a cake shop, not in a gym. He disgusted Greg.

He remembered overhearing the chubby guy saying that his girlfriend had given birth to their baby nearly two years ago and she wanted to get married. This guy was saying that he did not want to marry her.

'It's only a fucking piece of paper!' he told his companion. 'It would be a waste of fucking money,' he continued in an alcohol-slurred fashion. 'Fuck me, she's fucking let herself go... if you know what I mean.' A drunken laugh followed.

Greg heard him say how his money was his own. The child, his child, was of no importance and he referred to the baby as a 'pain in the arse,' and a 'fucking mistake.' The guy he was having a drink with felt a little uncomfortable at the way his drinking buddy was talking loudly and sometimes even shouting. Other people in the pub could hear their conversation. The way Greg saw the situation, that guy had made his bed so he should shut up and lie in it! Nobody made him sleep with that woman. Nobody else was at fault. He was the one that got her pregnant. *It takes two to tango.* After all, they did not have to keep the child.

The chubby guy went on by saying that he had given her a smack in the mouth to shut her up, and that he had taken the last of the child benefit money so he could go out and get drunk.

'When I get home...' the chubby guy said, 'I'll give her a good seeing to,' he laughed. 'She knows that I can't handle the baby fucking screaming all the time.'

That was what made Greg think about that particular guy, what he said, all of it made Greg want to go over to him and give him a smack in the mouth to see how he liked it! A bit of reflection and a sharp shock is was what he needed.

'But what day was it that I'd seen that fat fucker in that Pub in Baker Street? – Friday, maybe Saturday? And who was the guy he was drinking with? Who else lived in the house with the chubby guy, his girlfriend and the baby?' Greg had a lot of answers to find!

Chapter Two

It was the morning after…

As Greg opened his eyes, it all came flooding back and his recollection of the previous night's events began unfolding in his head. A massive adrenaline rush passed through him.

All the planning, all the times he had held his own private dress rehearsals, the secret way he had picked his victims, through their own self-selection. All the time the motive in his mind was the same; it never changed or lost focus. It was *murder*!

Greg was a very popular guy. His full name was Gregory Jason O'Hara. He was twenty-three and lived in a small flat in Raglan Court, Wembley Park, North London. The flat was not his, he leased it. Greg thought highly of his landlord; the rent was reasonable, any repairs were carried out with the minimum amount of fuss and Greg was shown respect and privacy. The truth was that Greg had only met his landlord once.

Greg was just about six foot tall, weighed about twelve stone and was in very good shape. He was very proud of the fact that he had passed his driving test on his first attempt. He owned a van due to his need to transport large loads. It was a white Ford Escort. It looked like a standard van; Greg had not made any very noticeable modifications.

He was not a bad-looking guy, though the small scar under his right eye sometimes made him feel a bit paranoid. He got the scar in a fight when he was younger. A guy had pushed into Greg in a burger bar, late after the pubs had kicked everyone out. Greg was trying to get a snack whilst on his way home with some friends, when a guy behind them in the queue kept nudging Greg in his back. There was an exchange of words and the guy punched Greg, cutting him just below his right eye. The guy was wearing a chunky ring. A lucky punch! Although Greg did not retaliate at the time, he got his revenge a few weeks later when he saw the same guy on his own. The guy was drunk; Greg was sober. It was easy for Greg to even the score. Greg believed that you should never get mad, you should get even.

Greg's mother and father had moved back to Ireland and his younger sister went with them. That was nearly four years ago, though Greg still missed them all greatly.

Ireland was the country of Greg's birth. He was born in a city called Cork. Cork is the Irish Republic's second largest city, situated on an island between the two channels of the Lee River. The family home, a modest two up-two down terrace was all they could afford at the time, as Greg's father was the only breadwinner in the household. The mortgage repayments stretched their already elasticised budget. The property was ideal for a new family starting up but was never meant for the long-term. The small yard at the rear would never have been large enough for Greg to spend his playtimes and the house soon became overcrowded once his sister arrived. It was then that Greg's parents decided to sell up and make a new life in England. The small amount of money they had made from the sale was just enough to get the O'Hara family of four on the ferry, with a little left over to enable them to set up home on the mainland.

Greg only had patchy memories of his birthplace. The tall statue of Father Matthew, the founder of The Irish Temperance Movement, St. Anne's Church where he had been christened, the English Market which his mother would push him around in his pram where it seemed that everyone knew everyone. A large city of over twelve million souls, Cork was a friendly place; people always seemed to find the time to ask after the well-being of others and were always willing to lend a sympathetic ear. Greg's mother often took him to Bishop Lucey Park. The vast greenery offered him the freedom to run free as far and as fast as his little legs would take him 'Slow down, Greg!' his mother would call out. Greg had inbuilt selective-hearing at a young age, and would be unable to hear his mother, his pounding heart muffling all outside noise.

Greg's parents had come to England not long after his fourth birthday. His sister, Elise, was three years his junior. They had first settled in Kilburn, North West London. Kilburn was known to most Londoners as 'Little Ireland,' this was because most of the people living in the area were either Irish settlers looking for work, or direct descendants of those who had previously migrated from the Emerald Isle.

They moved in to a terraced house on Dyne Road, just off the Kilburn High Road, using some of the capital from the sale of the home in Ireland to pay for the rental deposit. Greg's father saw this as a step down as they did not own the property but renting privately was the only option open to them at the time. It was not long before Greg's father had a full time job, and enough money saved to place a small deposit on a three-bedroom house in Wembley Park. They moved three years later. Oakington Crescent was a very quiet residential area and the large rear garden was perfect. The O'Hara stamp soon made the place feel like home.

As the years flew by, the time arrived for Greg to leave school and he got himself a job working for Brent Borough Council as a refuse collector. The money was OK. Greg was fairly bright but, more important than that, he was very streetwise. The work kept him active – easy Monday to Friday stuff. The money was always in the bank on time. Greg had worked for the council for five years, though not always in the same role. It was only the first two years that he worked on the bins as a refuse collector. It was OK, but you had to work as a part of a team and you had to work at the pace of everyone else in the team. When a job as street cleaner became available, Greg filled out his internal application in record time. His two years of service, along with his unblemished record, put Greg head and shoulders above the other applicants. The money was about the same but it meant that all the older guys could no longer bully him. Though that was during work, if they tried that outside work it would have been a different story.

In the evening, depending on how he felt, Greg would sometimes go to the gym and work out. He was a great believer in self-discipline. He did not smoke and only drank alcohol at weekends. Even if he went for a drink with a few friends during the week he would not drink alcohol. Greg thought of himself as a bit of a boxer, he had a speedball in his room and had gained a large collection of archive boxing videos. He worshiped Mike Tyson. Iron Mike had pure punching power!

Greg left home a few months after his eighteenth birthday. He found a one bedroom flat in the same area he had grew up in. The flat was in Raglan Court, on the Empire Road, still in Wembley Park and a few minutes' walk away from the family home. Everything about it was perfect.

'If you like it, you should take it,' Greg's mother told him.

'What do you think, Dad?' Greg asked his father.

'It's clean, and the location is great. But, son, I'm not the one who's going to have to live there, am I? I agree with your mother, if you like it, you should take it!' his father said, smiling.

His mother and father had helped him in all that they could. They gave him bedding, pots and pans and even a kettle along with other things he needed to set up his new home. Greg enjoyed the privacy as well as his newfound independence.

As the months drifted along, Greg made his new home very welcoming and a nice place to be.

Greg was not seeing anyone at the moment. He was straight, though he had some gay friends. He had been dating a girl for a while, though as the time drew nearer for his plan to hatch he ended the relationship for obvious reasons. Karen Hogan was a lovely girl; she was twenty-seven, a little older than Greg was. Karen still lived at home with her mother in Kingsbury, a nice, almost suburban area in North London. Her mother's three-bedroom semidetached house in Elthorne Road was close to a huge park – Kingsbury Park. The allotments opposite meant the area was a quiet residential one.

Her parents had lived in the property all their married life. They moved in to the ex-council property and rented for the first few years and then bought it when Maggie Thatcher introduced the *right to buy* act in the late eighties.

Karen's father had died when she was six and her mother had never got over his death, or even bothered with men since her husband died.

She was a tall, leggy kind of woman. Her long blonde hair, green eyes and slim-line figure drew many admirers. Greg was never the jealous type. When other guys looked, he took it as a compliment. The twenty-seven year old had her head well screwed firmly on her shoulders. She had a great job, also with Brent Borough Council, in the planning department in the same office block as Greg. This is where they met. Karen was the only girl that Greg ever felt serious about. Before that he had had a string of one-night-stands. Karen was only meant to be a one-night-stand but the sex was out of this world. Their relationship had lasted about eighteen months. Greg had told Karen that he felt suffocated and needed some space to breathe. Karen knew that when guys tell you that it just means they are bored with you, though this was not the case. Greg had other reasons for ending their relationship just over six months ago.

Chapter Three

It was heading for half six when Greg got home. He had spent longer than planned at the gym. He quickly popped the oven on while he checked his mail and then his emails. He always looked forward to getting emails from his family in Ireland. His sister would send him photographs of the place and of herself so that he could see her growing up. Greg did the same. They had grown closer since she had moved away. Their sibling rivalry had faded as their bond grew stronger.

Once the oven light had gone out, Greg put some oven chips in, making a mental note of the time. The oven chips needed twenty minutes and the left over pizza from the night before only needed a couple of minutes in the microwave so he had time for a quick shower and a shave. Once he was showered and had dried himself, he ran into the kitchen and switched the oven off and set the microwave.

Whilst eating, Greg pondered what he was going to wear. His plan was to follow the chubby guy home so that he could find out where he lived. It was Friday and Greg did not have to go to work on Saturday. Even so, he planned on not having too much to drink. He needed to stay alert and remain focussed. He would not draw too much attention to himself.

The capital was full of loners. After all, this was London; nobody would think of bothering to notice a guy on his own, and nobody would bother talking to him either.

Greg felt safe in the knowledge that he would not stick out in the bustling crowds. He needed to be careful about what he wore, he did not want to look out of place. This hunter needed to blend in, to look like any ordinary guy simply out for a pint at the end of a hard week. So it had to be something not too light or bright, he would need to be able to follow this guy without being noticed. The night air temperature may drop so he would need to be warm enough for any journey.

'Dark jeans and a plain long sleeved top I think,' he told himself, as he continued eating his food.

There were a lot of closed circuit television cameras around the whole of London. The guy may not live in the area. He may have to use public transport to get home, or to another place, where he can continue his evening's drinking.

'What if he were to jump in a taxi?' Greg asked himself – his nerves beginning to get the better of him.

If that were to happen, Greg would have to go back to the drawing board, he would still be spoilt for choice. Well, he was in the capital, and there were well over a million likely candidates.

Greg closed the front door to his flat and inserted the key to engage the deadlock. He walked down the stairs, out the main door and made his way to the tube station. Greg's nearest tube station was Wembley Park. He opted for a single ticket as he was unsure where he would end up making his way home from. As he walked down the stairs to the platform he kicked the litter that cluttered his way. Greg quickly checked which line would be arriving first. The Jubilee line would be the slower option as there are so many tube stations before you reach Baker Street Station. The Metropolitan line only stopped at one other station before it got to Baker Street, though on some occasions it did not stop at all. The overhead display started to flash.

Platform 2. Terminating at Baker Street will arrive in 2 minutes.

Greg knew that platform two was the Jubilee line, though this did not seem to matter as this hunter was not in any great hurry, he was enjoying it. After all, he did not know if his intended prey was going to be in that particular pub. Greg had decided that if the chubby guy was not there, he would pay that pub visits at other times, on other days. It seemed to Greg that it would be fruitless to visit other pubs in the area as he may miss him by minutes, or even seconds. Most of the pubs around there, like The Globe, were so big and busy that he could actually be in there and not be seen. This could make it very difficult for Greg to be one hundred per cent sure if his first intended victim was in there or not – it could all be subject to change.

Greg quickly walked over to a guy who was selling the evening newspaper and bought a copy so that he would have something to occupy his mind during the journey.

'Thank you, sir,' the elderly newspaper vendor said as he handed Greg a copy, allowing Greg time to pay.

Greg simply paid the man and then smiled as he readied himself to board the train.

As the train pulled into the station, Greg tried to position himself so that he would not have to walk too far to the train doors when the train stopped. The train stopped and the doors opened. To Greg's horror, it was only Karen sitting in the carriage he was going to get on. He quickly changed his route though it was too late, Karen had seen him.

'Hey you!' Karen shouted.

Greg had no choice but to turn and looked at her.

'Hi…' Greg said almost awkwardly.

Karen could see that Greg was feeling a little uncomfortable, though she could not understand why. 'Come and sit with me, we have some catching up to do,' Karen said patting the seat next to hers.

Greg decided to accept Karen's kind invitation – after all it was part of their no hard feelings deal. Though all the time he was trying his best, to avoid eye contact. He felt that she could see straight through him and even guess what he was thinking.

'This is a bit awkward,' Karen said.

'Why's that?' Greg asked foolishly.

'Well, we haven't seen anything of each other since we split up, and we've bumped into each other when we're both going on a night out,' she replied.

'Is there any reason why we should have seen anything of each other?' Greg questioned.

'Well, no… but I thought that when we split up, we were still going to remain friends…'

'We are friends,' Greg responded with a snap.

There followed an uncomfortable silence.

Greg's mind wandered off and without warning he found himself reminiscing; fantasizing about the intimate side of their past relationship, accidentally undressing Karen with his eyes.

'Where are you off to tonight then?' Karen asked, breaking the silence that briefly distanced the pair.

'Just out for a drink, don't even know where, till I get there,' Greg answered, non-committal and cagey.

'Where's the destination on your ticket?'

'Well, I've got a one way ticket to Baker Street. I think I might wander around there, see what's going on and who's about. I might go over to Covent Garden later, but who knows?' Greg thought that would throw her off the scent, just in case she tried to find him later on that evening.

'Who are you meeting up with then?' Greg asked, wanting to shift the spotlight on to Karen.

'I'm meeting a friend from work. She's going on a first date and thought it would be a good idea if she dragged me along and he's dragging a mate along with him – a kind of double date thing. Safety in numbers. The unlucky guy won't know what he's in for,' she quickly answered, adding an uncomfortable laugh.

'Why should he be unlucky?'

That was the response she was fishing for – exactly what she wanted to hear, music to her ears.

'Well, I didn't mean it like that, I…' Karen stuttered.

It was unusual for Karen to have run out of words, even though it was what she wanted to hear, she was now feeling shy, almost embarrassed.

'Any guy that ends up with you will be lucky. It's just that I don't think that I was meant to be that guy so, before you say it, no, and yes I am still very sorry that I hurt you and no I'm not seeing anyone, and no, I'm not interested in seeing anyone at the moment. I want some time on my own. I need to sort my head out and maybe in time… well, you never know!' Greg halted himself, not wanting their conversation to change. Not wanting to spark any animosity. 'Who knows?' He smiled as he touched her hand gently, his softer feelings trying to surface.

'You still feel that you need time, even after six months?'

The addition to Greg's little speech had made Karen confused.

'Yeah, I still need time and, as I said, who knows?'

This had messed up all of Karen's emotions, leaving her a little upset. Even though she was pleased with the fact that he was not seeing anyone, and that there may be some hope for them in the future, she felt confused.

The truth of the matter was that Greg knew that with his plan beginning to unfold he did not have a future. He only had a future for as long as it took the authorities to catch up with him. Greg had accepted that. He had no choice. Anyone who was setting out to do what he was planning had to look at the real picture. One day he would get caught and one day he would be spending some time at Her Majesty's pleasure. Although he had considered that and the possibility of being caught, he had always believed that as long as he controlled the game, his capture would not be for a long time yet. He planned to have a long career in his newly chosen profession. The control would only be his if he kept a firm eye on the ball.

Karen looked at Greg, never being one to feel comfortable with uneasy silences, she thought that she would try to keep the conversation going by changing its direction.

'How's work then?'

'Work is great. Me and my cart, we have a great day, rain or shine,' he replied with a pleased look on his face.

'Doesn't it get boring?' Karen enquired.

'No. Every day I know what I'm going to be doing. My day is planned. I know where I'm going to be stopping for my tea break, lunch and so on. On every other Tuesday I know that I'll be finished at half three. I think I've got the best job going!'

'I couldn't do it,' Karen said shaking her head.

'I hated the bins. I couldn't have hacked that for much longer!' Greg said with conviction.

'You hated the guys you worked with, you didn't hate the job.'

'Yes, I suppose that's true. Though I didn't hate them all, just the mouthy bastards. You know who I mean? Like that old fucker, Norman. What a wanker. I'd love to see his wife. I bet she bosses him round the house all the time. I bet he's well under the thumb so he takes it out on everyone else. That's why he's such a wanker!' Greg paused for a moment, in order to control his interior anger from surfacing.

'You got on well with Martin though didn't you?' Karen asked trying to steer him away from his anger.

'Yeah, Mart's a real diamond. I haven't seen him for yonks though. I think I'll give him a bell next week and see if he wants to meet up. I wonder if he's still with that girl. She was a right nagger. I bet she even nagged in her sleep!' Greg said with a smile on his face, adding his comical giggle again.

His laugh was something that Karen had always found sensual. Unknowingly, Karen burst out laughing and Greg could not help but join in. For a brief moment, they both forgot about the past although the moment was only short lived.

'Do you think Martin will turn out like Norman when he's older?' Karen asked, bringing the pair back to reality.

'I fucking hope not!' Greg said, still laughing.

'Where's he living now? Martin, I mean.'

'I think he's still in Neasden, above that chip shop.'

'I bet the smell must make him constantly hungry?' Karen said, rubbing her stomach.

'Mart reckons that he can't smell the chip shop from his flat but I don't believe him, do you?' Greg replied.

'How's your flat? Are you still in Raglan Court?' Karen enquired, choosing to ignore Greg's previous question. Martin was no longer of no interest to her; their conversation was now flowing, making her feel close to him once again.

'Yeah, I'm still there and it's pretty much still the same. I've got a new television now. A state of the art surround sound monster. I've connected my Xbox to it. It's fucking wicked!' Greg said proudly.

'You've wanted one of those for ages,' Karen laughed.

'I know. It cost nearly a grand. My dad sent me some money and told me it was to get something for the flat. He gave me a right bollocking when he found out I'd bought a television with the money though,' Greg smiled, shrugging his shoulders in a confused manner.

'Well, you only live once, so why not have the things you want. Anyway, your dad did say to buy something for the flat, and you did,' Karen smiled.

'Yeah, you're right. That's what I told him, but he was having none of it. It took him ages to calm down. Mum was OK about it though,' Greg said as though he was trying to justify his extravagant purchase.

'Good for you!' Karen said, as she winked at Greg. 'Here's an idea – why don't we go out sometime, as friends. There's no reason why we shouldn't, is there?' There was a hint of nervousness in Karen's voice. But she thought it was a reasonable question.

'Why not? Though, don't start getting any silly ideas in that head of yours, my girl!' he replied smiling.

Karen was not sure what he meant by that so she played it cool.

'I have no idea what you are implying, my boy,' she replied giving a childlike smile.

'Just friends then?' Greg confirmed, giving a cheeky smile.

'Yes,' Karen answered, 'give me a bell, and we'll arrange it.'

'Cool. Where are you living now?' Greg replied.

'I'm still living at home with Mum… I know I'm too old to still be at home, but you know what my mum's like?' Karen snapped sounding pissed off but still smiling.

Karen felt embarrassed by the fact that she was still living at home with her mother. By now she should have a place of her own – maybe have settled down and started a family of her own.

It was guilt and a sense of duty that kept her there, holding her back. Unable to move on with her life, she felt trapped; stuck in a rut she was unable to get out of. Though, deep down, she knew that her mother would have to cope if she chose to fly the nest. It was something to do with Karen's own gremlins. For reasons only known to her, she felt insecure. It may be because she lost her father at a very young age and she felt that if she left her mother, she would lose her as well. It was Karen's own self-inflicted little rut. Her demons were her own.

'Where are you getting off then?' Greg asked, thinking it was a question he should have asked earlier.

'Stockwell,' Karen replied, 'I'm jumping on the Victoria line at Green Park,' she confirmed.

'Oh,' Greg sighed.

'Why did you ask that?' Karen asked, putting her question to Greg. She was hoping that he would maybe want meet up with her later.

'Just wondered…' he replied in a manner that implied he had asked the question simply out of polite conversation.

'How about you?' Karen asked fishing for more information.

Greg knew that Karen had already asked him that question, though in a different way. He wondered if she had asked the question again just as to try to continue the conversation or if she was checking up on him. Deciding to play it cool, he answered. 'Baker Street is where I'm going to start my evening,' implying he was heading for a good night. In a way he was, he was finally starting his investigation in to where the chubby guy lived. To Greg, this was an exciting time. Investigation may not be the right word – research was more the right terminology.

'I have no idea where I'll end up though!'

'Are you meeting anyone?' Karen asked anxiously.

'Sort of,' Greg replied.

'I don't understand!' She seemed bemused by his answer.

'Well, I haven't arranged anything with him; I'm just hoping that he'll be there. If he's not, then nothing ventured and all that.'

Karen was pleased that it was a guy Greg was meeting because she thought that he still had a twinkle in his eye for her. The way their conversation had flowed made Karen feel like he wanted to talk to her and that he was starting to enjoy her company again. She had also felt the sexual chemistry return.

'Haven't you seen him for a while then?'

'No, I haven't. Not for ages,' Greg replied.

'Who is he? Do I know him?'

'No, you don't know him. Anyway that's enough about my plans, who are you planning to meet?' Greg replied, not wanting Karen to know too much.

She had made him feel like she was giving him a grilling. He knew she had already told him of her plans, though this was a way for Greg to do a bit of fishing of his own.

'I lied to you earlier, just to test the water between us. Sorry!' Karen said, the smile dropping from her face, 'I'm really meeting an old friend. We were at school together. We got in touch through that web site, *Friends Reunited*, Alison contacted me, and we've agreed to meet up after all these years. I hope she hasn't changed too much.'

'I hope you have a good evening,' Greg said implying that he had already forgiven her for lying to him. Greg felt that Karen was a little nervous about meeting up with her old school friend after all this time.

'I bet she's as excited or as nervous as you are,' he said, thinking he would try to set her mind at rest.

'I'm not nervous!' Karen snapped.

'Don't give me that, that's a load of bollocks and you know it! I'd be shitting myself,' Greg felt a little angry with the way that Karen had snapped at him. After all, he was only trying to be sympathetic and set her mind at rest.

'I'm just a bit apprehensive, that's all. Wouldn't you be?' Karen fired back, trying to justify the way she had spoken to Greg previously.

'Apprehensive? That's just another way of dressing it up to me, and it means the same thing if you ask me,' Greg said with a smug look on his face, like the proverbial I told you so.

A short silence followed with Karen not wanting to admit her nervousness and Greg not knowing what to say. It felt just like old times.

'I bet your mate from school is just as apprehensive as you are, so stop worrying,' Greg said, deciding to break the deadlock.

'OK, I'll try,' Karen replied, trying not to smile.

It was then that the train pulled into the station. Karen glanced out of the window noticing that this was where she needed to change trains.

'I still love you. Please call me and we'll meet up,' she said softly as she stood up from her seat.

'I will,' Greg replied without thinking, not allowing himself enough time to digest what Karen had just said. 'What did you just say?' he enquired, feeling his guard lower for a brief moment.

'You know what I said,' Karen blushed. 'Promise me Greg!' Karen added in a sexy way that only Greg could understand.

'I'll give you a bell soon,' Greg replied, unable to cement the promise that Karen had demanded.

The doors closed and the train started to pull away. Karen was still standing on the platform, frantically waving. She was shouting something, though her attempts to communicate were in vain. Greg had no chance of hearing her given the surrounding noise.

Unknowingly, Karen had made Greg feel a little embarrassed by the way that she had attracted so much attention toward them. It had made him feel like the whole world now knew that, in the past, he had hurt Karen, and, even now, after all this time, she was still hurting. He had no idea that Karen's feelings for him still ran so deep. Greg thought for a short while about whether or not this was a good thing. Maybe he could use Karen as an alibi: start seeing her again – but this time it would be much slower. Would she become too clingy? He would need her to understand this, though in a way that she would believe that the slower pace was a joint decision. His time would no longer be his own. If only he could somehow see her on his terms – when he wanted. He needed to dictate the pace. Both his sex life and his ego would get a massive boost. He made a decision that he would phone her, lay out the bait, and she would come running. This was not part of his original plan, though adaptability is always a much-needed strength. Adaptability eliminates the need to panic. Being able to think quickly and be flexible whilst wholly dedicated to your goal gives any career criminal the clarity to avoid conflict with any authority.

Greg knew that he would have to lead more than just a double life. Karen could be a very useful tool, an ironclad alibi.

As the train slowed, Greg glanced out of the window. He had reached his destination. He had not heard the driver announce that the train would be terminating. In a dreamlike state, he cut off from the real world, mentally adding to his already thickening plot. As he stood up, an elderly man spoke to him.

'Call her. She is obviously mad about you. You'd be a fool to let her slip through your hands!' the elderly man told him.

The man looked very well presented – perfectly groomed. His age was tricky to guess, but late sixties would have been a safe bet. His grey hair, though receding, had been slickly combed back. His carefully shaped moustache suited him. It looked like it belonged. The pinstriped suit he wore with a plain white shirt and colourful bow tie made him seem almost eccentric – the patent black leather shoes complemented his attire perfectly.

Greg looked at him in utter amazement and responded, 'Would you want her back?' he paused. 'She slept with my brother, and he gave her clap.' Greg kept a straight face, and looked hard at the elderly man.

'I'm sorry, son!' the elderly man replied feeling a little deflated by what Greg had told him.

'What you sorry for?' Greg questioned.

'Sorry that she did that to you!' he replied, trying to be tactful, though by this time the elderly man was feeling uncomfortable.

'No, she didn't, I haven't even got a brother. I'm just winding you up. Now piss off and mind your own business!' Greg said laughing, 'you nosy old fucker!'

The elderly man glared, only briefly, at Greg before snapping, 'You foolish boy!' and storming off making large striding steps as he did. Greg's laughter grew louder.

Greg left the carriage, made his way up the escalator and continued until he reached the exit. On his way past, he gave the ticket collector his ticket and then continued to make his way outside. As he exited the station, he looked across the road and there it was – The Globe Tavern. Built in 1735 it was full of character and the ambience was that of a busy friendly place. From the outside the forecourt beer garden was large in capacity, having a big seating area, as well as plenty of standing room.

He paused, though only for a moment, whilst he looked to his left and then to his right as if to confirm that he had arrived.

Chapter Four

Baker Street was a busy place, full of tourists as well as people who either lived there or were just passing through. There were also those on a night out, like Greg, or at least that was what the unsuspecting public thought.

Greg crossed the busy main road, Marylebone Road, not bothering to use the pelican crossing. As he walked through the already open main door, he found himself pausing without realising again, though only for a few seconds. This pause allowed him time to soak up the atmosphere, a calming atmosphere that had kept itself alive for centuries. The noise of simple chitter-chatter with added laughter made any visitor feel instantly welcome. Greg could smell the history of the place, especially now the smoking ban had come in to force. The place was buzzing – packed to the rafters.

'Perfect,' he told himself, 'no one will remember seeing me in here!' He negotiated his way to the bar, squeezing and pushing his way through the crowd. Once there, he waited his turn to be served. He made a couple of unsuccessful attempts to jump the queue. A young-looking barmaid from behind the bar looked at Greg.

'Yes, what can I get you?' she asked, showing her almost perfect teeth as she gave her best, professional smile.

Greg lent forward on the bar, closing the gap between them and replied, 'A pint of Fosters.' There did not seem the need for politeness.

'Coming right up,' the barmaid replied, her smile remaining the same. Greg gave her a flirtatious wink.

The barmaid placed his pint of lager on the bar and said, 'Anything else?'

This time Greg just responded with a simple nod of his head, 'Your phone number.'

'That's three quid for the Fosters, and you'll have to try harder than that if you want my phone number, cheeky,' the barmaid laughed as she held out her hand.

Greg gave her the right money. 'You can't blame a guy for trying,' Greg replied as he picked up his pint and took a big gulp.

'Well, sometimes persistence pays off,' the barmaid chuckled as she fluttered her eyelids.

Greg gave her another flirtatious wink before turning away in order to survey his surrounding area to see if the chubby guy was in there. He looked hard; it was no good. The pub was far too busy, far too full. Greg decided to circulate.

Once Greg had reached the bottom of his pint, he proceeded to make his way back to the bar but, just before he got there, he felt as though he was being shoved from behind as if someone was pushing him forward.

'Come on, get out of the way!'

He automatically knew the voice and turned round so that he could confirm the identity of the owner. He could not believe his luck. It was the chubby guy. Greg looked at him and the chubby guy glared back.

'WHAT?' the chubby guy shouted.

'Take it easy, mate,' Greg said looking the man up and down and then shaking his head. He had other plans for him and this was not the time or place.

'DO YOU WANT SOMETHING, WANKER?' the chubby guy asked Greg, still shouting in an aggressive manner. Other people in earshot deliberately moved away.

'Just for you to take it easy,' Greg replied, choosing to remain calm.

'Get out of my fucking way then!' the chubby guy ordered, deciding to lower his voice as he continued trying to push his way past.

Greg's calm demeanour quickly evaporated. The lava that ran through his veins started to boil. He repeatedly told himself that revenge was always a dish best served cold and never too sweet, though he was not willing to allow this fat fucker to push in front of him at the bar.

'Wait your fucking turn!' Greg told the chubby guy.

As the chubby guy turned away to walk to another section of the bar, he grinned at Greg, and said, 'Fuck you, you toss-pot!'

'Mess with me and you fuck with the wrong person!' Greg said calmly, blowing the chubby guy a kiss.

The chubby guy turned, and looked at Greg. He paused in his stride and said, 'I'll see you again, you faggot!'

Greg looked back at him with a crazed look in his eyes, 'You can bet your fucking life on it!'

The ironic thing was that the chubby guy did not realize that Greg meant it. It was all part of his plan. The only thing on his mind now was that if he followed this guy home now, the chubby guy would think that Greg was going to jump him.

'What do I do now?' he said to himself, as he tried to calm the internal rage that swept its way through his veins.

Greg decided to allow time to dictate his next step. Nothing was ever set in stone and if it meant he had to instigate their next dialogue, he was willing to do so. He would have another pint and wait for the chubby guy to make his move before making his decision on whether he should follow him or not. It was still early, so he had plenty of time to consider his options.

As he reached the bar, the same barmaid looked over at him. As she placed a pint of lager on the bar, smiled and said, 'Three quid handsome.'

'Here you go,' he replied handing the barmaid a ten pound note. Within seconds, the barmaid placed Greg's change in his hand.

'Thanks,' he said turning away; trying to focus on where the chubby guy had gone. The barmaid was of no interest to him anymore; he needed to concentrate on his mission.

'Ignoring me now?' the barmaid asked.

'Well, either you're gonna give me your phone number or not. I've asked you for it but, listen sweetheart, I'm not gonna beg you for it!' Greg replied, turning to face the barmaid as he spoke. His brash reply was deliberate, fully intending to put the barmaid off.

'Here you go,' The barmaid smiled, as she gave Greg a piece of paper. 'Call me, and we'll see what kind of a man you are between the sheets – bad boy or...?'

'We'll see,' Greg smirked, snatching the piece of paper out of the barmaid's hand, kissing the paper before slipping it into his back pocket.

'We will,' the barmaid replied as she walked away in order to serve the hordes of thirsty customers that lined the bar.

As Greg casually pushed his way through the bustling bodies that crowded the bar area, he noticed the chubby guy standing by a fruit machine. Unable to avert his gaze, eye contact was made. Greg decided not to look away and continued to look over at his intended quarry; the chubby guy did the same. A few seconds passed then, out of the blue, the chubby guy beckoned Greg to go over to him.

'What does he want?' Greg said under his breath, 'Only one way to find out. Here goes.'

'Sorry about what happened earlier, mate,' the chubby guy said with a hint of nervousness, 'over at the bar I mean.'

'Forget about it,' Greg replied, deciding that brushing the matter aside would be his best course of action.

'Let me buy you a pint, just to show that there's no hard feelings,' Greg said, trying to break the ice.

'Yeah, OK... I'll have a pint of Fosters,' the chubby guy replied.

Greg did not understand what was going on, though he thought it may pay dividends to play along.

As he made his way back from the bar, it started to make sense all of a sudden. The chubby guy was all mouth; when Greg told him that he could bet his life on bumping into Greg again, the chubby guy had lost his nerve and thought that he had better somehow make peace with Greg. That was why he had called Greg over – to offer an olive branch.

It was obvious to Greg that the chubby guy may try to befriend Greg which would save Greg a lot of time.

'Are we cool now?' the chubby guy asked. He questioned whether or not Greg had forgiven him for his foul-mouthed outburst.

'Yeah, we're cool.' Greg liked his directness.

''Thanks for the pint!'

'That's OK, mate. Let's forget about earlier,' Greg smiled encouraging further conversation.

'My bird has been giving me a load of shit at home. Sorry if I took it out on you.' The chubby guy seemed to be acting very humble, even if he was trying to pump his chest out.

'Forget it. I'm Greg by the way. What's your name?'

'I'm Brian. Pleased to meet you Greg,' Brian said, as he quietly breathed a sigh of relief.

'Do you live locally?' Greg asked, trying to continue the conversational flow.

'Swiss Cottage. How about you?' Brian replied. An uneasy pause had jolted him in mid-sentence.

'Neasden,' Greg replied, deciding that everything else he was going to tell Brian would be fabricated. 'What do you do for work then?' Greg asked deciding that he would play the old, question for a question game with Brian. Well, why not? He had to find out as much as he could, and if that meant spending a few hours with the guy, then so be it.

'I sell cars. I'm a sales supervisor,' Brian boasted. 'I specialise in the used car market. I earn bucket-loads!' Brian was in his element, his favourite subject: his job, his bullshit and himself. 'I'm based at Wandsworth, my boss, who's also my best mate – have you seen him in here with me before?' Brian's words racing out of his mouth, his grammar clumsy.

'I don't think so,' Greg answered.

Greg knew it could have been the guy he had seen Brian talking to the last time Greg was in there, but he did not want to cut Brian short.

'Well, he's my gaffer. Anyway, he begged me to go over and wake those toss-pots up at the Wandsworth site, so I did! That was about a year ago now. I haven't looked back. He wants to make me the sales manager over there but he reckons I'm too young, and he says that I need to mature my management skills first. See, I was crap at school and he gave me a job when I left school. I was out the front one Saturday morning, just giving a few of the motors a leathering, cos that's what I did, I just kept the place clean and smart looking. Anyway, this mug walked up. I could tell he was a mug, just cos I can spot a mug punter a mile away! Anyway, right, I sold this right nail. This motor had come in on a part exchange, right. How the fuck was I supposed to know? My gaffer was gonna scrap it. Honestly Greg, it was a right piece of shit. Anyway, right, this mug walked in and asked me about this motor, I told him it was shit hot, and if he wanted it he'd have to cough up five hundred quid! He looked at it for about three seconds and bought it. Can you believe that?'

'You sound like you were born to sell motors, Brian!' Greg knew that this story had bullshit written all over it. That did not matter, he was happy to listen. He just wondered how many times people had sat through this story thinking the same thing.

'That's what my gaffer said,' Brian continued, 'I had to carry on keeping the place looking smart, but Gaza, that's my gaffers name, Gaza, anyway, Gaza said that I could do a bit of selling only on Saturdays only cos I wasn't old enough to sell motors. I was just a kid back then.' Brian paused to gulp down the rest of his pint in a truly gluttonous fashion. 'You have to be over eighteen to sell motors you know. See, I was only sixteen so I just helped out in the selling side on Saturdays until I was eighteen. Then Gaza said even though I was shit hot, and born to sell motor's, I had to go through all the training like the other lads had. I was training the bloke who was supposed to be training me!' Brian laughed loudly, and then started to cough, 'fucking fags!' he cursed.

'How old are you then?' Greg thought he would try to move the conversation on.

'Thirty, why? How old are you?' Brian replied, sounding a little defensive.

'I'm twenty-three,' Greg openly answered. 'You said your bird was giving you shit.'

'Yeah, she's still a fucking kid, only nineteen. You're not long out of nappies yourself, are you?' Brian said whilst sniggering to himself. He did not answer the question; it was as if he did not hear it. It was as though he switched off once he heard Greg's age.

'Thirty is still youngish though, mate.' Greg needed to keep the conversation going. He had already pondered the idea of simply walking away but he knew that would have been far too easy as well as a mistake. 'My turn now, do you want another pint Brian?'

'Yeah, OK.' Brian had taken Greg's comment about his age well, complimentary. 'Would you get me a cigar whilst you're up there? I'll give you the money for it.'

It was as if Brian was disappointed that Greg was so young. It was not as if Greg looked older than his years. Though, in a way, Greg made Brian feel younger, or maybe it was just the alcohol having its desired effect.

When Greg returned, Brian was talking to someone on his mobile phone. Greg just sat down, put Brian's pint of lager in front of him and placed the cigar next to it.

Greg waited for Brian to finish his conversation and wondered how Brian could hear the person on the other end of the phone with all the background noise that was going on.

'Stupid fucking bitch!' Brian said, ending the call abruptly.

'Here you go,' Greg said, pointing to the cigar on the table. 'Everything OK?' Greg asked.

'Yeah,' Brian replied, pausing for a moment.

'If I can help, mate…' Greg jumped in.

Brian disregarded Greg's offer and simply decided to continue, 'She's got the hump cos I told her I was gonna be out all night!'

Greg felt uncomfortable, though knew that he was controlling the game.

'Where are you off to?' he enquired.

'We, mate, we're gonna knock these back, and then we're gonna fuck off to a little boozer just round the corner from my gaff.'

'Sounds good,' Greg half-heartedly replied.

He had been given no choice, he had to go. This would be an ideal opportunity for him to find out where Brian lived.

'I'm gonna have to pop home to get some more money so we can have a proper session,' Brian said, smiling at Greg.

'Fuck it, why not?' Greg said, building Brian's gluttonous excitement.

'I'm going outside to smoke this,' Brian said picking up the cigar.

Greg stood and followed Brian outside.

He did need to find out where he lived, though he did not want to meet Brian's girlfriend before the time was right. He would need to think quickly in order to avoid meeting her.

'I don't want to be the cause of a row between you and your bird, mate,' Greg said trying to be diplomatic. 'If this is gonna cause problems for you...'

'She'll be all right. She's got no choice, I wear the trousers in my house and she'd better fucking realise that.' Brain paused to light his cigar using a lighter he had found in one of his pockets. 'I'll knock the fucker into her. Fuck her. Bitch does my head in!' Brian said with a mixed look on his face, smoke bellowing from both his nostrils. It was as if he got some kind of enjoyment from disrespecting his girlfriend, the mother of his child.

'Hey, listen, mate, I just don't want to upset anyone or cause any shit for you at home. Anyway, we can always do it another time, if that would make things easier?' Greg was trying to calm Brian down a little.

'Things have never been better, mate. She should know me by now. If she doesn't like it, she can always do what she normally does – nothing,' Brian laughed. 'Anyway, it's been decided, right. I've told her now. If we don't go down my local, well, she'll think she's won and I can't let her think that she wears the trousers, can I?' Brian said in a tone that suggested that the matter was closed – his male pride was on the line.

'It's your round when we get there then Brian,' Greg smiled, as he gave Brian a friendly shove, 'Come on, drink up.'

'OK, mate... *Lager, lager, lager, lager, SHOUT! I'll have a whiskey drink, and a cider drink, a lager drink...* I've forgot the rest of the words.' Brian laughed, halting his tone deaf singing. 'I'm gonna have a piss before we go, mate,' Brian told his new drinking buddy as he swaggered away, back in to the building, heading in the direction of the men's toilets.

Greg decided to wait outside, watching the city types boasting and bragging how well their prospective careers were going. The suited young men eyed up the women as they gulped down their imported bottled beer whilst sucking on their Marlboro cigarettes. The women sipped down their large glasses of French wine whilst knowingly flirting with the bulging wallets.

Brian returned, almost losing his footing when he missed the step down as he exited the building. To Greg's surprise, he handed Greg a pint of lager.

'I thought we were going.'

'One for the road,' Brian said, slurring his reply. 'Can I ask you a personal question?'

'Yeah, why not?'

'Why are you being so friendly to me? You aren't fucking gay, are you?'

'You bumped in to me and then called me over Brian. Maybe I should be asking you that question?' Greg replied.

Brian froze, his manhood in question, he did not know what to say.

'I'm only fucking about!' Greg said laughing loudly.

Brian joined Greg's laughter. 'You had me going for a minute there!' Brian said, still laughing. It took the two men a few minutes to stop laughing.

'What do you do for a living then?' Brian asked.

'I'm a civil servant,' Greg replied.

'What the fuck does one of those do?' Brian asked.

'I can't tell you that, mate,' Greg said whilst gulping a mouth full of lager.

'Why can't you tell me?' Brian seemed shocked that his newfound friend would not tell him what he did for a living.

'If I could I would, mate, but I can't,' Greg said feeling this could drag on and become a bit tiresome.

'How can you say that? Work's work,' Brian seemed to think that Greg did not trust him. 'Civil servant... don't make me laugh.'

The truth of the matter was that Greg's employment grade did come under the civil servant umbrella, so he was telling the truth in a roundabout way. It was Brian who was bullshitting about his job, though it did not bother Greg. It was unimportant.

'Put it this way – if people could just simply get on with their lives, abide by the laws of the land...'

'What do you mean – the laws of the land?' Brian said, hijacking the conversation. 'You fucking Old Bill or summit?'

'OK, for instance, I bet you drop litter all the time.' Brian nodded his admittance. 'Well, littering the capital is a criminal offense. Don't get me wrong and, no, I'm not Old Bill or anything like that, but it's my job to make sure our capital is kept clean and a nice place to live. Without the dirty lazy fuckers my job would be much easier, but it's not, so I just get on with it and keep smiling.'

There was a long silence.

'Come on, we'd better drink up and get going,' Brian said, still having difficulty digesting Greg's speech. Greg simply smiled, remembering what he was doing there in the first place.

'I don't care what you do for a living. I think you're a good bloke. It's just that I'm still none the wiser to what you do,' Brian said shaking his head, 'but fuck it, I think you're an OK guy.'

Greg acknowledged Brian's sad attempt at an apology with a single nod of the head. Brian thought that he had offended Greg and was trying to think how he could tell him that he didn't mean to upset him without sounding soft.

'Listen, mate' Brian said, 'I'm sorry if I said something wrong... I'm just not very good at trusting people.' His words caused him to choke a little.

'Forget it, listen, I'm not gay and I'm not Old Bill. Let's get out of here and you can take me to that boozer of yours.' Greg smiled whilst brilliantly hiding his disgust for the man.

Brian did not have many friends. Well, the truth was that he did not have any and that was no surprise when you think of what a nasty person he was. He had told so many lies throughout his life that even he was not sure what was fact and what was fiction anymore.

Brian tried to put on a hard man image and sometimes he got away with it. This was only because of his size. He was no athlete but he was tall, around the six-foot mark. A morbidly obese man, his body odour stuck to him like chewing gum on the bottom of a shoe. Personal hygiene had always been at the bottom of his priority list, alongside his long-suffering girlfriend and his child. It was evident that this man had never done a single day's physical exercise in his life. His diet of junk food, beer and nicotine had taken its toll – poor health was the result of this lethal cocktail. He was trying to quit smoking and had now turned to rolling his own cigarettes and only smoked cigars when he was out drinking to portray his fake image. The only reason he decided to roll his own cigarettes was so that he had more money for booze, not to boost the household economy.

His job did not give him a good income. He was not a sales supervisor. Sadly, he was still doing the same job as when he started. He chose to wear a shirt and tie to work to keep up his bullshit image. Once he got there, he would put on his overalls and get cleaning. That was why he found it difficult not to be envious of other people, the city types. He would see them in The Globe Tavern throwing their money about, buying huge rounds of drinks, never seeming to worry about the vast amounts of money they were putting behind the bar. This was also why Brian was such a bastard to his girlfriend. Brian was the kind of guy that blamed others for his own failings in life. Brian's parents knew that he would never amount to much, so in a way, they could say that he had never disappointed them. They kept their expectations low. They had feared the worst for their son, anything else would be a bonus. Their son had never paid them a single bonus.

Brian's girlfriend was as much of a loser as he was. Her name was Sharon; she was nineteen, eleven years younger than Brian. She was as useless as Brian. Sharon could not cook, clean or do any domestic chores, not that she ever tried to. She was lazy and did not bother with cleaning or the upkeep of their home. Sharon was like a lot of young mothers. All she needed was a kick up the backside. She needed to raise the bar, set her sights higher. Sitting around the house, smoking cigarettes and watching daytime television was as high as her bar got. It was this that infuriated Brian so much. He did not love her and she did not love him, they were both too naïve to understand the true meaning of love.

Brian met Sharon and got her pregnant in record time. They had met at a party Brian had gate-crashed. Sharon was stoned. Back then, she smoked copious amounts of pot. The drug had left her in her own zone and not completely aware what was going on in the real world. Brian saw her as easy prey. Taking advantage of her drug-induced slumber, he forced himself on her and, nine months later, a reminder of that night popped in to the world. Brian, to his credit, chose to stand by the mother of his child, though regretted his decision every day. Getting Sharon pregnant was a complete accident, just another statistic. Brian only stood by Sharon because she was his first real girlfriend and his first real sexual experience. His naivety regarding unprotected sexual intercourse had bit him on the arse. Sharon had always chosen to blank the experience out. In the eyes of the law, she could have cried rape. Brain was a very lucky man. He could be in prison now, not freely living his sad life.

An uncle of Brian's owned their family home, but had since emigrated to Spain. His expat uncle had let them live there because it served his double edged business sword. The first was mainly through pity and it made perfect business sense. They lived in the property more or less rent-free. His uncle was pleased that someone was living in the house. The property being occupied would deter would-be vandals and potential squatters. Though, as time went by, Brian, being the simple-minded man that he was, erased this from his memory.

Greg looked at his watch and thought that this would be their last drink as time, as well as licensing laws, would not permit them to have another in this particular pub. He had already agreed to accompany Brian to his local watering hole in Swiss Cottage.

'Have you seen the time?' Brian asked.

'Yeah,' Greg answered. 'I've had a thought, mate. Haven't you got work in the morning?' Greg asked, pointing out the obvious.

'Yeah I've got work, but I drink seven nights a week. Getting to work has never bothered me. I'm always up before the alarm. It doesn't matter how slaughtered I've been the night before,' Brian replied while giving a belly laugh, 'I never miss a day's graft. The place would grind to a halt if I wasn't there!'

'All right,' Greg replied, his thoughts were elsewhere. They had moved on – jumping slightly as to what *The Ultimate* had planned for Brian and whether Sharon would be strong enough. She did not have a choice; adaptability was man's strongest attribute. Greg would make sure that her test was carried out and he knew she would pass with flying colours. He would make sure that was indeed what was going to happen.

'All right you poof?' Brian said laughing, 'We can carry on when we get to my house. I've got loads of beer in the fridge!' Brian said.

Greg knew that Brian was just being a glutton, and that he never drank for enjoyment. After all, he was a slob!

Greg only planned to walk up to the door of Brian's house, not go inside, as he did not want to meet Sharon. Greg would wait outside whilst Brian went in his house to obtain more drinking money.

Brian was talking, though Greg could not hear a word of what Brian was saying as he was too wrapped up in his own thoughts.

'Are you fit then?' Brian asked.

'Yeah, always, mate, let's get out of here. I'm knackered!' Greg replied.

They both stood up at the same time and made their way to the exit. Greg let Brian take the lead and tried to dictate the pace from the rear to stall him and give himself more thinking time.

'Come on, mate. What you fucking about at?' Brian said.

'I'm right with you,' Greg replied.

They both made their way across the busy main road and into the train station.

'Don't bother getting a ticket, I never do,' Brian said, with an element of excitement in his tone.

Brian walked straight through, passing the guy collecting and checking tickets and Greg followed.

'Tickets?' the ticket guy asked.

Brian did not even look, though Greg glanced back.

'Where are your tickets?' the ticket guy asked again, though this time he was more aggressive – shouting and demanding to see their tickets,

Greg stopped. Brian had seen that Greg had stopped, so he stopped as well.

'What you doing?' Brian asked.

'I'm going to shut this fucker up!' Greg replied.

'Listen, mate, I don't want any trouble, but if you want to travel on the train, you've got to pay,' the ticket guy said.

'You lot really piss me off!' Greg started, his state of mind blurred his clarity. 'Who do you think you are?' His anger was building. 'Why don't you just leave people alone, but no you can't. Some idiot tells you to wear a uniform and you think you're the fucking law, don't you?'

'No,' replied the ticket guy, 'I'm just trying to do my job, mate. I must remind you that all these stations are covered with CCTV cameras so please don't do anything stupid. Now, are you going to buy a ticket before you travel on the train. If you don't, I'll have to report you to the London Transport Police.'

'What you stop for?' Brian asked. 'Come on let's buy a ticket and fuck off.'

'Come on let's go. I've had enough of this idiot!' Greg replied.

'Don't forget your ticket!' the ticket guy said sarcastically.

They decided to buy their tickets, though Greg did have to pay for Brian's. It was the mention of the CCTV that changed Greg's mind. As he was purchasing their tickets, the two men heard a train approach one of the platforms.

'Come on, I think this might be ours,' Brian grunted.

Both men hurried their way down the two flights of stairs, with Greg having to slow his pace in order for the morbidly obese Brian to catch up. As they drew closer to the platform, they noticed that it was indeed their train.

'Told you,' Brian said, as he fought to get air back in to his lungs.

The train doors opened and Brian bundled his way into the carriage, not bothering to let the passengers inside the carriage alight. Greg waited and then followed.

Brian looked up at Greg from his slumped seating position opposite. His face was bright red and his eyes were almost half-closed. Still struggling to get his breath back, he was unable to speak.

The carriage they were on was empty apart from the two of them.

'You all right, mate?' Greg asked, thinking that Brian looked rather drunk.

'Yeah, I'm all right,' Brian paused, 'it's the others,' Brian said with a little chuckle, following his attempted quirk.

'Is that the best you can do?' Greg said in a way to suggest that Brian's attempt at humour was not very good.

'OK flash, let's hear one from you!' Brian said defensively.

'OK then,' Greg smiled, 'What do you call a man standing in-between two houses?'

'How do I know?' Brian replied, slightly over enthusiastic.

'Ali!' Greg shouted with a roar of laughter.

Brian looked at him with a puzzled, lost look on his face.

'I don't get it,' Brian said innocently.

Greg stopped laughing, paused and looked at Brian. Then, all of a sudden, Greg started to laugh again. After a couple of minutes, Greg said to Brian, 'What do you call a man with a number plate on his head?'

Brian simply shrugged his shoulders.

'Reg,' Greg announced, though this time he paused his laughter.

Brian belched, 'I needed that,' Brian said loudly. 'Better out than in,' Brian concluded, choosing to ignore Greg's last joke.

Their train journey would not take them very long as Swiss Cottage was only a couple of stops away from Baker Street.

As the train was preparing to stop at Swiss Cottage Station, Brian had already left his seat and was standing by the doors, ready to depart the train.

'Come on, mate,' Brian said.

Greg looked up at him, said nothing and rose from his seat.

The pair travelled up the escalator and made their way to the exit.

'Tickets please,' an Asian guy said as he folded his crumpled newspaper, placing it on a shelf in his ticket booth.

Greg turned to Brian and said, 'I've got our tickets.'

Brian gave a gesture with his hands as if to indicate that Greg was free to take control of the situation.

'We haven't got any tickets,' Greg told the Asian guy.

'Why not?' replied the Asian guy.

'The ticket guy at Baker Street told us not to bother because there wouldn't be anyone at this station collecting tickets.'

The Asian guy looked at Greg, 'You're having me on aren't you?' he said with a smile on his face.

' No, mate, straight up. That's what he said,' Greg was enjoying this.

'I will tell my supervisor at the end of my shift. In the meantime, you must pay me please… two pounds each please.'

Greg reached into his pocket and pulled out two travel tickets.

'Here you go, mate,' Greg laughed.

'A clown, hey?' the Asian guy said joining Greg's laughter.

'Sorry, mate, I was just pulling your leg,' Greg said, winking at the Asian guy.

'No problem,' the Asian guy replied, as he started unfolding his crumpled newspaper.

Brian and Greg walked out of the train station. Greg paused to let Brian lead the way. The two men walked in almost complete silence. Brian's mind seemed to be away with the fairies whilst Greg's mind remained focussed on the here and now. Every now and then, Brian would make a comment, mainly because he found being quiet hard. His mouth had always ran away from him. Putting his mouth in to action before putting his brain in gear was simply an occupational hazard for Brian.

'I'll wait out here, mate,' Greg said, 'that way we'll get to the boozer quicker.'

'OK, I won't be long.' Brian walked up a few stairs and banged on the door, too lazy to use his own set of keys.

'Come on!' Brian ordered.

Through the frosted glass, a silhouette in the shape of a female approached. It could only have been the abused Sharon. The door opened, an exchange of words could be heard before Brian disappeared inside the building. Greg waited, surveying the lay of the land – the surrounding area.

***

'I haven't got any money Brian!' Sharon yelled.

Greg could not help but overhear the heated exchange inside the building.

Sharon looked downtrodden. Her hair was untidy; her clothes looked as if their better days had passed by a long time ago. Her faded, creased, shapeless baggy RELAX T-shirt looked as if it had outlived its sell-by date and hundreds of hot washes and spin cycles. The black well-worn leggings clung to her thighs; her idle weight gain gave them a much harder life than they deserved. As she opened her mouth, her nicotine stained teeth aided her halitosis. The bags under her eyes gave her a well-worn appearance.

'Course you fucking have! What about the family allowance? That came today!' Brian growled in response.

'That's for nappies!'

'You don't need any more nappies. You've already got a fucking cupboard full!'

'They're not for me, you idiot!'

'Just give me the fucking money!'

Sharon ran out of the hallway back in to the living room. Their young baby had been woken by the couple's arguing and had started to cry.

'I'll see you later,' Brian growled as he snatched the money from Sharon's purse.

'Don't be too late,' she pleaded as she picked up her baby.

'Don't fucking tell me what time to come home,' Brian spat, slapping Sharon with a thunderous clap.

'Don't hit me. Please don't hit me!' Sharon begged trying to hold on to her baby whilst absorbing the blow Brian had administered.

'If you behave, I might come home early. But you'll have to make it worth my while.'

Sharon did not answer at first, the idea of Brian laying his grubby, sweaty hands on her, turned her stomach. 'Stay out as long as you like,' she said, grimacing.

Brian left the room, opening the front door. Sharon was quick on his heels. 'Bring your mate back with you, and I might let him fuck me!' she scowled.

'You'll pay for that, you fucking bitch!'

Sharon slammed the front door; their baby's crying faded.

Greg knew that although Sharon may have seen him, she had not heard him speak.

Brian trembled with anger. Sharon had stood up to him, she always did, but she seemed to be getting tougher these days.

'Women...' Brian commented.

'Looks like you've got your hands full there, mate.' Greg could not help Sharon at this time, her time to help herself would come.

'Tell me about it, mate. But she's nothing I can't handle. I had to give her a slap before she'd let me have my fucking money – cheeky slag. A few more fucking slaps is what she needs. That'll sort her out!'

It was not long before the two men had arrived at their destination. Brian entered the pub first, followed by Greg.

'We all right for a late one?' Brian asked.

'Of course you are, big boy!' A slutty-looking over-the-hill woman replied from behind the bar.

'Two pints then Trace… are your tits getting bigger?'

'No, they've always been this big, cheeky, and don't ask to see 'em either. I'll flash 'em to your mate for a fiver. Where do you come from, handsome?' Her attention now focussed on Greg.

'I'm not from round here Trace,' Greg smiled.

Trace had bought The Cottage – a small run down backstreet pub, after returning from her short emigration to Tenerife. Previously married to a local East End mobster, she had decided that the Mediterranean life was no longer what she wanted. She packed her suitcase and returned to England. Her divorce settlement was just enough for her and allowed her to buy The Cottage. Now in her early fifties, she looked liked she had been tangoed. Her fake sun bed tan, bleach-blond hair, hoards of yellow gold combined with her oversized breasts seemed to appeal to most middle-aged men. Though, for a man with high standards, Trace would be lucky to get a second look.

'I know that. Do you have a name?'

'Greg's one of my best mates, Trace,' Brian lied, interrupting.

'Well, Greg, do you wanna spend a fiver?' Trace said, trying to flirt as she placed two pints of lager on the bar.

'No offense, but I've never paid to look at a bird's tits before, Trace, and I don't intend to start now!' Greg replied, giving her a smile followed by a wink.

'I like you Greg,' Trace said, winking back before turning away to pour herself a large glass of wine.

Looking around, Greg noticed that the place was not overly busy, though being tucked away meant that The Cottage was the type of public house that would never attract new clientele. It was more of a locals only place. If you were not from the area, you would never know it was there.

During the rest of the evening through to the early hours. Brian got increasingly drunk, as did Trace. Before Greg had realised, The Cottage had only three people keeping the bar busy, and Trace was one of those people.

'I'm glad your mate's pissed off to the loo Greg. I'll get rid of Brian and we'll have a nightcap. What do you say?' Trace asked, thrusting her cleavage at Greg.

By this time, Greg was flat on his feet. The alcohol had made its way around his blood stream four times over and Tracy's invite was a very tempting one, despite her appearance. He tried to think clearly and battled his alcohol-leaden thoughts away. It was no good.

'OK, what side of the bed do you sleep on?'

'I don't. I sleep in the middle,' Trace replied.

Brian staggered his way back in to the bar, his trousers wet where he had not managed the correct aim angle into the urinal.

'I'm closing up now, Brian.'

'OK, Trace. Drink up, Greg, we've gotta fuck off Trace is closing.' Brian's alcohol-filled grey cells would not allow him to comprehend that Greg was sitting next to Trace when she made the announcement to close the pub.

'Greg's gonna stay on and have a nightcap Brian.'

'You jammy bastard...' Brian slurred, 'give her one for me, my son,' Brian's vulgarity was not his fault, he didn't know any better.

'I will, mate,' Greg smiled.

'All right then, give me your mobile number and we'll meet up for that piss up you said we'll go on!' said Brian trying to hide his disappointment, wishing it was him staying for the nightcap.

'OK, mate. Ready?' Greg said as he prepared to give Brian the Radio One flirt-divert number.

'Yeah, go on then.'

Greg read out a number that he had memorized from listening to the radio.

'Thanks mate,' Brian said, between hiccups.

The two men shook hands and went their separate ways.

Trace bolted the only entrance, turned to Greg and beckoned him to follow her up the stairs by the side of the bar. It was not long before they were both naked and sexually fulfilled.

On the train home, the next morning, Greg did not feel any sense of guilt by the way he had slipped away, leaving Trace still sleeping with a smile on her mascara-soaked face. He thought about Karen, though only briefly. He could not help feeling a massive sense of achievement. Greg had managed to find out so much information in one night. He knew where Brian lived, as well as who else was living there, Brian's girlfriend's name, her age and that Brian had no friends.

This was going to be easy, though Greg knew it was impossible for him to think like that. That is how others before him had been caught.

'You must never become sloppy!' Greg told himself, over and over.

The hard work was now about to begin. Greg had to find out if Sharon had a routine – an evening routine.

Greg already knew that Brian's evenings were spent in the pub that was the same day in, day out. Greg had to watch Brian though, he may have spoken to Sharon like she was shit, though was it another story at home and was that why he hit her and treated her so bad? Greg had witnessed a fracas of sorts take place during the previous evening. Greg had gained a lot of information from Brian, though Greg was unsure about the credibility of the information that Brian had given him. After all, Brian told so many lies that he did not know what was fact and what was fiction!

Chapter Five

Greg had not slept very well for obvious reasons. Despite her age, Trace was a bit of a whore in bed and had managed to zap Greg's energy reserves. The sleep he did have was alcohol-induced. He was feeling rough. His focus would not allow him to think about anything other than Brian.

As Greg was drinking the last of his second cup of tea, he decided that he would send Karen a quick text. He picked up his mobile phone and began to type.

Good morning. Hope u had a great night and your reunion went OK? We must go out sometime. Talk 2 u soon. Greg. X

Greg hit the send option and put his mobile phone down. As it was Saturday, he went into the bathroom and had a shower. Once he had finished, he shaved, brushed his teeth and got dressed. Greg then made himself another cup of tea. As he sat down on his leather settee, his mobile phone bleeped. He picked up his mobile phone. It was Karen answering the message that Greg had sent her earlier.

It must be a good morning! Good 2 c u again. School friend OK! Luv 2 go out sumtime SOON! Will talk 2 u anytime. Karen. XXX

Greg smiled to himself. He thought that he might text Karen again later and find out how keen she really was.

Today was going to be a busy day. Firstly, he would have to go through his plan in his head and roughly work out timescales. He would have to find out which day would be best. People's routines intermingle with other people's daily life. So he did not want anything that he did to set off any alarm bells. He needed to get himself away from there as quickly as possible. He also had to get rid of anything that could link him to the crime. He would have to formulate a plan that was foolproof. Greg's mind was racing now.

'I must not leave any evidence. Those forensic scientists are clever bastards,' he reminded himself.

He needed to get himself a special outfit, something that would cling to him from top to bottom; made of a material that would be easily wiped clean. He would need to be able to simply wipe away any debris should any blood or bone fragments land on him. Greg gave careful attention to what he was going to wear on his feet.

'Boxing boots,' he said to himself.

The great thing about boxing boots is that the soles do not have any tread so it would not leave a patterned indentation – only a plain footprint.

Greg thought that was a brilliant idea. He would get himself some cheap, plain, dark jogging bottoms and one of those hooded tops that the young skateboarders wore. They did a great job of concealing your face and would hide the fact that Greg was wearing a mask. Greg would wear his outfit under his loose overgarments. The mask would require a lot of thought. It would have to be a mask that was both easy for Greg to put on and take off, though difficult for anyone else to try to pull off. The internet was a great source of information. Greg started to think about what he would wear on his hands. Gloves were the obvious choice. The only thing about wearing run of the mill gloves is that the forensic scientists were very clever in pinpointing a particular make of gloves from a single fibre. There was also the choice of surgical gloves. Or maybe the internet would supply him with an alternative.

Greg had to think of ways to make it as difficult as possible for the authorities to track him down and catch him. He would have to stagger his purchases of all the tools and weapons of his new-found trade.

He knew that he would have to overpower his victims so that they would not question his authority. He would have to take control and maintain that control throughout the ordeal. Fear would be his stealth.

Greg decided to drive to Brent Cross, a large shopping centre near Colindale, North London, which was next to the beginning of the M1. Brent Cross was a good place for Greg to buy the things he needed without sticking out from the crowd. Greg knew that he would have to be willing to travel and even alter his appearance as he may be caught on CCTV in the various shops and stores that he would have to visit. Greg would also have to visit some DIY stores as tools made very good weapons. He needed rope and some strong tape. He had heard that type of tape called duct tape, though that must have been from a film he had seen. He purchased a simple knife set for the kitchen. He would be able to use the various knifes, or at least his victims would use them.

Whilst at Brent Cross, Greg decided to have his hair cut – just a trim.

Greg was sitting in the barber's chair when he overheard a couple of guys talking about going to a fancy dress shop as they needed some costumes for a birthday party. Greg thought that the fancy dress shop could hold the answer for a couple of ideas that Greg had. He needed a mask and some props to help him change his appearance. Greg also planned to visit a few of the charity shops. You could find all kinds of great things in those kinds of shops, the kinds of things that Greg could use and the people that worked in those kinds of shops were all volunteers, semi-retired or even retired. He was confident that they would not remember him, though he still had to remember that more or less all shops now had CCTV installed.

Once the hairdresser had finished cutting Greg's hair, he brushed Greg's neck, took away the gown and gave Greg a tissue. This was all done in a single well-rehearsed move.

'That'll be twelve pounds please, sir!'

Greg gave the guy fifteen pounds.

'Keep the change. Buy yourself a beer tonight!' Greg said with a flashy tone in his voice.

The hairdresser looked at Greg. 'Thank you, sir. Enjoy the rest of your day!' and, without pausing for breath, the hairdresser turned away. 'Who's next?'

Once Greg was outside the hairdresser's he paused to get his bearings. After a few moments, Greg made his way to the fancy dress shop to research what they had to offer and the layout of the shop. Greg did not plan on purchasing anything else today; he wanted to know exactly where he was going to get his tools of the trade from. He needed to know the layout of each shop, so that he could pin point where the security cameras were, and conceal his true identity.

After a couple of hours, Greg returned to where he had parked his van. He had one more stop. It was on the way home anyway, so it was not out of his way. The place he wanted to visit was a very big DIY superstore. By this time, Greg was feeling very hungry, so he thought that he would also call in at McDonald's, though he never went through the drive-through as he felt they would tamper with your food. Greg always sat down and ate inside the restaurant.

Greg ordered his food, the young girl asked for payment, Greg obliged and the girl then gave him his order.

'Please enjoy your meal,' the young girl said.

The girl serving him looked and sounded as though she had missed her last couple years at school. Deep down, she must have regretted her stupidity and her deepest wish must be to turn the clock back.

Greg did not answer her. He just felt sorry for her. She was obviously working very hard and trying her best. Greg thought that she could not be any older than seventeen and she was on the minimum wage. That was what wound Greg up the most. All the money that the McDonald's Empire was making in pure profit and the way it showed appreciation to its loyal, hard-working staff was ripping them off! At least his job was well-paid and he did not have to work as hard as that poor young girl did – at least she was trying to contribute something back to society.

Greg sat down; his thoughts quickly changed to the journey of the day. He thought about the places he had been and then, all of a sudden, he began to laugh quietly to himself. He was thinking about the hairdresser that had cut his hair and how Greg had given him a three pound tip, and how the smile and thanks that Greg had received seemed to be false. Greg could not help thinking that the hairdresser was also unhappy in his job – maybe not unhappy in his job, unhappy in constantly having to chase the pound.

'How many haircuts would the hairdresser need to do before he started to make a profit?' he asked himself.

Greg thought that the next time he went there he would not give the guy a tip, though he would give him the same false smile and false gestures. Greg got pleasure from taking the piss out of ungrateful dickheads, as he liked to label them. He thought that people like that should be happy with what they had got because there were people out there with a hell of a lot less. Most people could only ever dream of working for themselves, having their own business.

'You never know what you've got till it's gone,' Greg thought to himself.

Once Greg had finished his meal, he cleared his own mess away, got back into his van and drove home.

As he was walking up the stairs to his flat his mobile phone beeped.

'Ah a message,' Greg said out loud, both his hangover and Trace now a distant memory.

As he got inside his flat, he took his phone from his pocket and selected to read his message.

Hello u! Wen we gonna av this drink then? Finkin bout u. K. xx

Greg decided that he would amuse himself by answering a question with a question; play a little game.

He selected the reply option and began to type.

Well then! Wenz OK 4 u 2 buy me this drink then? Who r ya? XX

Greg giggled to himself, as he pressed the send button on his phone because he knew what Karen's response was going to be. Karen liked the fact that Greg was always joking, though he never treated her as anything less than a goddess. Karen knew that Greg respected her and that was why she could not understand him ending the relationship.

Greg's phone bleeped very soon after he'd sent his message.

'Wow you're on the ball!' he said.

R u going 2 b thirsty L8er? xx Karen's message read.

Always thirsty on a Sat nite! Why? XX Greg replied.

Greg did not get a reply from Karen so he assumed that Karen had got bored with the game. Then, out of the blue, his phone rang. Greg picked it up and looked at the caller display to see if it was someone he knew.

The display read '*HOT KAREN calling*.' Greg had not changed the caller I.D. Greg smiled, and then answered the phone.

'Hello?'

'Who are ya?' the voice at the other end asked.

'Who's that?' Greg asked, pretending not to know who it was.

'You know who it is, you cheeky sod!' the voice snapped back.

'If you are planning to buy me a drink tonight that's not the way to greet me, is it?' Greg laughed down the phone.

Karen thought that he seemed very relaxed compared to when they had bumped in to each other on the train. Then, Greg had seemed as though he wanted to be anywhere else but on that train with Karen.

'Who said I wanted to buy you a drink?'

'You seem very keen!' Greg replied.

'What makes you think that?' Karen asked, as she giggled.

'I'm the one who was supposed to phone you, not the other way round,' Greg said answering Karen's question for the first time.

'Wow, you actually answered one of my questions! Anyway, if I waited for you, I'd be waiting forever,' Karen giggled.

'How keen are you?' Greg asked.

'Not overly keen. Just at a loose end,' Karen replied. Her tone suggested that she was toying with Greg.

'Well, this call must be costing you a bomb... mobile to mobile... across networks,' Greg stated with a sarcastic, juvenile tone to his voice.

'How do you know I haven't changed networks and kept my number?' Karen answered.

'Maybe you have. But it still doesn't hide the fact that you're keen,' Greg replied.

The conversation seemed to be going full circle.

'How do you know that?' Karen asked, trying to make Greg play her game.

'I know you, that's why,' Greg felt on the back foot, 'How do you know I'm still with the same network? I may have changed networks and kept my number,' Greg said quickly trying to turn Karen's earlier question back on her.

'Cos I know you. Anyway, enough of the games. Are we going for a drink tonight or what?' Karen asked. She was beginning to think about how much this phone call was going to cost her if Greg really had changed mobile phone networks.

'I don't know... Hmm, let me think...' Greg was still trying to continue the game.

'Greg!' Karen said, abruptly, 'this call is costing me an absolute bomb! It's a simple question.' She paused, thinking that she might scare him off, coming on too strong or maybe rushing things. But they had been here before and he knew her well enough. 'Where and what time shall we meet?'

'How about the Punch and Judy?' Greg replied knowing that Karen was being serious.

'New Covent Garden?' Karen replied, wondering why they could not meet somewhere nearer to home.

'Why not? It's nice there,' Greg tried to explain his choice.

'It'll be packed and we live close to each other, why not meet up nearer to home?' Karen said wanting not to travel too far. The truth was that she was feeling tired but it was Saturday night and she wanted to see Greg.

'OK, where then?' Greg asked.

'How about... The Broadway?' Karen replied once again answering a question with a question.

'Yeah,' Greg answered, 'we like it in there.'

'At least we'll be able to hear each other talk in there?' Karen replied.

The Broadway was a very nice pub located in Kingsbury, close to Wembley Park. Greg would catch a train from Wembley Park and be at Kingsbury Station ten minutes later.

'What time do you want me there?' Greg asked.

'Is half eight OK?' Karen replied.

'Sounds good to me… see you then.' Greg was now bored with the conversation and wanted to concentrate on other things.

'OK. Don't be late,' Karen said sounding cheerful.

'See you later – eight-thirty on the dot!' Greg confirmed, before terminating their telephone conversation.

***

Greg found himself consumed with Brian, Sharon and their baby. Greg had thought that there must be questions that he still needed to find answers to, though at the moment he was unable to think of any.

Greg's plan was to gain entry into the house when Brian was not at home. He knew that Brian went to the pub every night and did not get back until midnight. So Greg had decided that he would get to Brian's house at around ten o'clock and simply knock the front door. As Sharon opened the front door, Greg would barge his way in.

Greg had made a mental note that the front door did not have a spy-hole so there was no way that Sharon could see who was outside without opening the door. Greg knew that before then, he would have to visit the house to have a look at the local layout. He would need to make a detailed escape route in order to make his departure without being noticed.

He would also need to think of a way to overpower Sharon very quickly, and with the minimum of commotion. He decided on using a tactic that has been used many times by the police. He would simply go for a surprise attack, using his strength to force her back in to the house. The surprise element would be enough to get the fear factor he wanted. Deciding where to hold both Sharon and the baby until Brian got home from the pub was another quandary. He thought that playing this by ear was the best tactic. Then he would need to overpower and control Brian; brute force would be the way. Once Greg had achieved all this, he would then have to force Sharon to kill Brian. 'That,' Greg thought, 'would be the easy part.' He would simply place Sharon in a predicament. If she did not kill Brian, the consequences would outweigh the alternative. The path was already laid out for her – not for her, for her baby. Her maternal instincts would ensure that she put her baby first.

Greg had not planned further than that. He knew that he would have to see how events went and adapt.

His getaway plan was simple: to slip away into the shadows.

Greg did not plan on killing anyone. Both Sharon and the baby would be left alive. It would take Sharon a considerable amount of time before she mentally returned back to normal. Her mind would not be able to concentrate in a rational manner. Her focus would be lost – though her maternal instincts, along with her newfound ability for survival, would suck her back to reality. What she would do then would be any one's guess.

Greg did not intend to kill any of his victims. His victims would kill each other and there had to be survivors. It would be the survivors who would be the common link between Greg and the authorities. He needed to be careful. It would be those survivors who committed the murders, not Greg. With the lack of evidence, along with an almost invisible trail, the link between Greg, the survivors and their victims would be untraceable. Greg would need to remain anonymous.

His anonymity would always be intact – the costume and mask would ensure that his features were never revealed. Once in character, his voice would be that of his alter ego, as if the two people within him had come from completely different back grounds.

Greg thought that, in this case, the young baby would have a better start in life if its mother and father had no input in its upbringing. The father would be deceased and the mother would be safely locked away, at Her Majesty's Pleasure.

If the child were raised by either, or both, parents the child would end up a clone-like version of them. All the bad, inbred antisocial behaviour, neglect and turbulence would continue to fester and the cycle would continue. The poor child would not have a chance to integrate with modern society. After all, we do not choose our parents, they chose us. We have to work and make the best hand from the cards we are dealt. If we are dealt a bum hand, why not fold and demand a re-deal?

Chapter Six

Greg's mobile phone bleeped.

'Who's texting me now?' he thought. It was Karen.

Please meet me outside the pub. K. XXX

Greg thought that was a silly text as he would have expected to meet Karen outside the pub. But, knowing Karen as he did, he decided it would be better if he let her know that he was already planning to wait for her outside the tube station. He sent her a reply informing her of his plans.

His thoughts went back to Sharon, Brian and their baby. He couldn't get them out of his mind. He thought that the whole ordeal would have to be controlled by him even down to how long it would take from start to finish. Time, though, was on his side.

Brian would get home at around midnight; Greg would have to work fast to ensure everything was in place for his return. Though not too fast, otherwise Brian would not be truly sorry. Once Brian had returned home, it would be Sharon who would need to take control – she would be Brian's executioner. That was if she had the nerve. It was a gamble, but Greg knew what she would do.

Brian would need to suffer maximum discomfort along with excruciating pain before he died. Brian needed to understand why this punishment was being dealt to him, why it was in this way and why the mother of his child was his killer. There had to be a purpose to it all.

When Sharon was later questioned by the police, she would have to explain why a complete stranger had forced his way into their house and forced Sharon to kill the father of her child. The fate of both Sharon and the child was in the hands of the authorities.

Greg would need to make Sharon understand all of this, before Brian's imminent demise.

Greg glanced at the watch on his wrist and realized that it was time he started to make himself something to eat before having a shower and meeting Karen. He had not given any thought as to what to wear. He had not done any ironing for nearly a week now and the heap of creased clothes was piling up.

Greg decided that he would find the easiest things to iron. It was not as if he needed to impress Karen, after all they had done this once before and Greg was not going to let Karen come on all heavy. It was just a casual sexual relationship and Greg was going to let Karen know that, though in his own subtle way.

Chapter Seven

Greg was already outside the tube station when Karen arrived.

She had the look on her face that suggested that she had got the cream and was not sure if what was happening was real – it all seemed real enough. Greg was there, looking as dapper and as handsome as he always had done, in Karen's eyes anyway.

'You're eager,' Karen said, as she approached her date.

'No, Karen, you're normally late!'

Greg took Karen's hand, leading the way, as they both made a beeline across the busy main road, dodging the oncoming traffic.

Kingsbury was busy, bustling like the rest of the outskirts of the capital. Most pubs, clubs and restaurants centred around the busy tube station. Kingsbury Road served as the main thoroughfare through the town.

The Broadway Public House sat almost opposite the busy tube station. Situated next door to an impressive multiplex cinema, which boasted twelve separate screens. As the couple arrived outside their destination, Karen looked at Greg, readying herself to say something.

'Let's get inside. It's too noisy out here!' Greg said, whilst he opened the door to the public bar.

As they walked towards the bar, Greg nudged Karen.

'What are you drinking?'

'White wine, please.'

'OK, small or large?'

'Large of course,' Karen smiled.

As they reached the bar, after navigating their way through the bustling crowed – Greg started to wave a twenty pound note in the air in order to attract the attention of one of the bar staff – it worked.

'Yes, mate,' one of the barmen asked.

Greg ordered a couple of drinks, paid the barman, then turned to face Karen.

'Shall we find a table and sit down?' Karen asked feeling a little enclosed, the bar area was crowded, with no elbow room.

'Yeah, good idea.'

Greg followed Karen to a table situated in the corner of the bar. They sat down.

'I want us to lay down some foundations Karen,' Greg said, as the pair sat.

Karen gave a puzzled look, though did not answer.

'I want to take it slow... I don't want anything heavy... No repeat of where we went wrong... Am I making sense? Bloody hell, this is hard!' Greg took a gulp a beer.

'Why complicate things, Greg. Let's take it a day at a time. I know that I smothered you, and that was why you finished with me.'

'You...' Greg tried.

'Hold on a moment. If you want something casual, that's cool. But, if we are going to be shag-buddies, then you only shag me, and I only shag you. I don't want you shagging any other birds, is that clear? They'll be no bed-hopping Greg! I don't want you giving me an STD or anything else for that matter.'

Greg was shocked. It was as though she had read his mind.

'That's exactly what I want. Not the bed-hopping, I just don't want us living in each other's pockets. It's not as if we own each other, but we aren't having an open relationship either.'

'So you want a casual relationship without the strings or the infidelity?'

'Yeah, that's exactly what I want, if that makes sense?'

'To me it does – as long as we understand each other.'

They both chinked their glasses and kissed. The pair enjoyed talking about everything and nothing. As the conversation deepened, Greg and Karen completely lost track of time, forgetting if either of them may have wanted to go on to another pub – the area was awash with quaint establishments. The little bubble they had been locked in burst when the barman rang the bell for last orders.

'Do you want another one for the road?' Greg asked Karen.

'No thanks. But you go ahead if you want one.'

'Nah, I won't have another on my own,' he smiled, 'I've had enough to drink for one night.'

There was a pause, an uncomfortable silence. Someone had to ask the question. Greg decided that as he was the man, it had better be him.

'Do you fancy coming back to mine?'

'OK,' Karen replied. 'I suppose we'd better consummate our shag-buddy type of relationship,' she said giggling with a sheepish smile.

They stood up, left the pub and headed for the tube station, hand in hand.

'Are you hungry?' Greg asked.

'No, I'm fine, are you?'

'Nah, I thought I'd be a gentleman, that's all.'

'What, and offer me a kebab?' Karen laughed.

'They sell burgers too,' Greg replied, joining her laughter.

They continued their journey to the tube station and boarded the train that was already waiting at the platform. During the short journey, they both sat close to one another in silence, arms wrapped firmly, kissing at intervals. No need for conversation.

As the train stopped at Wembley Park Tube Station, Greg waited for Karen to step out of the carriage first. He followed her closely, eyeing up her firm buttocks.

The walk from the tube station to Greg's flat would normally take approximately ten minutes. Though they were not in any particular hurry.

'It could be worse,' Karen said.

'What? It could be raining!' Greg replied, patting Karen's bottom.

'No,' Karen smiled. 'It could be snowing,' she replied, patting Greg on his bottom.

The pair continued walking down Bridge Road, the long hill from the station made the walk pleasurable. Navigating their way across the main road, they arrived at the entrance to Greg's flat.

Walking through a gap between two high walls where a gate used to be, they followed a path that led to the main communal doors. It was covered by security cameras – although they had never worked and were mainly there as a deterrent. At least the intercom worked.

Using his key, Greg opened the main door and pressed the energy-saving timer switch with his elbow whilst he held the door with his other hand.

'Forever the gentleman,' Karen commented, giving a squeaky giggle.

'Some things never change,' Greg smiled.

'The same can be said for people,' Karen quipped.

'People change, it's only to what degree,' Greg smirked.

Once the pair had reached the front door to Greg's flat, they paused.

'You don't have to stay. It's not…' Greg began.

'I'm here and I do want to stay and, yes, I know it's not too late to change my mind.' Karen kissed Greg on his lips. 'Second time round so it's not unchartered territory for either of us, is it?'

'Like we agreed, one day at a time.'

Greg inserted his key into the lock, turned it clockwise and pushed. The door opened; Greg paused, allowing Karen to walk in.

'I don't think the old place has changed too much?' Greg said, closing the door behind him using his right heel.

Karen had already switched on a couple of lamps in Greg's living room and sat down before he joined her.

'What would you like to drink?' Greg asked, smiling at Karen.

'Nothing. Take me to bed and have your wicked way.'

Karen stood and waited for her man to approach – her heart raced, pumping faster and faster.

Greg could feel his manhood swelling, his heart beating louder than a bass drum. They met half way across the living room and began to kiss passionately. Greg gently took Karen's hand and led her into his bedroom. She had been here before. Privately, she remembered the first time – she shivered like a nervous twig, afraid and excited by what he might do. These were joyous memories, memories of finding womanhood, finding her inner-self.

Once they entered the bedroom, they paused and looked at each other, admiring the view.

'Kiss me,' Karen commanded, in a soft tone.

They kissed with tremendous passion, undressing each other as though the stop watch was ticking. They fell on the bed and made love.

Chapter Eight

The sound of the radio woke Karen from a restful sleep.

'Good morning. Did you sleep well?' Greg politely enquired.

'Yes, I did – did you?'

'Not bad. I forgot you snore though,' Greg laughed.

'No I don't, you cheeky sod. Where's my tea?' Karen snarled, giving Greg a playful slap across his back.

'On its way, would you like any breakfast?'

'Nah, just tea please. Thanks for last night Greg – no regrets?'

'Not a single one. I'd forgotten how good I was,' he tried to lighten the subject and redirect it.

'Oh that... I'd forgotten about that. It doesn't stick in my memory,' she laughed.

'Ha, ha, you're not funny. What are your plans for today?' Greg had plans of his own, and time was of the essence.

'I had forgotten how comfortable your bed was, nothing else.' Her laughter had now diluted to a big smile. 'I'm going to take my mum out for some lunch.'

'That must involve some form of shopping, knowing your mum.'

'No, she's going to the cemetery first. So I'm going to meet up with her.'

'How long is it now?'

'It still feels like it was yesterday, the way Mum carries on.'

'I didn't mean it like that. I was only asking...'

'Oh sorry... I know. It just gets too much.'

'Hey, let's forget I asked. Now shut up and drink your tea.' Greg tried to lift the conversation by sending a wink Karen's way.

Karen responded by sticking her tongue out then winking back at him. They took turns using the shower, Greg shaving whilst Karen showered. When they were both ready to face the outside world, Greg kissed Karen.

'See you soon,' Greg smiled.

'OK. Thanks again stud. I had a great night!'

'Go on then, you'd better piss off,' he said whilst her gave her a kiss on the lips.

Karen gave Greg a knowing look – the kind of look that confirmed she was at ease with things.

The door closed and she was gone.

Greg concentrated on doing his normal Sunday morning domestic chores and then he spent the whole of Sunday afternoon on the internet. He had found a website that allowed you to download aerial maps of whatever area you wanted. This would prove to be invaluable, as he would be able to plot his getaway route.

Greg's mobile bleeped. It was a text message from Karen:

Thanx Pee Wee xx

He laughed. Deciding not to reply and returned to his work.

Greg needed to set up some kind of timeframe. He had thought about this quite a lot. Though he would not be wearing a watch, he would still need to keep it militarized. It was a time governed exercise.

Greg was astonished when he glanced at the clock. He had been sitting there for hours. He could not understand where the time had gone. It had flown by. He quickly set about choosing what he was having for dinner. Lunch had passed without notice. He put two large potatoes in the oven and decided to have another shower to clear his head. He needed to think of a way to commit his first crime and be sure that his alibi was completely watertight. He could not think of anything else.

'That's it,' he said to himself whilst looking at his reflection in the bathroom mirror, 'I'll invite Karen over for dinner, slip some sleeping pills in her food and Bob's your uncle!'

He decided that he would have Karen stay over for the night. That way, he could drug her and have enough time to slip out, put his plan in to action and return home. If questioned, Karen would swear blind that he had been with her all night.

'You're a genius, and handsome too,' he told himself.

Karen was a deviation from the original plan. Now he was seeing Karen, a few things would have to change. Progress dictates change.

Greg had also decided, during doing his internet research, that he was going to get most of the tools he needed from eBay. By doing this he could cover his tracks. There were account settings where he could keep his purchases private – allowing him to bid anonymously.

***

During the following weeks that passed, it appeared to the outside world as everything was normal but, behind the scenes, things were ticking along nicely for Greg. He had obtained a number of necessary items and also been able to do a few dummy runs and accurately time them. Everything was now in place, he felt ready. He was ready.

He thought about the French serial killer and tried to imagine how he felt. Greg knew his crimes were premeditated but the Frenchman's had not started that way. Greg imagined himself as nomadic; a truly individual vigilante. He tried to think and cover every angle, every eventuality that he thought might happen.

'Not long now,' he told himself, as he looked at his masked reflection in the mirror.

Chapter Nine

Greg pressed the speed-dial on his mobile and waited for the person on the other end to answer.

'Hello,' said a feminine voice.

'Hello, Karen. What are you up to this Saturday, any plans?'

'Nothing solid planned, only shopping with Mum. We're going up Oxford Street during the day. Why? What do you have in mind?'

'So you're free in the evening?'

'I most certainly am,' her fake casualness barely concealed her eager anticipation.

'I was thinking of inviting you over to mine. I thought it was about time I cooked for you. What do you say?' Greg enjoyed the way Karen tried to play her harmless games.

'What... you cook for me?' Astonishment echoed in her voice.

'Yeah, I'll cook for you. Try not to sound so shocked,' he laughed. 'What do you think?'

'I think it's a great idea. I'll stay the night if you like. You cooking for me?' she giggled, 'I can't believe it... let me get a tape recorder!'

'You're not funny. I don't know why you try to be funny. You should leave that to the professionals like me.'

'Who told you that you were funny?'

'You did.'

'It must have been at a weak moment, or maybe I was just being kind,' she giggled.

'Are we on for Saturday?' Greg did not have time for this.

'Yes, course we are! What are you going to cook me then?'

'Firstly, is there anything that you don't eat?' Greg was hoping that Karen had not done anything silly, like stopped eating meat.

'I've cut down on red meat, though I've not cut it out completely.'

'That's not a problem. So that's settled then. Oh you'll just have to wait and see. I hope you'll be impressed.'

'What time should I get to yours then?'

'Six, or there about, is that OK?'

'Sounds great, I can't wait. I'd better bring my camera,' she said laughing.

'You're still not even slightly funny. Remember, I'm the funny one.'

'If you say so.'

'I don't know why you're still laughing, I might surprise you.'

'I'll see you Saturday, Gordon,' she said, referring to Gordon Ramsay.

'But it's heavens kitchen in my flat, love.'

'OK, I'll place my digestive system in your hands,' her giggles returned.

'See you Saturday then,' Greg replied softy.

'I'm looking forward to it already.'

With that, he hung up.

***

Greg had decided to cook chicken in an aromatic sauce. The sauce would act as a smokescreen for the sleeping tablets that he was going to put in her food. He had already decided against putting anything in her wine as this could prove to be tricky, as well as high risk. What if, after a few, he drank from the wrong glass? What if she noticed? Far too many risks. By drugging her food he could be sure that she had ingested the required dosage. The marinade would ensure that she would not be able to taste anything untoward. He had a lot to do.

Saturday arrived in record time. Watching *Soccer AM* with his mug of tea, he was not concentrating on what was actually going on on the television, he was miles away. Tonight was the night. He was ready, ready to start his reign.

Greg decided to spend the remainder of the morning and much of the afternoon preparing for the evening's events and the night that was to follow. He marinated the chicken and placed it in the oven at medium temperature. He was careful to make two separate marinades, one of them had an extra special ingredient. He prepared all the vegetables. A simple prawn cocktail would suffice as a starter, with ice cream for dessert. Two bottles of wine were chilling nicely in the fridge.

Greg then decided that he would need to sort his kit out for when he went to Brian's house. He had been able to purchase an all-in-one PVC suit from a guy in Belgium, via an auction website. This also avoided the need for gloves, as the body suit covered his hands. He had gone with his original idea of wearing black leather boxing boots. His mask was an absolutely amazing find. Following his purchase of the PVC body suit, he asked the seller if he knew anywhere that did masks. The seller gave Greg the information of his contact in the United States. Greg could not believe his luck. These people e-mailed him a catalogue of all the kinds of masks that they supplied. Greg had e-mailed them back with his exact requirements. Within the quoted time, Greg received the mask and, to his amazement, the mask was exactly as it had been described – like a second skin.

Greg had also managed to source some sleeping tablets from the dark side of the world wide web. Although the only medicated sleep-enhancing drug he was able to purchase, with no-questions asked, were only to be used by veterinary surgeons. Further investigations revealed other medical suppliers who practiced the same no-questions business ethos.

Greg had taken time to complete a handful of costume changes and dress rehearsals, timing them on every occasion. The only thing that was worrying Greg was how hot he would become if in costume for longer than planned. Indeed, he would need to exert a certain amount of physical force. His adrenalin and blood pressure would kick in and escalate. He would have to be careful not to overheat or dehydrate. Maintaining his health would be vital to keeping a calm state of mind and optimum brain function.

***

Greg stood in front of his ironing board, wondering how long Karen would be knocked out for. He did not know how much of an effect the sleeping tablets would have on her. Maybe he should have had a dummy run.

'No,' he thought firmly.

There was no way. Nothing would delay his plans. He did not want to put it off any longer.

***

Karen walked up the main doors and pressed the intercom button for Greg's flat.

'Hurry up, I'm starving,' she laughed into the intercom.

'Come on up, greedy,' Greg responded. His hands shook with excitement.

Karen opened the door, allowing it to close behind her. Walking up the stairs, she started to sing, though not loudly. It was a song that she had heard on the radio – a song that was being played over and over.

As she stepped out of the elevator, she noticed Greg was already waiting for her, standing in his doorway.

'Hiya,' Greg greeted, giving Karen a peck on the cheek.

'Hello you, what you been up to today?'

'I've been busy cooking and preparing for tonight, why?'

'Just being nosey… is that OK?' She smiled.

'Course it is. How did the shopping go?'

'Going shopping with my mum was a stupid idea. Oxford Street was manic. I could not move. Tourists everywhere you looked. I'd had enough after five minutes, but you know my mum and her marathon shopping expeditions.'

'Sounds like you could do with a drink. What do you fancy?'

'What's on offer Pee Wee?'

'Don't start that again,' Greg joked. They both laughed.

'Let me think,' Karen replied, as she took her shoes off.

'Are you going to let me know what you want to drink or not?'

'I fancy a cold beer. Have you got any?'

'Yes, of course I have.'

Greg returned with a cold bottle of beer in one hand and a glass in the other.

'Here you go.'

Karen poured the contents slowly in to the glass, she then took a big gulp.

'Looks like you needed that,' Greg smirked.

'That's just the ticket. Cheers. Aren't you having one?' she asked, before taking another thirsty sip.

'Yeah, I think I'll join you,' he laughed, 'I've got mine in the kitchen.'

'You'd better bring me another, if that's OK. I've almost finished this one.'

'No worries,' Greg replied from the kitchen.

'Shall I put some music on?' Karen asked before an involuntary belch escaped.

Greg did not reply, his mind was elsewhere... Not long now. 'If she continues to knock the booze back like this, she'll be out cold for hours,' he said to himself, out of Karen's earshot.

Standing in the kitchen, his nostrils took in a waft of the chicken that was slowly cooking in the oven. The marinade was potent by now and he felt his taste buds salivate. He quickly checked the progress of the chicken – making sure that Karen's chicken looked exactly the same as his. There was no difference to the naked eye.

'Shopping with my mum is enough to drive anyone to drink,' Karen said loudly, making her voice heard over the music she had selected.

'There's plenty more where that came from. So kick back, and chill out,' Greg said walking back in to the living room. 'Jamiroquai, excellent choice,' he smiled.

'You are an angel when you wanna be,' Karen commented, blowing a kiss.

They continued drinking and talking. Greg was on tremendous form. Karen could not remember laughing this much for a long time.

'Right... prawn cocktail to start, madam. Please be seated,' Greg playfully announced, inviting Karen to the small dining table, trying his best to mimic a comedy waiter.

Karen followed Greg's instruction, taking her drink with her. She enjoyed this side of Greg's personality.

Greg's flat was too small for a full-size dining table. He had found his miniature version in a camping shop. Although he was used to eating his food on his lap, when he had company for diner, he always got his mini dining table out.

The pair were completely relaxed in each other's company. Greg decided to continue his comedy sketch – awkward moments never arose.

'Prawn cocktail, hey? You have been a busy boy.'

'Enjoy,' he said, handing her the starter in a controlled clumsy manner. 'I can speak English,' he smiled, 'I read it in a book.'

'This is delicious,' Karen said, between her bouts of laughter.

'Why thank you, madam.'

'What's that other smell coming from the kitchen?'

'You'll have to wait and see.'

Once they had finished their starters, Greg took the empty dishes away and returned with their main courses. Karen could not believe her eyes. The smell took her back to Spain. She knew that for someone who was trying to be casual about their rekindled relationship, Greg had worked very hard to impress her and gone to a lot of trouble. She also knew that the only way she could return the favour would be to cook for Greg. As she still lived at home, this was completely out of the question – her mother would continuously interrupt them. She adored her mother, though sometimes her overpowering nature was smothering.

'Here you are madam – compliments of the chef,' Greg said, placing Karen's main course in front of her, followed by another cold bottle of beer. 'I hope you like it, if it tastes funny let me know. You see, chef has never cooked this before, so...'

'Stop flapping,' she said as she took her first taste of the chicken. 'This is beautiful. I have never tasted chicken like this before,' Karen was genuinely astonished.

The texture of the almost sweet marinade danced across her taste buds. The chicken flaked and then melted on her tongue. The asparagus, surrounded by button mushrooms, accompanied the dish superbly.

'Excellent, I'm glad you like it. I was worried that I might have cocked it up,' Greg joked.

The relief that Karen could not taste the sleeping tablets, which he had secretly crushed into the marinade, had made him feel proud. This was working. She was eating the contents of the dish with unreserved enthusiasm.

They continued eating and filling the gaps with small talk – reminiscing about times gone by.

Once they had both finished eating, Greg took the empty dishes back to the kitchen.

'I haven't got anything much for pudding. I hope you don't mind?'

'Greg, I couldn't eat another crumb, honestly,' Karen replied, yawning.

'You tired?' he asked, already knowing her answer.

'Yeah. I dunno what's come over me. Being dragged around Oxford Street must have taken its toll,' Karen replied, shrugging her shoulders and slurring her words slightly.

'All that shopping with your mum, hey?' Greg smiled, returning a shrug of his shoulders.

'Yeah, I suppose your right.'

'Would you like another beer, or something else?'

'Oh, go on then. I hope you're not trying to get me drunk so that you can take advantage of me,' she replied, yawning again.

'I don't need to get you drunk to do that. Anyway you're too knackered aren't you?'

'Sorry… and…' she was unable to finish her sentence, another yawn had interrupted her in mid flow.

Greg walked back in to the living room carrying two cold bottles of beer.

'What time is it?' Karen asked.

'Almost twenty past ten.'

'Don't call me a lightweight.'

'Lightweight!' Greg interrupted.

'Thank you, I think I'll drink this and go to bed, if that's OK.' She was far too tired to appreciate Greg's humour. Disappointment was written all over her face.

Greg knew that she had been a little optimistic in thinking that she would stay awake long enough to finish her beer.

'Oops,' she slurred, almost dropping her drink.

'Come on let's get you tucked up in bed.'

'Sorry Greg, but I'm too tired for sex. Is that OK?'

'Yeah, course it's OK. You can make up for it another time,' he giggled.

Greg helped Karen in to the bedroom, allowing her to visit the bathroom on the way. He was not too bothered that she had neglected to brush her teeth. He wanted her in bed, asleep and off his hands.

Greg waited a short time, making sure that Karen was truly out for the night. He collected his large holdall and carried it to his van, placing it in the back, being sure not to make too much noise. Greg did not want to attract any attention. He had already decided that he was going to change once he had reached his destination, he couldn't afford to be noticed now.

There was plenty of room in the back of his van. He swiftly popped back inside the flat, just to make sure Karen was safely unconscious, then checked that everything was as it should be.

As it was now only twenty to eleven, Greg decided to wash all the pots and pans that were all over the kitchen. He then left the flat, closing the door gently so that it would not be heard by any of his neighbours. He got in, turned the ignition key and the van's engine fired up immediately. With a quick glance at the clock on the dashboard, he quietly drove away.

Greg deliberately parked his van two streets away from Tinckerton Street, so that it would not be spotted by any potential eyewitnesses, should the police carry out routine door-to-door enquiries.

He slipped into the back and removed all his clothes and

jewellery, until he was completely naked. He did not realise how tight the suit would feel now that the adrenalin was rushing through his body. He wanted the sweat to stop, it was hindering his progress. As he tied the laces, his hand shook. He tried counting slowly in order to slow himself down. His boxing boots were an excellent fit; he was careful not to put them on too tightly. He paused, looking at his trembling hands.

'Once I leave this van, there's no turning back,' he told himself. 'Am I sure?' he pondered. 'Fucking right I am! Time to slip in to character...'

Chapter Ten

Greg collected the tools he was going to need: two hammers, two knives, a meat cleaver, two sets of handcuffs and pepper spray. He had thrown the keys to the handcuffs away. He had no intention of releasing whoever wore them. He closed the door as quietly as he could, pressing the lock button on the key fob.

Staying in the shadows, Greg quickly made his way to Tinckerton Street, and then to number 54. As he approached the front door, pausing for a moment, he rang the door bell. No answer. He rang it again.

'She never goes out,' he thought.

He heard footsteps. The noise of the lock turning, etched a grin on his face.

'Who is it?' a gentle feminine voice asked as the door opened.

'It's the fucking grim reaper!' Greg said, purposely for effect.

The accent he had adopted was distinct and recognisably middle class. He pushed the door with his shoulder. The momentum forced Sharon backward, she lost her balance. She bounced off one of the walls in the hallway; the gravity sucked her to the floor. The whole thing had happened in a blur.

Greg wasted no time. He quickly bundled Sharon back in to the living room, pushing her with short, sharp jolts, though without any real force. She was not the true victim. Greg had impressed himself by how quiet he had kept her.

Once inside, Greg returned to close the front door with a swift kick. The door slammed. The neighbours would have become accustomed to this kind of noise if Brian had told the truth about their fights. Despite the bullshit, Greg had chosen to believe Brian on this occasion.

'Sit Down,' Greg barked. 'Where's the baby?'

Sharon pointed to another room. Her hand shook – she was far too petrified to speak. Her whole body trembled, consumed by fear. Sweat dripped its way down her back as goosebumps made the hairs on her arms stand up. She shivered.

'OK, Sharon, this is the drill. I'm not here to hurt you or your baby, but you must do as I say. Do you understand?'

She managed to nod. Fear surged through her body. Urine escaped without warning as it trickled its way down the inside of her legs.

'We're going to keep the noise level to a minimum, and that way we'll get on famously,' Greg continued to survey his surroundings.

Sharon simply nodded frantically, not knowing what was happening. She looked up at the silhouette – a male silhouette: medium height with an impressive athletic build. She could not work out what it was that the man under the silhouette was wearing, a kind of shiny black all-in-one suit. She tried to make sense of his face. Once she was able to focus through her tears, she saw that a mask was covering his true identity. She had seen her fair share of horror films, but she had never seen a mask like this before. It was as though it had been surgically implanted. A batman type of tool belt clung to his waist.

'It's plain to see that Brian knocks the fuck out of you. Isn't that so?'

She nodded frantically in agreement.

'How long do you think you can allow this to continue?'

'I don't know,' she squeaked sounding like the teenager she really was.

'It's up to you Sharon,' Greg noticed a clock sitting on top of the television. Time was ticking away from him. 'Would you like to get even or escape?'

This time she glared at Greg.

'Answer the fucking question.' He did not have time to pussyfoot around.

'What, are you here to save me from Brian?' her voice shook. 'Yes, yes! OK… Sorry… Please don't hurt my baby!' Sharon blurted out.

'Now we are getting somewhere. No, Sharon, I'm here to offer you the chance to save your baby. I'm going to offer you the opportunity to get your own back tonight. If you do as I say, I promise that I will not hurt any member of this household.'

'But I love him.'

'Tonight, Sharon, you are going to kill Brian.'

There was a heavy silence.

'How can I kill him? He's my baby's father,' she seemed confused.

'To stop being abused and to save your baby.'

Sharon became hysterical. Greg slapped her, though not firmly, more for effect than impact. She was stunned, her noise stopped.

She spoke. 'Why do I have to kill him? Why can't I just leave him?'

'Vengeance is yours. I bet you've thought about retaliating, but it is fear that stops you. It's that fear that stops you from venting your frustration. You no longer need to fear Brian; tonight you will turn the table on him. He will fear you.'

'What if I won't kill him? I don't know if I can!' her voice shook.

'You need to search deep within yourself; find the courage to stop all this. What I'm offering you and your baby is a way out, away from his evil neglect. You kill him and you'll both be free.'

Sharon was trapped – the rock and the hard place had become very uncomfortable. The choice was hers to make, there was no way out for her and she knew it.

'What has this go to do with you? I'm fucked no matter what I choose,' she rambled.

'I'm simply thinking of your baby; your baby's future. A future with Brian in it doesn't bear thinking about, you don't even want to contemplate it. Sharon it's an obvious choice. His actions have consequence. He needs to be punished.'

'I don't know if I can do it.' She urinated for a second time.

'Grow a fucking back bone! The shit's going to hit the fan when he gets home. How you choose to direct that shit, Sharon, should be your only concern. Protect your baby's future Sharon.'

'OK then… what should I do?' a whisper hissed from her lips.

Brian had never allowed her to make a decision herself, he bullied her – she was struggling. Her mind flickered, jumping from the broken sentences she was trying to make. Her emotions leaped as she felt her heart snap under the strain of the strings being pulled in every direction.

'Everything begins with choice, Sharon!' The calmness in his voice shot through her. 'I'm not here to choose for you, that's something you have to do,' he lied; he had no intention of letting Brian go.

'I don't think I have a choice… I don't want to do it, but I have to.'

'As you already know, Brian will be home soon. You can set your watch by him – very predictable. I'll get him into a safe state and the rest will be up to you.'

'How am I supposed to kill him, he's bigger than me?' her voice trembled as the reality of what she was about to do sunk in.

'You can use this hammer or this meat cleaver. Choice shapes everything Sharon. Your next choice is forever. What'll it be?' Greg asked, showing her the two objects.

'Fucking hell… I don't know. How do you know whether I can even do it?'

'If you don't, the stakes increase – Brian or your baby? Learn to live, or live to die, those are the choices. Quick choices have to be made.'

'Listen, I'm sorry for whatever Brian has done to you,' her saddened heart collapsed, 'but I know that he loves me; it's all my fault,' she sobbed, 'I should be a better person. He's the way he is because of me, he tells me that all the time.' Her bleeding heart weighed heavy. 'I can protect my baby. He would never hurt our baby.' Her ramblings only made her sobbing worse. 'I have always protected my baby from him. I can take whatever he gives me but I know you're right…'

'Brian or the baby?

Sharon looked up, astonished by her understanding of the threatening ultimatum she had just been delivered.

'Make a choice,' Greg snarled.

'Give me the hammer… I'll do it with the fucking hammer!' she snapped.

'That's more like it.'

'I have to protect my baby,' she repeated this like a mantra.

'That decision has changed your life. It will change the life of so many.'

Then followed a brief interlude of silence. Sharon had not thought about what would happen to her and her baby once she had murdered Brian. Greg had not allowed her the time. She had realised that she no longer loved Brian, though she tried fooling herself. She was beginning to look upon the man in the shiny suit as her saviour. He was giving her a way out, a way to stop the beatings and the abuse. Greg looked into the room where Sharon had indicated her baby was. Totally oblivious, the baby was sleeping deeply.

'If we keep the noise down, the nipper might sleep through all of this,' Greg said, closing the door to the room that separated the little soul from its mother's nightmare.

'Are you sick?' Sharon asked struggling to process it all.

'No, Sharon. It's you, and scum like you, who are sick. Why does Brian beat you and then fuck you? Why do you let him treat you like shit? You're the sick bastards not me!'

'If I didn't let him fuck me, he'd rape me… I can't control him, he's too strong.'

'What a sad existence for you and for your baby. You let a man who you don't love fuck you. You gave life to his child for fuck's sake, and you allow him to treat you like this – like shit! Is this the role model you want for your baby? The template for your baby's normalcy?' Greg knew he had struck a chord.

'What else am I supposed to do?'

'You look for a way out; you find your escape. You do exactly what you are about to do.'

'You are fucking sick!' Sharon trembled.

'We're not going over that again; remember promises can be broken... I could start with the youngest and work my way up. Well, I don't have to spell it out to you, do I?'

Sharon glared at Greg. He had forced her into her own personal hell. She felt trapped; there was no way out.

'I want to wake up from this bloody nightmare now.' Sharon was exhausted, worn down by it all. She knew that it was not going to end for a very, very long time. 'Forever is a long time,' she mumbled.

'You're not dreaming. This is all very real. You're going to have to deal with it; face it with open eyes and clear vision. Your choice has been made and you made it. Don't live with regrets. Live knowing that you saved your baby's life and your own.'

Silence filled the air as they both heard a key being pushed in to the keyhole. Greg pointed at Sharon.

'Promises and choices. Don't you make a fucking sound,' he told her as he quickly made his way to the front door.

The front door opened slowly as the drunken man wrestled with the lock. He was struggling to retrieve his key. Seeing double hampered his vision.

'Fucking shitty lock,' he burbled, his aggressive speech slurred. Brian finally yanked the key from the lock and stumbled backwards. He closed the door with an aggressive push, almost losing his balance in the process.

'Hey!' Greg said, in his middle class voice with a startling effect.

Brian turned to see where the greeting had come from. His intoxicated state of mind did not allow him to instantly recognise the owner's voice.

As Brian turned his head, he was blinded by a mass propulsion of liquid being forced in to his eyes.

'ARRHHHHH!' he screamed, 'What the fuck's going on?'

His question was unanswered.

'Brian?' Sharon called.

'This fucking stuff stings... I can't breathe! Help me Shazza!' His pleas were all in vain.

'Shut up,' Greg said calmly.

'You're fucking dead, you wanker!' The pain was evident in Brian's threat. He was still trying to act the big man.

Greg had heard enough and gave Brain a couple of sharp blows to his chest, using his clenched right fist. Brian fell to the floor with a thud. Greg rolled him over on to his stomach and, in a single manoeuver, pulled both his hands behind his back and handcuffed him. Brian continued to scream, puffing and panting, fighting to regain his breath.

Greg then put two layers of industrial tape on Brian's mouth. Brian was whimpering by now. The pain he was suffering had taken him to a dark, terrifying place. His eyes burned, he found it difficult to breathe and his nose was partially blocked from all the snot and mucus. The handcuffs had been applied tightly and he could feel pins and needles in the tips of his fingers. As he was knocked down by Greg's thundering blows, he banged his head on the radiator in the hallway.

Sharon had almost begun to feel sorry for Brian as she saw him lying there helpless, powerless and at the mercy of his fate. Until her memories of the beatings, along with the unlimited abuse she had received from the hands of this man, the father of her child, came flooding back with a sharp jolt.

'You have been treating Sharon like shit for far too long. Retribution is the order of the day here, Brian,' Greg paused, 'Sharon has been told her options and has made her own informed choice.'

Brian was trying to talk but the industrial tape was serving its purpose. Sharon remained silent.

'Make peace with your god, your demons and yourself Brian... Today is your last!'

Brian began to scream louder, his crying made his sorrowful existence seem putrid. Brian tried cowering away, wanting to blend in to his background and make himself as small as possible.

'Sharon,' Greg barked. 'Do it!' he ordered as he passed her a hammer.

Sharon took the hammer from Greg with both hands as she

weakly stood up, stunned by her own willingness to complete her task.

'What do you want me to do?' she asked in a quivering tone, 'I don't understand…' She had begun to cry, more than before.

'FINISH HIM!'

Sharon stood, surrounded by an almost pathetic aura. Shaking, quivering uncontrollably, her body started to shiver.

'Promises and choices Sharon. Do I have to remind you?'

Brian was still trying to plead for his life, although his words were unintelligible. He was completely wasting his time and making this harder for Sharon.

Sharon bravely stood over Brian looking at him, her vision transfixed on his cowering body. It didn't feel real.

Brain was trying to manipulate her, using cowardly body language. Greg took a step back. After all, this was Sharon's time.

'You fucking coward! I hate you.'

Those words gently tumbled from her mouth in a whisper. She took a deep breath and swung the hammer, griping it with both hands. A half-hearted, effortless attempt bounced off Brian's left shoulder. He screamed, more with shock than pain from the hammer's blow.

She looked at Greg, then at Brian once more. This time, she swung the hammer above her head and sent it crushing down on to the back of Brian's skull. Brian squealed. Her heart was trying to force its way out of her chest. Brian's body flipped over as electromagnetic pulses ran through his veins. Sharon raised the hammer again and screamed as she lowered it at speed. It was more of a wail of pleasure, pleasure at the release. She could not have agreed with the man in the PVC suit more, this was her statement; this was her fight for her own justice. Brian's body convulsed, sending him in to an epileptic fit. His body quivered totally out of control. As his body slowed and stopped, a smell filled the room as he lost control of his bowels. The urine rushed from his penis saturating his jeans. The hot urine was pungent. Excrement raced through his anal passage. The tape covering is mouth had fallen off; moisture had made the tape lose its adhesive tack.

Brian groaned. He was still alive. He begged for Sharon to stop, wanting her help.

She paused for a moment, looking at his blood-covered face, his saddened eyes and emptying soul.

Lying on the floor, Brian tried to curse Sharon, but his weak state only hampered his efforts.

'Give me the cleaver!' she ordered with pure dominance in her voice.

'Give me the hammer first,' Greg replied, reasserting his control.

Sharon obliged, exchanging the hammer for the cleaver.

Greg was in total disbelief. Sharon had become the hunter after being the prey for such a long time. She wasted no time, returning straight back to work – the job in-hand. She hacked at Brian's vastly mutilated body. Her clothes were saturated with his blood; fragments of his skull flew into her hair. Sharon was in her own zone, nothing else existed and she did not want to leave.

Greg, almost hypnotised, decided to slip away, making his way quietly out of the front door not bothering to close it behind him. He clocked Brian's mobile on the floor on the way out. It was not part of the plan but he slipped it into his pocket and walked out of the door.

Greg moved swiftly, remaining in the shadows until he had reached his van. His pulse echoed in the back of his throat. He felt almost sick, though pride over the way things had gone prevented him from vomiting. He felt a godlike pride pass through him. He paused as an acidic belch forced its way up his windpipe; a dribble of bile dripped from his lips. He climbed into the back of his van, removing his suit, mask and boots and hurriedly placing them in a transparent rubber bag. The bag had been supplied with the suit and he quickly sealed it shut. As he dressed, he was unable to shake the image of Sharon from his mind. With his heart pounding; his mind racing, he put the van in gear and pulled off. His eyes stung as tears welled their way from both tear ducts. He was shocked by his own sadness at what he had orchestrated. He hurriedly unwound his window and hung his head out, trying to refresh his lungs with the cold air but as more acidic bile shot from his mouth, his stomach ached as he retched.

Greg switched off the engine, along with the headlights and coasted his van to its parking position. Deciding to leave everything in the van till tomorrow, he entered the main building and his flat unnoticed.

Popping his head in to his bedroom, he quickly checked that Karen was still sleeping.

He undressed, stood under the jets of water from the shower head and squirted toothpaste in to his mouth. Suddenly, he realised that he had left one of his cleavers with Sharon. He panicked before he rationalised that it was no bad thing.

The police would not suspect a third party. Let the police sort that one out. He dried his body using a towel from the rail and then he slipped in to bed next to Karen. No one would ever know.

Chapter Eleven

It was the morning after the night before. Greg opened his eyes and it all came flooding back. As his recollection of the previous night's events unfolded in his head he felt a massive adrenaline rush pass through the whole of his body. He'd done it. All the planning, all the times he had held his own private dress rehearsals, the secret way he had picked his victims through their own self-section. All the time the motive in his mind was the same, it never changed or lost its focus – it was murder!

Greg sat up erect as he woke. He was surprised that he did not feel any guilt or remorse – maybe his guilt system had already flushed those feelings away. He knew that Brian had no chance of survival when he had chosen to slip away. Karen stirred and interrupted his thoughts, though she had no idea how dark they were.

'Good morning. I went out like a light. What time was it?' Karen asked, still yawning.

'Half ten-ish I think. How do you feel this morning?'

'Fine… apart from I've got a bit of a headache,' Karen mumbled.

'I'll get you a cup of tea. Do you want juice and some headache tablets?'

'Yeah that'd be great.' Karen placed her hand on her forehead and lay back on the pillow. She could not understand how she had slept for so long or why she felt completely drained.

'Put the telly on, will you?' Greg asked from the kitchen.

'Where's the remote?'

'It should be under my pillow. I'll be in in a minute, hold on,' Greg replied, as he juggled his way in the kitchen.

'It's OK, I've found it.'

Greg returned and gave Karen a glass of fruit juice and a packet of paracetomol.

'You'll only need two of those,' he said before she asked.

Karen passed Greg the remote control, Greg instantly pressed the standby button and a picture appeared on the screen. He then flicked through the channels until he found some news.

'Wonder how the football went yesterday? I didn't stay up to watch *Match of the Day* last night – I was worried about you,' he added as he walked back in to the kitchen, to finish making Karen's tea.

The other reason for his swift exit was so that Karen would not question why he had put the news on. Greg wanted to know if there was anything on the previous evening's events in Tinckerton Street.

He placed a cup of boiling hot tea on the floor next to where Karen was now propped upright on the bed, though still under the duvet. Greg walked around the bed and lay on top of the duvet. Karen slowly got up and went in to the bathroom to relieve her bladder, taking a pillow with her. Her attempt at using the pillow to cover some of her body bought a smile to Greg's face.

'Fucking hell,' Greg said trying to act astonished.

Karen rushed back in to the bedroom, pulling her knickers up en route.

'What's the matter?'

'Look!' was the only reply she got.

A reporter was commenting on a disturbing story. A nineteen year old woman, and mother, had violently attacked and mutilated her boyfriend in a frenzied attack. Their young child had been unharmed.

'The young child...' the reporter said, *'was sleeping in the next room when the attack happened. Tinckerton Street, here in Swiss Cottage, is a very quiet residential area and has not witnessed this kind of crime for over a decade. At the moment, the police have told me that they do not want to release any of the names of the family.*

This is an absolutely terrifying story. The young mother, who is now in police custody after being treated on the scene for shock by paramedics, is now helping the police with their enquiries. The young woman claims that a man dressed in a black plastic suit, wearing a mask, forced his way in to the property and threatened to harm her young child if she didn't kill her boyfriend. The mutilated remains of the man, who has been identified as the father of the child, have now been removed from the scene.' The reporter paused, in order to compose himself. *'I can say that, from what I have been told by a police spokesman, this was a very brutal, wild, frenzied attack. The child has now been handed over to the social services and placed in their care for the foreseeable future.*

Police are inside the property where this horrendous crime has taken place and have told me that the place looks like a slaughter house. We won't know what really happened until we have the results of the autopsy. Forensic scientists are on the scene; who only knows what they'll find?

The police are appealing for anyone who knows anything about this hideous crime to come forward. Anyone who has any information can either call the Crime Stoppers hotline or New Scotland Yard. Both numbers should be on your television screens. Let's hope that someone does. This is Terry Bane, in Swiss Cottage, reporting for Thames News.

'She must be a fucking nutter,' Greg laughed.

'How do you know she did it?'

'Come on – a bloke in a rubber suit… Did she say what planet he was from?' Greg began to laugh louder. Karen was not impressed.

'That poor girl, she's only nineteen and she's locked up and has no idea where her baby is and her boyfriend is dead… murdered! She must have seen the whole thing.'

'Yeah, of course she saw it. He was murdered by her. Best place for her – behind bars. Her baby's lucky that she didn't kill it. Do you remember that girl whose boyfriend was killed in a road rage attack a few years ago?'

'Yes, I can remember, why?'

'Well, she said that this guy got out of his car, battered her, then got back in his car and drove off. In all her interviews she sobbed her little heart out and everyone felt sorry for her. She fucking killed him; she's still locked up – doing porridge for it.'

'You've got a point, I suppose.'

'I know I have, you wait and see. When she gets sent down, I'll remind you how you felt sorry for her.' Greg lay back down on the bed with a know-it-all look on his face.

Karen hoped that Greg was right. The thought of someone like that roaming the streets sent a cold shiver down her spine. She decided that she did not want to think about it anymore.

'What you doing today?' Karen asked, changing the subject.

'Going to the gym in bit, watching the football later, bit of domestic stuff chucked in for good measure – the normal Sunday stuff, why?'

'I just wondered.'

'What about you – any plans?' Greg thought he had better return the question, show a bit of interest.

'I'm just going home to veg out I think – I dunno what Mum's doing,' Karen quipped. 'I'm first in the shower. You can make me a second cuppa,' she said whilst she leaped out of Greg's bed, taking a pillow with her, attempting to cover her breasts, not turning and throwing the pillow at Greg until she was almost out of the room. The pillow landed on his chest.

'You're a crap throw,' he laughed.

Greg did as Karen had told him to and made her another cup of tea; he thought that he would put some bread in the toaster, just in case she wanted something to eat before she left. He wondered how long it would stay in her system.

Greg started to think about the news story. He thought that the reporter had been very accurate with his coverage of the murder. Greg did remember the scene as he left. Sharon had made the room look like a slaughter house. Her manic butchering of Brian would have been impossible to clean up – even if she had the wherewithal to do it. Greg tried to imagine what had taken place after he had left. Though almost without control, his thoughts returned to the reporter – Terry Bane.

'He knows more than he's telling us,' Greg mumbled quietly to himself.

'That's better,' Karen said softly, walking back in to the bedroom using a small towel to dry the ends of her hair.

Greg had already returned and was laying back on the bed, staring at the television.

'Good. I've made some toast, there's marmalade, jam, Marmite, all kinds, help yourself. Did you want a boiled egg?'

He was fussing, and this was not like him. Karen had noticed a slight change in Greg's up and down tone.

'Tea and toast is fine, with a little marmalade… Are you alright?' she added.

'Yeah, I'm fine. Why?'

'You're fussing – stop fussing, it's not like you.'

'Well, I've matured! Anyway, I can't send you out to face the world on an empty stomach, can I?' he recovered quickly.

'Have you matured?' she giggled.

Karen sat quietly eating a slice of toast smothered with lime marmalade. That fantastic smell of freshly toasted bread filled the whole flat. That toasty morning smell made her feel warm and safe. Greg was singing in the shower; trying to camouflage his dark thoughts of the recent evening's events, telling himself that the sleeping drugs he had given Karen had passed unnoticed.

Karen decided she should get dressed and ready to leave.

Greg had exited the bathroom and was dressed in his gym attire before Karen, even though she had showered much earlier than him.

'Time for me to go,' she said. 'Sorry for crashing out on you, I'll make it up to you next time, I promise.'

They both hugged and engaged in a long kiss.

'Do you fancy doing something next weekend?' she asked.

'Yeah, that'd be cool; we'll sort something out during the week.' This was just how he wanted it. He needed plenty of space and time.

Chapter Twelve

Greg watched Karen until she was completely out of sight. He then made his way back in to his flat, making an important collection from his van on the way. Once back in his flat, he hurried into the bathroom and started to fill the bath with both taps running.

He held the plastic bag containing his PVC suit, mask and boxing boots. He then set about cleaning all the debris off the costume. He sponged the costume and face mask and used a nailbrush to scrub the soles of the boxing boots.

As he washed off the splattered blood and what appeared to be gravel, Greg realised that the gravel was actually fragments of Brian's skull. The water changed from a clear transparency to a soft pinky-red. Without control, he started to projectile vomit. It forced its way up through his digestive system like a volcano, scorching the back of his throat. His nose dripped and his eyes filled with tears. He broke down and started to sob.

Coughing and choking, Greg had managed to drape his head over the toilet and started to wipe the mucus that was now dangling from both his nostrils and the clear stream of salty tears that had flooded his eyes.

Attempting to compose himself, he returned to the task in-hand, trying to find a distraction in order to help him cope. Greg decided that he needed to remain on the bicycle because if he was to fall off and crash, he would be in danger of an emotional burnout and it would be impossible to get back in the saddle. He told himself he could do this.

Spitting venom, he was angry with himself for his weakness – as he considered his act of remorse. His bed had been made and the show had to go on. He forced his alter ego to resurface. He had to think about the next one, not look back.

'Hector,' Greg said, announcing the name of his next target through gritted teeth. 'Hector,' he snarled.

Hector was a fat, slobbish guy who drove a dust cart. He would lean out of the window of his cab taking the piss out of the young lads as they struggled to carry the heavy steel bins, full of other people's stinking garbage. Hector was known for proudly boasting about his escapades with young men, even though he was a married man. He had come to England from South Africa. Greg was not sure how long he had been in England. Hector had told stories of how his brother-in-law had constantly threatened him and it was Hector's wife who had intervened. She protected her lying, cheating homosexual husband.

Greg did not know if Hector's wife knew about his double life but he had decided that the time had come for Hector to face his brother-in-law alone, without the protection of his wife. There were many occasions where Greg had to be held back from attacking Hector, when Hector had gone too far. Greg always knew his day would come.

He had now entered the planning phase. Greg smiled privately; he knew Hector's clock had begun ticking. His time was almost up.

Chapter Thirteen

The phone on Terry Bane's desk started to ring. He tried to ignore it but the constant noise began to irritate him.

'Terry Bane,' he said in to the phone's receiver.

'Hi, Terry, great story, can we meet pal?'

'When?' Terry replied – he knew the voice.

'The sooner the better… do you fancy a pint?'

'Yeah, why not?' Terry replied, smiling to himself. Things had not changed.

'The Bidders Arms in, let's say, an hour?'

'Have one waiting for me, mate.' There was no need for goodbyes.

Terry Bane was now a reporter. He worked for *Thames News* and had been doing the job for nearly five years. He had previously worked as a high-ranking detective at New Scotland Yard. Terry had decided to leave his job at The Yard soon after his wife left him. At the time, Terry had been involved in a murder case – a very high profile murder case. It had been the ever-building media pressure that dictated that the case needed solving quickly. Someone had to be brought to justice and therefore Terry had to commit to working long hours to catch the culprit. This, in turn, had put a strain on his marriage. The pressure had become too much for his wife to cope with, forcing her to make a break from the whole thing that was smothering her life. She couldn't take it anymore and broke free.

She always knew that her husband did not have the luxury of a nine-to-five job. The constant phone calls in the middle of the night drove her crazy and they could never plan anything. Their lives seemed to become an ad-hoc existence.

Terry had taken the whole thing very badly. Once the case was solved and the killer caught, he resigned, though by then it was too late. This was another blow which struck him deep. He had lost his true love. It was this loss that pushed Terry over the edge; he began to drink excessively. He knew he was heading for the gutter if he did not pull himself together; a breakdown soon followed. With the help of his best friend and ex-colleague, James McFarland, Terry cleaned up his act and landed a job as a crime reporter at Thames Television. His background at The Yard had opened doors. He'd done the press a fair few favours in the past and it was time to call them in. Time had proved to be Terry's best ally, time to heal his broken heart, though the deep scars still remained.

Terry now lived with his new girlfriend, Natalie, and was very content with his life. He knew that his friend wanted to talk about the Tinckerton Street Murder. During the next hour, Terry prepared himself for his meeting.

As Terry was getting ready to leave his desk, his phone rang. He was going to ignore it but something told him to pick it up. A copper at heart, he couldn't ignore his gut feeling.

'Terry Bane,' he said in to the telephone's receiver.

'Hello, darling.' It was Natalie.

'Just on my way out to meet McFarland. Sorry sweetheart,' he apologised.

'Give James my love and I'll see you tonight.'

'OK, darling, sorry to have to cut and run like this.'

'No worries. Say hi to James.'

'I will. Gotta go… bye!' With that, the conversation ended.

Terry knew, and had never allowed himself to forget, how lucky he was to have met Natalie. She always seemed to understand; never questioned him. She trusted him completely.

Terry had met McFarland at Hendon Police Training College a long time ago when they had both joined the force. They had sparked an instant friendship, buddying up almost immediately. They clicked; thought on the same wave length. They were then stationed together and preceded through the ranks at more or less the same speed. They knew each other inside out. Once McFarland had moved from CID to New Scotland Yard, the wagers were flying thick and fast as to how long it would be until Terry followed him.

McFarland openly admitted that it was never the same after Terry left. They had remained great friends; nothing was going to change that.

Even though past evidence had proved that they were a very effective team, they were very different in the way they carried out their investigations. Terry was logical and methodical whereas McFarland was the bull in a china shop, seemingly wild but usually right. It worked. Results were results, and they were both in the results business.

Upon arriving, Terry paused for a moment. His heart started to race, he had not set foot in this establishment for a very long time. He slowly made his way inside. The Bidders Arms was a nice cosy pub, mainly used by people who worked in law enforcement or who were attached to it in one way or another. Police informers, solicitors who had crossed over to the dark, murky side of society.

Terry glanced around. The place had not changed in the slightest. A couple of prostitutes giggled at Terry, one of them flashed her breasts. Terry simply looked away, not interested. A couple of unsavoury faces from the past stirred the acid in his stomach. Terry had acquired an overwhelming hatred for corruption within The Yard.

'Terry... over here!' a voice called from a table in a quiet corner of the bar.

Terry acknowledged it with a simple hand gesture. As he sat down to join his friend, he was handed a pint of lager.

'Cheers,' James McFarland smiled, with a hint of a Scottish accent.

'Cheers. You're losing that accent, mate.'

'I know, I know,' he smiled. 'How's Natalie?'

'She's as great as ever. She sends her love by the way.'

'It's been a long time, Terry.'

'I know, too long. Listen, mate, I'm sorry for cutting myself off...'

'Shut up you fool,' McFarland interrupted. 'We're mates and, hey, I understand. It's what you had to do. Listen, you went through a shit time. Getting away was the best move for you. It was the coming back to London that surprised me.'

'I met Natalie, that's why I came back. Oh, and not to mention the fact that I am a Londoner. I could never stay away from the smoke.'

'Aye, it gets a hold on you after a while.'

'Cheers McFarland,' Terry said, raising his glass. 'Now what's this all about?'

'As if you don't know already.'

Terry looked at James McFarland. They knew each other better than anyone else, as if they were still playing their detective games.

'Tinckerton Street,' McFarland replied succinctly, confirming Terry's suspicions.

'What would you like to know?'

'Who did it?' McFarland laughed. 'I'm only joking. What's your gut telling you?'

'Fuck me, how long you got?' Terry smirked. 'But my gut is telling me one thing.'

'What's that?'

'It's telling me to tell you that I'm not coming back to The Yard.'

'Did I ask?' the Scotsman laughed.

'No you didn't. But you don't have to McFarland. I know you too well, mate. You've been sent to ask. I know how the wheels within wheels work. Don't treat me like a fucking amateur.'

'OK, OK. We need your experience. We are never going to solve this case with the fucking muppets that they've assigned. We don't even know if she's insane or not,' McFarland had a passionate side to him. He cared about the public, even if most of them hated him for the career he had chosen.

'Shit, shit, shit!' Terry spat, showing that he was not impressed.

'Calm down, Terry. I need you back on the team. You can lead from the rear. I'll take the front.'

'Natalie will have my balls. What about my day job?'

'That's taken care of, it's been called a "leave of absence",' McFarland smiled.

'This has come from the top and the people at Thames have been told – they have humbly agreed to our terms,' McFarland smirked.

'You sneaky bastard. I never had a choice did I?' Terry smiled. 'But I'll only agree on my terms.'

'And they are?'

'You get another drink in.'

'Fuck me, nothing's changed there,' McFarland joked.

'Seriously though, mate...' Terry added, leaning closer, 'one, I'm not directly reportable to anyone, but you. Two, I'm there in an advisory capacity. McFarland, I can't come back in full capacity – you understand... Natalie would worry. Mate, last time...'

McFarland smiled at him. 'I know, I know. Your role would simply be neutral. No rank, no warrant badge, on no one's payroll, reportable to me and no one else.'

They were so close that they could be themselves and they knew that if they pissed each other off, it would be forgotten five minutes later.

'I'll need to speak to Natalie first,' Terry said. 'Now tell me what you know.'

'OK. A large, mutilated white male died from being hacked to death with a machete and was found at the scene. This is the strange bit, the victim had been hit on the shoulder once and twice on the head with what seems to be a hammer or something similar. This has not yet been recovered. Their baby... hold on, you know all this!'

'So he was still alive before she started hacking him with the machete?'

'Yes, it seems so. She has admitted to the murder but she is sticking to her story that a man in a black skintight suit made her do it.'

'The baby was unharmed in the next room? I thought that was just what they had told the media, I didn't think it was true. This is a strange one, McFarland.' Terry seemed confused. 'I think we need to find out her mental state before we proceed. If she has a clean bill of mental health, we should be asking why this guy in a black skintight suit made her kill her boyfriend and why he chose not to harm the child. Did he use the child to force her actions? Why didn't he kill her boyfriend himself? Why didn't he just kill all of them? Does he really exist?' Terry was rambling now.

They both looked at each other, puzzled by what Terry had said.

'Another drink?' Terry asked, not bothering to wait for a reply. McFarland nodded anyway.

At the bar, Terry looked around; he was feeling a little uncomfortable. Ex-colleagues were looking at him, talking amongst themselves – though they all seemed too embarrassed to talk to him directly. The man behind the bar acted awkwardly. He even fumbled Terry's change.

As he sat back down he took his mobile phone out of his pocket and began to dial. He waited for a response.

'Natalie… Sweetheart…'

'Hello darling,' she replied.

'You know what I'm going to say?' he correctly assumed.

'Yes I do,' she replied, wearing a wry smile. 'You know I'll support you in whatever you decide, though I'm not going to lead a lonely life with you working all the hours.'

'Clear as a whistle. I'll help them with this and that'll be it!'

'Your choice, you have my full support though please remember what I've said,' she had firmness in her voice.

'Yes darling… thank you.' He ended the call.

McFarland waited for Terry to speak first.

'Did they have a landline phone?'

'Aye they did. That's another thing. Their landline is untouched. It worked perfectly. Normally that would have been ripped from its socket. That's why I'm not convinced Terry.'

'Or maybe the guy in the black suit was very confident. It's all too… We need to fill in too many blanks.' Terry shrugged his shoulders.

'Now you see why I need you. Things don't seem to add up.'

'Nothing is as it first appears McFarland. You of all people should know that.'

The two men finished their drinks.

'See you in the morning,' McFarland said.

'Are you picking me up?'

'Yeah. By the way, only the top brass know about this.'

'Why doesn't that surprise me?'

'See you at your house in the morning then,' McFarland confirmed gripping Terry's hand firmly as he shook it.

***

As Terry walked back into the Thames Television offices, he was greeted with a whisper in his ear.

'We'll call it a career break, a leave of absence.'

Terry turned quickly to see who the comment belonged to.

'Thanks Dave,' Terry replied.

'Solve it, mate. Hey, and call me when you're ready come back,' Dave said, with his voice still lowered.

'I will and thanks again.' The two men privately shook hands so as not to draw any attention.

Terry spent the rest of the afternoon at home going over what he knew. He was trying to look at all possibilities but without a proper look at the scene of crime, he was still blind. He sipped the scotch that he had previously poured himself and fell deep in to his thoughts, reminiscing about cases that he and McFarland had worked on together. They had never left a case unsolved. They were legends, solving the case was his focus and also his fear.

A bottle of champagne appeared from behind the door.

'Congrats darling.'

'We need to talk,' Terry said with seriousness in his voice.

'You're covert, I know.' There was a hint of sarcasm in her voice.

'How did you know that?'

'Come on darling, The Yard can't be seen to have to beg an ex-one-of-their-own back to solve a case that has only just opened, it's because they've not got a clue.'

'Why didn't I see that?'

'You're a man. Now are we going to drink this bubbly?'

'Bloody right we are. Let's order a curry, we're celebrating!'

They continued their celebrations until the early hours, before they both decided that it was time they fell into bed.

***

Morning arrived unannounced. Terry's head throbbed unforgivingly. Once Terry had shaken off the alcohol-induced cobwebs, he kissed Natalie. She was still in a sleep-like coma, completely unaware of her lover's departure.

McFarland picked Terry up as promised and they headed for the scene of crime. They both separated once at Tinckerton Street, preferring to do their own investigating and pooling resources later. This had proved successful in solving past cases. Even though the crime scene was no longer fresh, Terry was still able to look at most of the important things. All the time he was taking notes, questions were popping up in his mind. He was also interested in reading Sharon's statement, to see whether she was telling the truth. So many questions, he knew that he was going to have to interview her himself at some point, to freshen his investigation.

He noticed that there was a single partial footprint, though there was no pattern on the sole of whatever made the mark. He quickly snapped a picture with his digital camera.

'Hold on a minute, sir,' said an uniformed officer.

'That's OK officer, he's with me,' McFarland snapped at the uniformed officer, giving Terry the thumbs up.

Terry returned the gesture and continued. He could not understand where the hammer had disappeared to, that is if it was a hammer. He was going to have to wait to see the coroner's report, whatever it was. Where was it now?

'McFarland,' Terry called.

'Yes, mate, what is it?'

'I've hit a dead-end. I'm going to have to see the girl's statement. Have you received the coroner's report yet?' It was as though he had never been away.

'I've been here with you so I'm not sure about the coroner's report. I can get you a copy of her statement though.' A plain expression covered his face.

'What's that smell?' Terry enquired. They both looked at the uniformed officer.

'What smell, sir?' he answered uncomfortably.

'Can you smell that?' Terry asked.

'No, sorry, sir,' he replied plainly.

Terry continued sniffing, tiptoeing around like a basset hound, hoping that he would be able to pinpoint the smell.

'Let's go. I need to see the girl's statement and check if the coroner's report has come through,' Terry instructed. 'Thank you,' Terry said to the uniformed officer.

The officer nodded politely.

Once the two men were outside, and out of earshot, Terry told McFarland what he required.

'I'm not going back to the office McFarland. I don't want anyone at The Yard knowing I'm on-board. I need you to e-mail me a copy of the girl's statement to my private e-mail address, and a copy of the coroner's report in the same e-mail would be nice.' Terry gave a knowing smile.

'Aye, that's fine.'

Terry then told McFarland that once he was done at The Yard, he wanted him to go home and pick up his toothbrush.

'You'll be staying at mine tonight, mate,' Terry told McFarland.

Terry also needed to clear all of this with Natalie, though he knew she would not mind. She would accept it as a one-off.

'I'm going to have to talk to the girl, you know,' Terry announced.

'Not a problem. When?'

'Tomorrow morning. You can clear it while you're at The Yard.'

It was normal for Terry to take the lead; assume command. He was like a dog with a bone – the only difference was that Terry never buried his bones, he would gnaw them, until there was nothing left.

'I'll drop you off on the way,' McFarland said.

'OK,' Terry replied, climbing in the passenger seat.

Terry checked the time – to his surprise, they had been at Tinckerton Street for just over two hours. The day was still young.

McFarland drove away as Terry put the key in his front door.

He went straight into the kitchen and made himself a cup of coffee, stuffing a handful of biscuits in his mouth during the process. He could not believe his luck when the phone rang. He tried to swallow the contents of his mouth and darted to the phone. He missed it. His mobile phone rang and he removed it from the inside pocket of his jacket and answered it. By this time his mouth was empty.

'Hello.'

'Hi darling, it's Natalie.'

'Hi darling. I've got a favour to ask.'

'I can read you like a book, Terry,' Natalie giggled.

'Wait till I've asked. How do you know what the favour is?'

'I know you, Terry Bane. Is James going to stay at ours, or are you staying at his?'

'McFarland is staying here... if you're OK with it?'

'I know you've already told him, Terry,' her giggles continued. 'Listen, darling, I've had an idea. You've already invited James to stay tonight. And I know you'll both be working on this case and downing copious amounts of booze. If I'm there, I'll get in your way and be bored. So I've decided that I'll give Mum a call and let you boys get on with whatever you get on with. I'll spend a few days at Mum's. That way I'll be less of a distraction. I hope that's OK.'

She knew that Terry would have to agree. She had done what she did best, she had taken a decision and then followed by asking the question as if to turn the tables – textbook Maggie Thatcher. Natalie knew that Terry admired Maggie, so would never disagree when she used Maggie's negotiation techniques.

'Great idea, thanks for being so understanding, sweetheart.' Softness did not suit him.

'I'll call you,' and with that she was gone.

Terry knew that his lady was not impressed and that she was only testing him.

He uncontrollably drifted back to his thoughts though he was never alone. His counsellor had taught him that.

Terry sat in silence, thinking that McFarland seemed to be taking a long time. Logging on to his laptop, Terry was able to watch the video footage broadcast by other news channels. Most of them were like-for-like. They gave him nothing new. Frustration was beginning to blur his train of thought. He started to prepare dinner, cooking made him feel relaxed and when he was relaxed, he could think more clearly.

Terry rarely watched the television. When he did, he mainly watched current affairs and the news, the rest of the world never interested him. It was Natalie who was a self-confessed soap addict. Terry found the soaps fascinating, though never enough to offer him the same escape as it seemed to offer the millions of other hooked viewers.

When he told Natalie stories of his detective days, he would insist that to be a successful detective you could not afford an imagination – it was removed once you had secured your promotion and discarded your blue-bottled uniform.

Terry had been productive with his culinary and his logical skills. As McFarland arrived, dinner was ready to be served.

'Perfect timing,' Terry said as he opened the front door.

'Great, I'm starving. What is it?' McFarland replied, trying to look in the kitchen.

'Wait and see, you nosey bastard,' Terry chuckled.

McFarland sat down in the living room and, as Terry finished serving up the food, Terry switched on the radio for any snippets of news that may filter through. They ate quietly; the sound of the radio could be heard in the background from the kitchen.

The two men cleared their plates as if they had not eaten for a week. Both men read as they ate. They read the pathologist's report as well as going over Sharon's sketchy statement.

'I'll wash, you dry,' Terry suggested.

'Let's do it!' McFarland replied, mimicking the movements of a commando in action.

'What's on your mind?'

'Too much, they've managed to overlook too much,' Terry answered, wearing a troubled look.

'Tell me more.'

'In a minute, let's get this out of the way first, mate.' McFarland did not reply. He knew when not to push Terry.

Once they had completed the task, both men returned to the living room. Terry collected two cans of beer on the way.

'Cheers, now tell me more,' McFarland said, making himself comfortable. It was going to be a long night.

'Right, the victim was killed by being hacked to death by a machete. We know this because Sharon was still holding a machete when she was arrested,' he paused, 'and the only prints found on the machete belonged to her. The victim had suffered three blows from a blunt instrument, believed to be a hammer, one to his shoulder and two to his head. The pathologist confirms this in his report.' He stopped to look at Sharon's statement and to take a large swig of his beer. 'OK, where is the hammer?'

'Shit, you're right. How did I miss that?'

'Now, in her statement she mentions this guy in a black shiny suit.'

'Yeah. Ha, ha, ha – out there I think,' McFarland could not contain his emotions.

'I don't think she is, mate,' Terry replied bluntly. 'Who would make something like that up? Hold on; listen to my theory so far. Only one of the weapons used has been recovered. Sharon had not left the premises to dispose of the hammer because why only get rid of the hammer? If she had, she would have got rid of the machete at the same time. She has not denied that she actually did kill the victim. We need to get her state of mind checked out. I need to talk to her,' he concluded.

'Let's see what the shrink says. She saw her this afternoon – last thing. I've told her to e-mail me the results. All my e-mails will be automatically forwarded to you whilst we're working on this case Terry,' McFarland said flatly.

'Once this case is over, I'm off back to TV land, mate.'

'We make a great team, Terry.'

'I know we make a good team, mate. We might be chalk and cheese, but don't think you can reel me back in because I'm a bit drunk, I won't soften McFarland!'

'We locked some evil fuckers up in our time, Terry.'

'I don't wanna talk about it.'

'We only ever did our job!'

'They didn't teach us half the shit we got up to at Hendon, McFarland. Maybe you can block your mind off to it, but I can't. There's innocent people locked away, and we made sure they went down for something they didn't do.'

'Fucking hell, Terry, we only did what we had to – what we were ordered to do. We had no choice. We didn't make those decisions, they came from above. I can't believe you're still carrying this guilt around, mate.'

'My demons...mine and yours; remember, they're mine and yours.'

'I don't feel any fucking guilt Terry; your demons are your own. Fucking move on – I have!' McFarland growled. 'Let go of your fucking excess baggage, Terry!'

'What if I can't?'

'Terry, let it go, leave it in the past.'

'Not this time, McFarland.'

'You don't think the girl did it, do you?'

'No I don't... well at least not on her own. Whoever aided her or...' Terry paused, 'or forced her actions, will be the only fucking arrest we make. Are we on the same page here McFarland?' Terry said, gritting his teeth.

'Clear cut Terry, fucking clear cut.'

The time seemed to have run away from them. Both suffering from too much alcohol intake and tiredness they said their goodnights and went to bed.

Chapter Fourteen

Hector Hylie was an overweight man of South African descent. Aged forty-two, he looked older than his years. He suffered from bad health due to his mammoth size. He had met and married Mandy in a short time span after arriving in the UK. Mandy had fallen for Hector's accent rather than his looks and, back then, Hector had a great sense of humour, though once he had married Mandy, all the niceties diminished. Mandy was ten years his junior; therefore easier to manipulate and control. Martin, Mandy's brother, three years older than his sister, was completely different. It may have been the environment that he worked in. It could have been that he knew his brother-in-law better than his sister knew her own husband. Martin had threatened Hector on a number of occasions and was not bothered who had overheard. Hector used to brush off Martin's threats, knowing that Martin would never do anything that would upset his kid sister.

Hector was bisexual, though his wife never knew her husband's dirty secret. He would frequent gay bars in order to quench his hunger, picking up young gay men and fulfilling his needs before slapping them about and leaving them a little worse for wear.

The thing that angered Martin the most was the fact that Hector boasted on a Monday morning at work, completely unashamed, without thought of who may be in earshot. Being related to the man was bad enough, but what made it worse for Martin was that he had to work with him.

When Martin informed his sister of her husband's advertised conquests, his reports landed on deaf ears. Martin's frustration grew, along with his sister's tunnel-vision. She loved that man, or at least that was what she wanted the outside world to believe.

Martin, himself, was in a relationship and had a four-year-old son. His girlfriend, Lisa, who he loved, knew what buttons to press. Lisa was 29-year-old devoted mother. He wanted his sister to have the same life that he had built with Lisa, though he knew this would never happen while she was still married to Hector.

Greg, on numerous occasions, had wound Martin up about his brother-in-law, trying to ignite the fire inside him. Greg had increased the pressure once he had decided that Hector was going to be the next victim. Pulling at Martin's anger strings, he goaded the man, only for effect though. Greg wanted others to see the rage Martin had for Hector. Martin was going to be the catalyst in Greg's flawless plan.

Greg had been closely watching Hector's movements for a while, though only on and off. Greg knew enough. He had a rough idea of where and when he was going to pounce on Hector. Greg's only other obstacle was to get Martin where he wanted him. There would need to be a delay between the two. After all, Greg could not be in two places at the same time. Greg had a contingency plan should the first fail. The police were going to be far too busy to spot what was going to happen next, though once it had, they would then link the two. The roller coaster would then be off and running and Greg's fun would not be limited.

Chapter Fifteen

Terry stood in the hollowness of the interview room, waiting to meet Sharon. He felt as though he was being held back until he spoke to her. He needed to analyse her mood, her demeanour, her remorse – guilty or not. Whatever the case, he needed to see it for himself, with his own eyes. He stood by the two-way mirror drinking his cup of coffee. He scrutinized his own reflection and felt nervous. He had never interviewed a female killer before, they had all been men. This was different though, he felt that she was firstly a mother and, accidentally, a lover but a murderer nonetheless. The report on her mental health and state of mind had come back clean. She was fully compos mentis.

A door opened and McFarland emerged.

'Right then, this is where we are,' McFarland said, firmly. 'She and her brief have been told that you have been called in from outside. Her brief has been informed of the sensitivity of your involvement in this case and the whole investigation. Terry, he's a bit of a tosser so be careful how you word your questions. Her brief has also been told that your identity and involvement in this case is completely confidential – without prejudice,' McFarland smiled. 'Please take your time, we're in no rush.'

'I'll fuck off if you like and you can sort this shit out yourselves,' Terry's nerves were beginning to show.

'Sorry, mate, I didn't. Take a deep breath – this is your show.'

'Forget it, let's do it!' Terry said placing his hand on McFarland's shoulder.

Both men waited a couple of minutes for Sharon and her solicitor to enter the room. McFarland had instructed the

Duty Sergeant to switch off the CCTV. They both sat down and McFarland introduced the pair for the benefit of the tape. The tape was not switched on.

'Sharon,' Terry began 'How are you? Are you being treated OK?'

She raised her head and answered 'I'm fantastic Mr Bane. How are you?'

'Sorry Sharon, I didn't mean it to sound like that.'

Sharon shook her head slowly. 'Do you think I'm barking mad like the rest of them?'

'No, I don't, and neither does anyone else. I think that you should tell me what happened and, with your help, we can work as a team and get this mess sorted out.' Terry's voice remained in a low soft, sympathetic tone.

'I'm Mr Barnford, Sharon's solicitor. My client has been over and over her statement on more occasions than we care to remember.'

'I'll end this interview then, you'll get your fee, Sharon can go to prison and I'll be home in time for the football,' Terry said, quickly.

'Hold your horses here Mr Barnford. We're here to help your client. We want to unfold the true events of that night,' McFarland said, backing his partner.

'Mr Barnford,' Terry interrupted, 'this is a criminal investigation. Your client is in serious trouble. Questions need to be asked and, in turn, answered. If you're advising your client not to participate in helping us with our enquiries then, Mr Barnford, that makes things even more interesting.'

'How so Mr Bane?'

'Withholding evidence, perverting the course of justice... need I go on?' Terry now had the bit firmly between his teeth.

'He is right Sharon, but it's your call,' the young solicitor nervously pointed out.

'Let me paint things more clearly for you Sharon,' McFarland said interrupting things slightly. 'Perverting the course of justice, in English, Canadian, and Irish law – Article one-three-nine of the Canadian Criminal Code, is a criminal offence in which someone prevents justice from being served on himself or on another party. It is a common-law offence. It carries a maximum sentence of life imprisonment, although no sentence of more than ten years has been handed down in the past one hundred years. So help us, to help you.'

'I've got nothing else planned. Go on then,' she said, shrugging her shoulders.

'My client wishes to continue,' the young solicitor said unnecessarily.

'Great,' McFarland said, impatiently.

'Sharon, please tell me about the man in the shiny suit,' Terry asked.

'I don't know what it was made of. It was shiny, like school shoes. He spoke funny, he kept talking about choices and how choices affected everything. He messed with my head. Telling me that I had a shit life and so did my baby... He told me that I had to kill Brian to save my baby.'

'Did he threaten you or your baby?'

'No... I'm not sure. He mentioned promises and that they could be broken, I'm not sure.'

'What promises?'

'I don't know, as I said, he messed with my head.'

'Take your time. Would you like something to drink?'

'Water, could I have some water?'

McFarland stood up and used a phone that was mounted on the wall by the door. He spoke quietly in to the receiver and replaced it just as quietly, once he had finished talking. A few moments later, a plastic jug of water arrived accompanied by four plastic cups. McFarland filled the four cups with water before returning to his seat.

Sharon drank the entire contents of her cup in a single gulp. Her solicitor refilled her cup.

'Sharon, I have read your statement over and over. There seems to be some blanks I need filling. I understand how painful this must be for you but I need your help.'

'I think you're the first person I have spoken to since I've been in here that I trust Mr Bane. I'll answer your questions. But please... don't rush me.' The sorrow in her eyes told Terry she felt alone.

'OK, Sharon, please tell me what happened.'

'I was sitting watching the telly. I was a bit stoned, but not out of it. The door went and I answered it. The guy in the black shiny suit forced his way in and forced me back into the living room. He knew everything about us Mr Bane – about my baby, about me, about Brian,' she paused for no apparent reason.

'Please continue.' Terry was listening hard.

'He told me that I had to kill Brian to save me and my baby. Then Brian came home. We heard his key in the door.'

'Why did he tell you that?' McFarland interrupted.

Terry glared at him.

'Brian used to abuse me. Come home drunk – he always came home drunk… and raped me, did horrible things, made me do horrible things. The man said that one day Brian would get bored with me and turn on my baby and make my baby do horrible things.'

'How do you think he knew those things?' McFarland returned Terry's glare.

'I don't know. Brian was known for his big mouth and his bullshit. Maybe he told him.'

'Were you having an affair Sharon?' McFarland continued.

'You're having a laugh. My fanny and my arse are red-raw, my tits are covered in bite marks and the rest of my body is black and blue – I'll fucking show you if you don't believe me? I'll never go near another man for as long as I live.'

'There won't be any need for that Sharon!' Terry said, hijacking proceedings.

'Go easy please gentlemen,' Sharon's solicitor asked, his face a picture of horror.

'My partner will select his questions more carefully in future,' Terry said in an apologetic nature.

'I'm sorry Sharon, but questions need answering.' McFarland's sad attempt of an apology was accepted.

'Sharon, please continue,' Terry sympathetically prompted.

'He told me to choose what I was going to use to kill Brian,' she said as a long tear tricked down her cheek.

'Where did this choice of weapon come from?' Terry enquired, wanting to carry on, to continue her flow.

'He was holding them.'

'What was he holding?'

'A hammer and a machete, they were the only things he offered, but he was wearing a belt, and he had all sorts of stuff.'

Terry looked at McFarland and smiled.

'What weapon did you choose?'

'I panicked and took the hammer.'

McFarland smiled and asked, 'Did you use the hammer?'

'Yes, but...' Sharon paused and looked at her solicitor.

'We can take a break if you need one,' Mr Barnford told his client.

'No, I'm fine,' she shuddered. 'I hit Brian with the hammer and the sound made me feel sick.'

'How many times did you hit Brian with the hammer?' Terry needed to know.

'I wasn't counting... not many.'

'Then what happened?'

'Brian kept moving, trying to get away from me, but he couldn't.' Sharon glanced at McFarland. 'I couldn't hit him any harder. I tried, but he wouldn't die.' Her tone seemed slightly frantic. 'So I told the guy in the black suit to give me the machete,' she paused and sipped some water to take the bitter dryness away from inside her mouth.

'It's OK – take your time,' Terry said, trying to understand how lost Sharon was and how she had become the person in front of him.

'He gave me it, but I had to give him the hammer first... I...' Tears filled her eyes, without sobbing, she continued. 'So I went back to Brian, and hit him with the machete. I caught him across his back. He was yelling at me, but I couldn't hear a thing,' Sharon glanced back at McFarland, wiping her eyes.

'Can you tell me what happened to the hammer please Sharon?' This time McFarland asked the question.

'I don't know. He must have taken it with him – that guy.'

'Are you pleased that Brian is dead?' Terry enquired.

'I don't know to be honest. I've not thought about it. I've been fucking busy.' Her tone suggested harshness and was full of hatred.

'What happened next?'

'I must have hit Brian loads of times because when I stopped, there was blood everywhere. And I mean, fucking everywhere.' Sharon laughed, nervously. 'I… all of a sudden stopped and sort of forgot where I was. Then it came back to me – I thought it was a dream.'

'A nightmare?' McFarland said, interrupting.

'I suppose, I don't know. The fucking mess, that's all I kept thinking about, the fucking mess. I knew I had to call the police. It was then that I noticed he had gone. There was no sign of him – it was as if the air had swallowed him. Well, I didn't hear him go, but then… I had zoned out,' she gave another nervous laugh.

'Do you take drugs Sharon? And I don't mean the type of drugs you'd get from your local GP,' Terry asked.

'I smoke weed, if that's what you mean? But I already told you I was a bit stoned Mr Bane,' Sharon replied sarcastically.

'Do you take any other drugs?'

'No… not anymore.'

'Do you drink alcohol when you are smoking weed?'

'Yeah, course I do. Listen, I'm not making this shit up.'

'I don't believe you are Sharon. I just need to cover every angle,' Terry smiled.

'Were you the only person to hit Brian?' McFarland interrupted.

'What – with the hammer, or the machete?' Sharon snapped.

'Either!'

'Yeah, he only hit Brian with his fists.'

A brief silence followed.

'When did he hit Brian?'

'When Brian walked through the door. He sprayed something in his face; Brian screamed, saying it stung like fuck and that he couldn't breathe. The guy didn't listen. He punched the life out of him. Brian didn't stand a chance.'

'What happened then?' Terry asked, leaning forward.

'He dragged Brian in the living room, handcuffed him to the radiator and stuck some tape around his mouth – telling him to shut up.'

'What stood out to you about this guy, Sharon?'

'He was powerful; in control. He knew fucking everything, everything. He never lost it, he never shouted once.'

'What do you think he would have done if you had said, "no"?'

'Fuck knows, but... I think he would have been angry. I didn't want my baby hurt.'

'Can you describe his accent?'

'Let me think... Irish-English – well-spoken... posh... very calm not angry.'

'Young?'

'I don't know. How could I know that?'

'Any gravel in his voice?'

'I don't know... sorry.' Sharon looked at her solicitor – puzzled.

'My client has answered all your questions. Unless you have any further questions...'

'Yes, one more,' McFarland interrupted. 'What's his name, Sharon?'

'Who's name?' Sharon replied.

'You know, the guy in the black suit.'

'I don't fucking know his name. He didn't fucking exactly introduce himself,' she said, shaking with anger.

'Thank you Sharon,' Terry said.

'Interview terminated at eleven thirty-one,' McFarland said, pretending to switch off the tape recorder.

Terry remained seated as McFarland used the telephone on the wall to alert the uniformed officer, waiting outside the room, to escort Sharon back to her custody-cell.

As Sharon left the interview room, she turned and looked at Terry. Although she did not speak, Terry knew she was begging for his help. Terry gave a placid smile in return.

'Do you believe my client?' Mr Barnford asked as he stopped and turned towards Terry.

'Yes, I do. I also work on facts, which we are short of at the moment.' Terry paused. 'Can I ask you a question, Mr Barnford?'

'Be my guest.'

'How old are you?'

'I don't see that question relevant, Mr Bane.'

'OK, do you believe your client?'

'Yes, I do.'

'The reason I asked your age was to see what experience you had of cases like these.'

'I'm twenty-seven.'

'Why did you agree to represent Sharon?'

'I was the only one available.'

'Mr Barnford, are you hoping that we are going to get your client off?' McFarland growled.

'No Detective – that's my job,' the young solicitor snapped.

'You seemed shocked by some of what Sharon said.'

'Horrified,' McFarland added.

'Have you any idea of the magnitude of a case like this?' Terry continued. Sharon's solicitor acted embarrassed, avoiding eye contact with either men.

Terry was not going to allow himself to be drawn. 'Good day Mr Barnford.' The young inexperienced rookie solicitor left.

'What do you think now? Now you've had chance to talk to her, to meet her,' McFarland asked Terry.

'That smell I couldn't identify, that was pepper-spray. Someone else was there at the time, a third person was involved. Who and what the connection is I'm not sure of at the moment. Her solicitor won't help her. He was far too quiet – waste of money.'

'Fresh out of his nappies. Are you going to talk to her again?'

'Yes, we are. I'm going to have to see what develops first though.'

'You're fucking nuts. We can't afford to sit on this Terry,' McFarland could not believe his ears.

'I need her to ask to speak to me – allow her time. She's the only credible witness.'

'She fucking did it Terry.'

'Her hand was forced.'

'Do you think that she planned to kill him? Do you think the third person may be her lover?'

'No, I don't think she planned to kill Brian. Her story is not elaborate enough, though, it's also slightly fractured. Where's that fucking hammer? Someone took it. We only need to find out who that was – simple really,' Terry said, shrugging his shoulders.

'Where do we look next?'

'Listen, my Scottish friend, you know that I already think that Sharon is telling the truth. We have a massive fucking problem roaming our streets. Yes, we've got a fucking psycho walking the streets of London and we haven't got a fucking clue how we're going to stop him!'

'We need a lucky break. We must have missed something.'

'The only thing we don't know is who the fuck he is going to choose next.'

'So you think this wasn't a one-off?'

'No way – the planning was far too immaculate for it to be a one-off.'

'Right, I'd better go and report where we are with this case to our lord and master.'

'OK, mate. I'm going to go home. Try and make sense of all this.'

'I'll see you later,' McFarland said, trying to remain positive.

***

Terry got home and drifted off into a world of his own, lost within his own thoughts. He remained completely baffled by Sharon. Why had she not asked about her baby? Terry had checked that she had not been placed on any medication. And the state of her mental health had proven that she was completely, without question, compos mentis. He continued to read his notes, scribbling and adding to them as he did.

Chapter Sixteen

It had been seven weeks since Sharon had killed Brian and the media frenzy that had surrounded the case had all but died down. New Scotland Yard had reached a dead end and had nothing new to report. A single tabloid newspaper reporter had decided to keep a hold of the story and kept writing about how the police had tried to dilute the events that had taken place on that horrific evening – provocatively telling his readers that the police needed a fresh killing in order for them to find the mysterious man in the black suit. New Scotland Yard had unsuccessfully applied for a gagging order, stating that the reporter was trying to ignite a fire that they were trying to keep under control.

***

Greg had kept his relationship with Karen on an even keel – seeing her regularly and treating her well. On a couple of occasions they had double dated, making up a foursome with Martin and his girlfriend. Greg needed to be seen socially with Martin and Martin would not be suspicious if he asked him to go for a drink without their girlfriends.

***

Greg had been busy formulating Hector's abduction and subsequent demise. A disused multi-storey car park, located just on the outskirts of London, well out of the way, was going to be the venue.

Greg had decided to leave as much distance between his victims as possible – though only in a geographical sense. Once everything

S. J. Wardell

was in place, he would strike – no time limits, no calendar to work to. Greg did not want to leave the police any clues as to the where and when. No habitual trail was going to lead them to him.

Greg had visited the venue on more than one occasion, keeping an eye on any activity in the area. He also wanted to make sure that everything was in place. The multi-storey car park had been sold to developers and was due for demolition. Greg researched the demolition planning consent application on the internet. There were not any immediate plans to demolish the structure as fresh building plans had neither been passed nor rubber stamped. He had time, enough time.

The car park had five levels but only the lower level had been used by drug users and alcoholics. Vandals had also left their mark. Now the place was all but deserted. Greg had selected the fourth level for Hector's final resting place.

He decided that he was going to grab Hector a day earlier than Martin, as timing was everything. If he rushed it, he risked being seen and blowing it and there was a big chance of both men getting away. If that happened, he would have to stop – abort, for risk of getting caught.

With his stopwatch running, Greg had completed his own time trials to calculate how long it would take him to cover the distance between Hammersmith and the disused car park. He was thorough and tried out two separate routes at the approximate time of his planned abduction. He carried out this exercise from his own flat too. He would use the AA's online route planner on both evenings in order to assess whether roadworks or diversions affected either of his chosen routes, just in case he needed alternative options.

Hector had proved to be a creature of habit. Every Friday, he would frequent a well-known gay bar in Hammersmith. The Penny Farthing was a nice friendly place in the centre of Glenthorne Road – a detached building with a large car park at the rear of the building, perfect for Greg.

Greg witnessed Hector leave with his quarry and walk around to the rear car park. The area looked as though it had been tailor-made, out of sight from the big brother – CCTV. Hector and his boy would fornicate before Hector would get violent, though this would never last more than a couple of minutes. This was followed by an exchange of verbal abuse and then Hector would leave.

Greg had decided to snatch Hector on the following Friday evening and Martin on the Saturday. Greg had previously arranged to go out on a heavy drinking session with Martin.

Chapter Seventeen

Greg stood waiting in the darkened shadows. He had no idea of the time, but he knew it was late. He must have been standing there for almost an hour. His heart raced; his stomach acid danced. He could taste the bitterness at the back of his throat. Trying to calm his breathing, he counted slowly in his mind and attempted to sing a slow melody. His adrenalin had already kicked in. Recalling his utter hatred for the South African, he pumped himself up, raising his aggressive side and calling his alter ego to surface.

As predictable as ever, Greg noticed two men leave The Penny Farthing – one of them was Hector. Both men were staggering, holding each other up whilst kissing. Greg watched patiently – waiting for his time to pounce. He followed both men with his eyes as they engaged in a sexual activity. Greg waited for the men to finish. He saw his signal when Hector started to hit the young man. Screams came from the young man, begging his attacker to stop. Greg heard Hector's laughter in between verbal abuse. Hector's time had arrived.

Greg sprinted over to where the two men were. Pushing the young man out of his way, he hit Hector with a forceful punch to the side of the head, sending the overweight man crashing to the floor. Greg turned and faced the young gay man, who had got back to his feet.

'Go,' Greg told him, using a middle class tone to his voice – the voice of his alter ego.

'Don't hurt me. Do what you want to me, but please don't hurt me.' The young man was terrified by what he had just witnessed, although he saw the man in the shiny black suit and mask as his saviour.

'Go. Fuck off and clean yourself up!' Greg ordered with an aggressive tone.

'Thank you,' the young man replied, not knowing what to say as he made his getaway.

As Hector raised himself to a kneeling position, a lightning kick removed the air from his lungs. He coughed and spluttered, fighting to find the stolen air as his eyes filled with tears. He crashed back down onto his stomach, wincing with the pain and clutching his chest.

'STOP, STOP!' he pleaded, still trying to replace the oxygen missing from his lungs. 'What do you want?' he pleaded.

Greg walked slowly around the overweight South African and waited until the man was on all fours. From behind, Greg released a pulverizing kick which landed perfectly, crushing the man's genitals.

'I want you,' Greg answered bluntly.

'What do you want?' Hector begged, as he winced in agony.

'I applaud you Hector, you take a beating well – like a man, but you're not a man, you're an insult to all men.'

'What are you on about?' Hector asked, trying to get to his feet.

'Don't get up!' Greg warned.

Hector decided to listen to his attacker's advice. He stayed on the ground adopting a sitting position as this guy did not look like he was joking.

'What do you want?' Hector asked, in a sheepish manner.

'I want you. I have to deliver you to someone.'

'Do I have a choice?'

Greg appreciated the sarcasm in Hector's question. 'Everything begins with choice, Hector. Yes, you have a choice to make and that choice will shape the rest of your life. You can choose to resist – bad choice in my opinion, run – another bad choice – or surrender. Whatever you choose, you need to make it quick. Time is of the essence Hector. One thing is certain though.'

'What's that?'

'You are coming with me.' There was a definite authority in his voice. Greg was already holding a leather-bound, tightly stitched cosh which he swung, striking Hector on the back of his head.

'Lights out Hector. We'll talk later.'

Staying in the shadowed boundaries of the car park, Greg dragged Hector to his van. The back doors had been deliberately left unlocked. Greg bundled the slobbish oaf into the back of his van, used zip-ties around Hector's wrists and ankles, placed duct tape over his mouth and a cloth hood over his head before closing the rear doors firmly.

Once in the front, Greg removed his mask, started the engine and drove away in an unhurried manner in order not to attract any attention. During the journey to the disused multi-storey car park, Greg could hear the dull sound of movement in the back of his van.

'Good, that will make things easier at the other end,' Greg thought with a smile.

The journey time matched Greg's calculations exactly. Greg slowed the van, applied the handbrake and got out. He needed to open the gate that the building contractor had erected to keep trespassers out. On a previous visit, Greg had swapped the padlock provided by the building contractor, for his own. The padlock snapped open and the gate followed the momentum. Greg got back into the van and drove, exiting the van to close the gate behind him. The van stopped on level four. Greg opened the back doors with caution. Hector remained still.

Greg hit Hector with a thunderous blow. The crunch he felt under his knuckles confirmed that two of Hector's ribs had crumbled under the force. Hector coughed, his mouth filled with blood.

'Just to let you know where we stand,' Greg said.

Hector tried to reply but it was no use, the duct tape covered his mouth and muffled his words. The hood hid the tears of pain in his eyes.

Greg dragged Hector forward.

'I'm going to free your legs. Don't do anything foolish that might make me regret my generosity.'

Greg sliced through the plastic zip-tie, freeing Hector's legs.

'Stand up and walk,' Greg ordered.

Hector did as instructed – still walking, staggering and stumbling. Once they had reached a previously designated area, Greg threw Hector to the ground. Handcuffing both Hector's wrists and his ankles, Greg sliced through the zip-tie that had bound Hector's hands then removed the hood that covered his head. Hector squinted, trying to focus, navigating his vision through the darkness.

'Where's your mobile?' Greg enquired, ripping the duct tape from his quarry's mouth.

Hector winced against the sting of the adhesive being forced from his lips.

'In my pocket… it's in my trouser pocket, front pocket,' Hector replied.

Greg placed his hand in the pocket he had been directed to and removed Hector's mobile phone. 'You won't need this anymore,' Greg told him assuming his alter ego's voice.

'Where are we?' Hector enquired.

Greg moved close – the big South African was truly petrified. The fear set deeply through his eyes, the window of the soul.

'You can ask me as many questions as you like,' Greg prompted.

'Who wants me here?'

'I do.'

'You said that you were delivering me to someone,' Hector was confused enough already and this was not helping him make sense of his predicament.

'I want you here, but the truth is, he doesn't know you're here yet.'

'I don't understand,' he said confused and dazed. 'Am I going to die here? Is he going to kill me here, God damn it?'

'No not yet. Let me explain. You are a married man, your wife, bless her, defends you to the hilt, even though, in her heart, she knows what an absolute bastard you are. You treat her like shit. Tonight, after fucking that guy, you would have gone home and smacked your wife around a bit, and then you might have decided that you wanted to fuck her too. You didn't even wear a condom when you fucked that guy and you wouldn't even wash your cock before shoving it up your wife, you piece of shit!' Greg was beginning to lose his temper, he paused, gathered himself. Control was everything.

'How do you know so much about me?' Hector enquired.

'I know everything Hector.'

Hector cursed to himself.

'You would have beat that guy up if I hadn't intervened. Have you not heard of AIDS? Your wife may have contracted the virus because of you, your kids could even have it. All the people you have had sexual contact with may have contracted the aids virus from you. You, Hector, may be responsible for all their deaths. Do you give a fuck? No you fucking don't.' Greg stopped abruptly, as he felt an overwhelming power of dominance.

'You're going to kill me aren't you?' Hector blurted out in panic.

'No, I've already told you I'm not, that's the job of the person you'll be meeting tomorrow. That's if he decides to do it. We'll have to leave that for tomorrow.' Greg stopped speaking and walked away. He felt like a giant, no more than a giant, a god.

'Where are you going?' Hector's fears grew.

Greg returned a couple of minutes later, holding a bottle of vodka.

'Who are you? Why are you doing this to me? What is that for?' Hector rambled.

'It's for you Hector – I'm going to help you drink it,' Greg decided to only answer Hector's last question.

Greg then broke the seal on the screw cap on the bottle. He grabbed Hector's head, pulling it back sharply. Hector opened his mouth, gasping for air in order to soften the shock. 'Drink up,' Greg said whilst pouring the transparent liquid down the South African's throat without concern. The liquid oozed from the corners of Hector's mouth. Hector desperately fought for air, swallowing the alcoholic spirit seemed the only answer, but the more he swallowed, the more the burning alcohol flowed. Greg forced Hector to finish the whole bottle – a whole litre of vodka was now racing its way around the South Africans bloodstream.

'Stop, please!' Hector choked, before vomiting.

Greg did not reply. He quietly stepped back, avoiding the substance that had projected its way from Hector's intestines. Hector's eyes glazed over, his head throbbed; the pain from the rest of his body had diluted. His vision wobbled, his surroundings shook and everything seemed to vibrate. The back of his throat stung; the acid contained in his vomit stuck. Coughing, he tried to clear his airways. His eyelids started to feel heavy. Unconsciousness followed.

Greg crouched over the unconscious South African and rolled him over onto his stomach. Greg removed a small tube of Super Glue and emptied the contents along the crease that ran down the centre of the seat of Hector's jeans. Rolling Hector's completely limp body onto his side, he placed the empty vodka bottle in the crevice, forcing the crease into Hector's anal crack. The Super Glue served its purpose. Greg smiled, deciding not to replace the duct tape, in case Hector was to vomit again. The South African choking to death on his own vomit was not part of the plan.

***

Greg arrived home carrying his sports bag. He quickly had a shower. Sitting in the living room he checked the time. Almost five-thirty, time had escaped him; he was exhausted. His bed begged for his company.

Chapter Eighteen

Greg stirred from his less than restful sleep. Tossing and turning, his mind was unable to relax, filled with thoughts of Sharon, Brian, Hector, and now Martin had found his way in. He decided to get up in order to shake away these intruders.

As he walked into the kitchen he checked his mobile phone; Karen had sent him a text.

Morning. Hope you had a good evening. Have fun 2nite. Looking 4ward 2lunch 2moro.xxx

Greg did not have too much to do today. He had arranged to meet Martin for a boys' night out though that was not for a good few hours yet. With trembling hands, Greg made himself something to eat. He was starving. He tried to navigate his way around his kitchen, his heart continued to race as the flashbacks blurred his vision. The moment soon passed as soon as his taste buds were engaged, his thoughts drifted elsewhere.

***

Uncontrollable shivering woke Hector. The concrete slab he lay on acted like a block of ice. His head pounded with a sharp jabbing needle-like pain. His sore ribs made breathing difficult and he felt a burning sensation from his groin. Something did not feel right. He rolled over and shuffled his left hand down to feel why he had a tearing sensation from his anal crevice.

'What the fuck?' His sense of touch informed him that a large bottle had been stuck to the area. It was at that moment that everything started to flood back. Tears filled his eyes and he sobbed without control. He knew this was going to be the last place he would ever see, there was no escape. Coming to terms with his reality was too much for him and he urinated on himself.

Hector looked around to try to understand his surroundings, but could only see a vast open space. He noticed a lone table, it looked steel. The table was located around twenty feet away, with a few items sitting on top. It was then he remembered what he had been told. 'Who else is that fucker bringing here?' he asked himself, as he desperately tried to formulate a means of escape.

***

Greg had a lot to do. Firstly, he had to pick up a package from an agreed meeting point – no questions asked. Greg's shady internet portfolio was escalating by the day. One dodgy contact led to another, and so on. Greg had decided that he was going to drug Martin once he had lured him back to his flat. His extensive research had given him the best possible drug, a date rape drug named Rohypnol. This particular drug, which has been readily available for many years, is intended for use as a surgical anaesthetic and muscle relaxant. However, with a strong enough dose, it would be possible to be used as a sleeping pill. The effects are almost immediate, starting within fifteen minutes of consumption and can last up to twelve hours if taken on an empty stomach. Martin's stomach would be almost empty, with only alcohol in his digestive system.

The effects of Rohypnol consumption are: sedation, difficulty with concentration, dizziness, poor balance and walking difficulties. When taken with alcohol, the cocktail proves much more potent – there is an increased nervous system depression, with symptoms such as confusion, loss of memory and thinking difficulties.

During later years, and because Rohypnol has long been used as a rape drug, a blue dye was added in order to make the drug more obvious and slower to dissolve. However, the blue dye cannot be seen in coke, red wine, or in coloured beer bottles. Rohypnol and other of its forms are readily available on the street, so the blue dye does little to limit its use as a drink-spiking drug.

Greg knew Martin well enough to know that Martin would not be able to resist an offer of more beer, a free curry, and a pornographic movie – which Greg would use to lure Martin back to his flat at the end of the night.

Chapter Nineteen

Walking at an almost leisurely pace, Greg listened to the passing traffic. 'The busier the better,' he told himself. Greg knew nothing about the person he was going to meet – only that they would know him. He had been instructed to carry a pink umbrella. He had purchased the umbrella en route. A French bar in Camden Town was where the rendezvous was to take place.

Greg arrived and checked the time. He was early, though not too early, only ten minutes which was good.

From the outside, La François looked like a pleasant, friendly establishment – modern with a hint of a yesteryear in the background. The furniture was very trendy, with leather and chrome armrests that matched the tables – immaculate. The paintings looked expensive, most displayed nude or scantily clad females.

Greg sat at an available table and tried to visually locate his contact.

'Hello, sir. What can I get for you?' a waiter enquired, with a hint of a French accent.

'White coffee please, mate,' Greg replied.

'One moment please, sir,' the waiter replied, before scuttling off.

As Greg turned his head back, away from the waiter, he noticed that a young woman had sat at his table.

'Sorry love, that seat's taken,' Greg said, smiling.

'Yes, it's taken by me. Nice colour, your umbrella,' the woman replied. Her accent was not easy to place.

The woman looked like she was lost, but only lost in a sense that she was dealing with a novice.

'I have something for you and you have something for me,' she said, returning a smile.

The waiter returned, delivering Greg his coffee. 'Can I get you anything madam?'

'Yes, coffee – white with sugar – brown sugar.' Her accent was more prominent; Turkish seemed like a safe bet.

'Thank you madam, one moment,' the waiter smiled, scuttling off again.

The woman looked at Greg, not leaving his eye-line; she placed a small Jiffy Bag on the table in front of him.

'Go to the men's and check the contents. Don't try to leave without paying, if you do I will fuck you in your head,' she smiled.

'You can't fuck what you don't understand,' Greg replied, returning a smile. 'Try ripping me off and I'll cut your tits off!'

Greg stood up and made his way to the men's toilet, once inside he locked himself in an available cubicle and checked the contents of the Jiffy Bag – it was all there. He went back to his table.

'Your turn,' the woman said.

Greg slid an envelope across the shiny table top. 'It's all there,' he told her firmly.

'I like to count – It makes me feel better,' she told him.

Greg looked at his coffee, his mind was now suspicious. He watched as the young woman openly counted the money. It was then that Greg knew that someone else in the bar was linked to her. He did not care who, but almost automatically he was planning his attack, should the occasion turn sour. He had become very organized lately.

'Everything is in order,' the woman told Greg. 'I don't have to fuck you in the head and you don't have to cut my tits off,' she laughed. 'Join me in a brandy?'

'I don't have time,' Greg told her.

'What a pity,' the young woman replied. 'OK, I'll buy your coffee then, Goodbye.'

Greg nodded his head politely and stood up, not bothering to pick up his umbrella – he was occupied surveying his surroundings. It was clear that he was not out of the woods yet. There was at least one other wolf in La François. He made his way to the exit and left, glancing back through the large panelled window. Greg was right to be suspicious; the waiter that had served him joined the woman and kissed her passionately. He thought it had been suspicious that the waiter had not returned with her coffee. Greg made his way back to the tube station – full-steam ahead…

Chapter Twenty

Greg had arranged to meet Martin in a pub called The Blackbirds on Blackbird Hill – halfway between Wembley Park and Neasden. That said, the meeting place was a little out of Martin's way as the pair were planning to move on to wherever the mood took them. Greg made sure that he had a dozen bottles of beer in the fridge, ready for when he and Martin returned. Putting on a generous amount of aftershave, Greg checked his hair, wallet, mobile phone and keys before leaving.

He was going to catch the number fifty-two bus which would drop him off outside The Blackbirds. The bus arrived, almost on time. Greg stepped on, paid the driver and found a vacant seat. To make the journey more pleasant, he decided to phone Karen.

'Hello,' he said.

'Blimey… Hello stranger?' Karen replied, sarcastically.

'Sorry, I know that I haven't been in touch all day, but…'

'But?' Karen snapped.

'But I've been busy!' Greg snapped back.

'You couldn't see me last night and you can't see me tonight because you're too busy.'

'Fucking hold on a minute, I didn't say I was too busy to see you…I said…'

'Save it Greg.'

'Save what? You know I've had this drink with Mart arranged for almost a fucking week now.'

'And?'

'And fuck all. I'm taking you out for lunch tomorrow aren't I?'

'I hope that you're not keeping me away at evenings for some other bird?'

'Don't be so fucking stupid.'

'I'm stupid now am I?' Karen giggled signifying that the danger was over.

'Saying rubbish like that, you are!'

'You on your way to meet Mart now?' Karen enquired, softening her tone.

'Yeah, I'm meeting him in The Blackbirds.'

'You blokes,' Karen laughed. 'You really know where to go, don't you? I was only pulling your leg babe.'

'Just because we're meeting there, it doesn't mean we're going to stay in there all night.'

'A tenner says you do.'

'Make it twenty and you've got yourself a wager my dear lady,' Greg smiled warmly.

'You're on, my dear fellow.'

'Here's my stop. See you tomorrow,' Greg announced.

'Have a good night – Love you.'

'You too,' Greg replied feeling slightly uncomfortable.

He stepped off the bus and checked the time; he was early for the second time that day.

The Blackbirds was not an impressive building to look at. The history of the building was, in fact, dull. Thirty years previously, someone had decided to purchase two of the neighbouring houses and join them making one single building. It had unimaginatively been named after the road the building was located on, Blackbird Hill. Inside, the building was completely different. You would be forgiven for forgetting where you were.

The open plan idea gave the impression of vast space. The bar was circled in the middle, almost like an island. There were no hanging optics, no unsightly mirrors. It was as though the place had been morphed from another time, a future-proof time.

Greg walked up to the bar and ordered two pints of lager. Once the drinks had arrived, he paid the barman.

'Has Mart been in?' Greg asked, on receiving his change.

'No, but I've not been on long. Do you want me to find out?' the barman replied.

'No, thanks anyway.'

'No problem.'

Greg left the bar and stood by a games machine, resting both his drinks on the top of the machine.

'Is that one for me?' a voice enquired.

Greg knew the voice. 'Course it is.'

'Cheers, mate,' Martin said, taking a large gulp, 'You wouldn't believe the day I've had.'

'Tell me,' Greg relied.

'Fuck me, where do I begin? You know that dickhead brother-in-law of mine, Hector?' Martin began, 'He never went home to my sister's last night... we all know where he goes on a Friday night.'

'Or, where he tells us he goes,' Greg interrupted, 'We all know how full of shit he is Mart!'

'Well, he never went home and no one's heard from him. His mobile is switched off, and, well, he's missing.'

'What do you mean "missing"?'

'I know what a wanker he is Greg. But it's my sister... The Old Bill have told her that he's gotta be missing for twenty-four hours before she can report him missing and, even then, they've told her not to hold her breath. Listen, mate, I know that he's a fucking loser but, at the end of the day, he's never stayed out all night. Alright, he may not get home till the early hours, but he's always got home.'

'What do you think's happened to him?'

'I think someone's beat the shit out of him and he's dead in a gutter somewhere.'

'Is that what your sister thinks?' Greg said, shrugging his shoulders, 'He'll be OK, mate, he'll turn up soon enough.'

'She's gone off on one, mate. She's between a rock and a hard place at the moment. I wish I could do more, you know?'

'You'll find him, I guarantee it Mart,' Greg smiled, secretly finding the whole thing amusing.

'Same again?' Martin enquired.

'Yeah, you downed that quickly, mate.'

'I needed it, mate, believe me.'

The two men continued talking, with Hector being the main topic of conversation. Time ran away from the pair of them.

'Listen Mart, I've had a great idea,' Greg said, placing his arm over Martin's shoulder. 'Why don't we move to a pub closer to mine – I've got plenty of beer in the fridge, a porno that I haven't watched, and we can grab a curry on the way. What do you think?'

'It's further for me to get home, mate,' Martin replied, slurring his words slightly. The background noise, along with the copious amounts of alcohol he had consumed hampered his hearing.

'Fuck it, you can stay at mine.'

'But we'll get a taxi from here, pick up a curry on the way, then it's beer, curry, and porn all the way!' Martin said, getting a little too vocal.

The pair continued to laugh and joke about times gone by, getting louder as the evening progressed, singing along with the jukebox, swearing at the fruit machine and telling adult jokes. A couple of times, the pair come close to causing more than an argument with some of the other customers. This is exactly what Greg wanted, he needed the attention – after all, they were friends on a night out.

'Get some shots in,' Martin told Greg. 'We're celebrating.'

'What we celebrating?'

'Friendship, being mates,' Martin slurred.

'Not a chance. That's it for tonight,' the barman announced.

'But it's not even ten o'clock,' Greg said.

'You two have had enough for one night, come on lads,' the barman replied.

'Never mind, there's plenty of beer at mine,' Greg told Martin, as he laughed.

'You phone a taxi and I'll nip for a piss,' Martin slurred.

'No worries,' Greg replied.

Greg stood waiting for Martin to return from the toilet, so they could leave the pub. He seemed to take forever, though he eventually appeared. He looked unsteady on his feet, swaying slightly as he walked.

'Come on. Our taxi's outside,' Greg told Martin.

The two men swayed together as they left. Once in the taxi, Greg encouraged Martin to sing along to a song that was playing on the taxi's radio. The driver did not seem to mind.

'If you're gonna be sick, tell me and I'll stop,' the driver told the drunken pair. 'Don't chuck-up in the back of my fucking cab – OK?'

'We're not gonna puke,' Martin replied, interrupting his singing.

Greg wanted, needed, the taxi driver to remember them.

They reached their destination. Greg carried their Indian meal. Greg paid the driver, giving him a generous tip for his troubles, for both the detour to collect their meal and for the aural abuse his eardrums had suffered en route. He would definitely remember them.

'Thanks mate, enjoy the rest of your evening,' the taxi driver gleefully told Greg.

Greg and Martin clambered up the stairs and bounced their way into Greg's flat. Once in, Martin fell on Greg's sofa with a joyful bounce.

'I'll get us some beers,' Greg announced.

Greg slipped into the kitchen and retrieved two chilled bottles of larger from the fridge. He had strategically placed two Rohypnol pills on some kitchen towel on the work surface, before dropping them in Martin's bottle of larger and waiting for the fizz to settle.

Martin had remained on the sofa, wearing a drunken smile, completely oblivious.

'Down in one,' Greg said, passing Martin the spiked bottle of lager.

'On three,' Martin said, adding a hiccup. Martin did the countdown and the two men raced, gulping the contents of each bottle down as fast as they could. They finished level.

Greg took both empty bottles back to the kitchen, placing them both on the work surface. He would need to dispose of the drugged bottle carefully later...

Greg returned with two more bottles, this time neither was

spiked.

'Where's my curry?' Martin cried.

'Hold your horses, I've only got one pair of hands,' Greg said smiling to himself.

As Greg entered the living room, he noticed Martin had slid down the sofa, in a doubled-over sleeping position.

'What are you doing? Are you alright, mate?'

Martin did not reply – he remained still.

Greg dashed to the kitchen, the clock was ticking. He knew that he had twelve hours. He needed to consume vast amounts of coffee in order to sober himself up and quickly switched the kettle on. Pouring generous amounts of milk into a large mug, along with two heaped spoonfuls of coffee, Greg proceeded to gulp down the contents. He rushed around in an almost frantic panic.

***

The following three hours were a bit of a blur. Martin had been securely placed in the back of Greg's van. His hands and legs were fastened by plastic zip-ties and duct tape was placed over his mouth as a precaution.

Once the pair had reached their destination, Greg donned his mask and retrieved Martin from his makeshift confinement, heaving the unconscious man onto his shoulder, fireman style.

Hector opened his eyes, 'Who's there?'

'Hector, I'm glad that you're still with us,' Greg replied, 'You might recognise this man – a relative of yours I believe,' Greg laughed.

'What the fuck is he doing here?'

Greg gently placed Martin on the ground, securing him by fastening a handcuff around his ankle. Greg then removed both zip-ties and the duct tape and slid his hand into Martin's trouser pocket, removing his mobile phone. Martin did not stir.

'What's he doing here?' the gravelly-voiced South African asked for a second time. He sounded like a beaten man.

'He's going to decide both of your fates,' Greg answered without making eye contact. Turning to the South African, 'What do you prefer, Beer or whisky?' he asked.

'Water… I don't feel like celebrating!'

'Just answer the question. Water was not on offer, Hector.' Greg's head turned sharply bringing Hector's pathetic body into his sight, 'I asked you a question, or do I have to decide for you?' he barked.

'I don't care – I don't have a fucking choice,' he replied, his whole body trembling with fear.

Greg turned away and went over to the table. Opening one of the draws he removed an unopened bottle of whiskey. He then produced a key and held it up.

'Use the whiskey to swallow this key. Don't try anything stupid, you will swallow this key – either the easy way, or the other way.'

The overweight man looked at him completely bemused as to why he was being asked to swallow this key. He was calling the shots and in a dominant position.

'You're going to have to help me, my hands…'

'Your hands are free enough. Don't fuck with me Hector.' Greg glared, before sending a thunderous open-handed slap across Hector's face. Hector's head rocked with the impact, his only response was a small shriek; his spine tingled with panic.

'You can let me go, please let me go. I will change. I'll do whatever you tell me to. I'm asking for another chance to save myself,' Hector begged.

'It's too far gone for that – there's no second chances in the game of life Hector.'

'I'm in agony, why the bottle? Why the bottle? Please take it out.'

'The bottle is to prevent you shitting out the key.'

Greg passed the bottle of whiskey to Hector and forced the key into his mouth. 'Swallow it!'

Hector started to cry as he placed the bottle to his lips and opened his mouth. Gripping his arm, Greg tilted the man's head back and began assisting with pouring the whiskey down his fat throat. Whiskey was overflowing out of the sides of Hector's mouth. He choked, trying to swallow the liquid as fast as it was being poured. He found it hard to breathe and tried to pull away.

'Enough,' Hector pleaded, gasping for air as he did. 'My head is fucking doing summersaults!' Greg did not have time to sympathise and continued to pour the remainder of the whiskey over Hector's head. 'OK, OK,' Hector screamed, as the alcohol started to sting his eyes.

Greg stepped back, just in case Hector was going to vomit.

'I think you owe it to me.'

'What do I owe you Hector?'

'Tell me my fate – please, think of my children, I'm a family man.'

'Martin is going to decide your fate. All will become clear when he wakes up. Until then, all you can do is wait.'

'Look at me, look will you? I've pissed myself, I'm fucking freezing and I'm starving. I will never go with another man, if that's why I'm here.'

'Hector, Hector, Hector,' Greg laughed. 'Who else can see you in this state? No one can. So no one gives a fuck what you look like. You've spent most of you putrid life in this state. Come on, let's be honest, personal hygiene doesn't rate high in your to-do list, does it? So why are you worrying about it now? A bit too late for that isn't it?'

'How long have I got? My family... what about my family?' Hector begged.

'Martin will wake up in a few hours, you can ask him. I'll be back to see you both later. All will become clear Hector. Try not to worry too much...' Greg replied, not answering any of the wasted questions he had been asked. Greg walked away...

Chapter Twenty-One

'What the fuck's going on?' Martin demanded, as he woke.

'Martin, it's me, Hector. We are prisoners.'

'What the fuck is going on Hector… and what the fuck are you doing here?' Martin demanded answers, his voiced raised, anger raging through his veins.

'Do you remember the guy in the black suit that they were talking about on the news? He bought us both here.'

'Fucking hell my head hurts. Why?'

'He didn't explain that bit. I think it's me he wants, you are just here to make up the numbers.'

'Fucking hell Hector, where are we? We need to get away. How long have we been here?'

'I've been here since yesterday… I think. You arrived a few hours ago.'

'You look like shit; you've been given a right fucking kicking,' Martin said, as he checked himself. 'He doesn't seem to have touched me.'

'That's why I said he only wants me!'

'Hold on a minute,' Martin sat up, 'I thought she was making him up, if it's the same guy, he made that girl kill her fella. Oh no – fucking hell Hector!' Martin panicked.

'You're here to kill me Martin. And there's no way out.' Hector said pointing to his posterior, 'It's a bottle and, yes, it's been stuck there. I've tried to remove it but it's too painful.'

'Why?' Martin gasped. 'What have we done?'

'It's me, what I've done, I think you're here for the same reasons he used the girl.'

'We need to stop him, to tell him to stop,' Martin said urgently.

'When he bought you here, he stuck that handcuff around your ankle and then made me swallow a key. I would place money that the key he made me swallow is the key to that handcuff and the bottle is to stop me shitting it out!'

'What are we gonna do?'

'Wait for him to come back. Listen Martin, I know I haven't been a brilliant husband to your sister, and I've not been there for our kids. All this is a little too late I know... but I have to make peace, there's no way that we can escape. I've tried begging him but he is cold. I have to face it, I'm going to die here. If you don't do it, he will. You might not have a choice – make no mistake. You have to do it, to save yourself.'

Martin couldn't take it in, 'I was out with Greg, but I don't remember getting back to Greg's. I was gonna stay at his... I don't remember leaving the pub... oh my fucking God, this must be a fucking bad dream.'

'He got me from around the back of The Penny. Listen, it's no secret that I swing both ways – Mandy knows, and always has done. He must hate gays.'

'I never thought it was true. I thought you were just a mouthy bastard!'

'It's common where I come from.' Hector coughed the pain from his broken ribs more potent now. 'I know that...what I'm trying to say is that Mandy accepts me for who I am.'

'That's fucking bullshit! If Mandy knew, you would have been history – and if I had known...' Martin started to cry, saddened by what he had just been told.

'Cut the bollocks Martin. Mandy would never have allowed you to do anything and you know that!'

'She's protected you for years Hector. But look where you are now – look where we are now,' Martin snapped, tripping on his words. 'This is your fault, you dirty bastard. I've been dragged in.' Once again, Martin paused, his anger intensifying his hatred for Hector. 'I'll tell him to fucking kill you; then my sister will be rid of you. I'll tell him that I ain't gay and he'll let me go. That shit ain't got fuck all to do with me.'

'Well, he seems to think it's got plenty to do with you, or you wouldn't be here would you? You stupid bastard!'

'No. If you fucking understood what your fucking arsehole was for, then neither of us would be here, would we? And he wouldn't have shoved a bottle up it, would he?'

'Be as angry as you want, it doesn't change anything. We're both here, and we ain't fucking going nowhere, unless he says so.'

'You know that, whatever happens, it's all down to you. It's your fucking fault.'

'I know one thing… he's not bothered what we think.'

Chapter Twenty-Two

Karen walked at a steady pace, making her way to the exit of the tube station.

'Hello sexy!' she called out.

Greg stood, casually leaning against a wall reading a newspaper. He slowly looked up on hearing Karen's voice.

'Are you catching up on yesterday's football?' she asked.

'Yeah, something like that – West Ham lost, again and Chelsea only managed a draw,' he laughed. 'How are you? You look gorgeous,' he added, as he gave her a full kiss on the lips, complemented with a big hug.

'Wow. I'm much better now. Did you miss me last night or something?' she asked, as she took hold of his hand, gripping it tightly.

They both started to walk in the direction of the restaurant.

'No!' Greg replied, teasing Karen with his answer.

'What did you get up to last night then?' Karen tried to keep the conversation going. 'You don't look too worse for wear.'

'Met up with Mart, stayed in The Blackbirds all night, so I owe you twenty quid.' He turned, giving her a kiss on her cheek. 'Mart came back to mine – we got a curry on the way, had a few beers at mine, before we both crashed out. Old Mart was up early though, gone before I got out of bed.'

'He must have had stuff to do?'

'You'll never guess what Mart told me about his brother-in-law.'

'Hector?'

'Yeah, Hector.'

'Go on, tell me.'

'Hector went out Friday night and hadn't been seen since.'

'What?'

'He hadn't gone home and Mart told me that his sister, Mandy, Hector's wife, had called The Old Bill.'

'Well, we've all heard the stories he comes out with.'

'That's what I said – I said that he's probably been beaten up or something.'

'When he does go home, he'll have some explaining to do,' Karen laughed.

Greg smiled to himself – Karen was eating out the palm of his hand. 'Yeah, I know, he's in deep shit!' Greg laughed as he opened the door to the restaurant and, being the gentleman, held the door open for Karen to walk through.

'Hello, sir, madam, have you a reservation?' asked a well-presented middle aged man.

'Yes,' Greg replied. 'Mr O'Hara, table for two for one o'clock,' Greg smiled politely.

'Yes, Mr O'Hara you are a little early. Would sir and madam like to have a drink at the bar while I check if your table is ready?'

'Yes, why not?' Greg smiled.

As the pair reached the bar, they could hear a man and a woman having a heated discussion. Karen looked at Greg and shrugged her shoulders. 'Leave it at home,' she giggled.

'Ignore them. What would you like to drink?' Greg asked.

'I'll have a dry white wine please,' Karen replied.

Greg ordered Karen's wine and himself a pint of lager. Moments later a waiter appeared. 'Mr O'Hara your table is ready. May I take your drinks to your table for you?'

'Yes please – and can you put them on my bill?'

'Certainly, sir.'

The waiter took their drinks, placed them on a silver tray and led the way. As they were being seated they could hear the heated conversation that Karen commented on at the bar. A couple seemed to be having an argument.

'Listen Brent, if you don't like it you know what you can do,' the woman firmly told the man sitting opposite.

'No, you listen to me Val, it is not happening,' the man replied, trying to stand his ground.

'Well, it's all a bit too late for you to decide what is and what isn't happening – don't you think?'

'We can sort this out. We always have in the past.'

'You think you can call the shots?'

'Listen to me, you silly cow. He who pays the piper, names the tune, just you remember that, hey?'

The whole restaurant could hear the couple though, for some reason, the staff were reluctant to ask the couple to keep the noise down.

Brent and Valerie Hope were a very wealthy couple, their money had come from Brent's software business which was doing as well as it ever had. Valerie was a lady of leisure. Brent had spoilt her from the day they married; she got whatever she wanted which was the main reason she stayed with him. He, on the other hand, worshiped the ground she walked on, she was a very attractive woman for her years. Brent had just turned forty and his wife was three years his junior. It was evident that a cosmetic surgeon had lent a hand in sculpting her statuesque figure.

'I'm telling you that if you don't put a stop to this, I will leave you,' Valerie told Brent.

'Leave me and you'll get nothing,' Brent snapped.

'I'll bleed you dry,' Valerie snarled.

'OK, time out. I can't understand why you two have to share your matrimonial problems with the rest of us. Can't you take your personal problems somewhere else and let us enjoy our lunch in peace?' Karen interrupted, she could not listen to any more.

'Mind your own business,' Valerie barked.

'We would love to, but you two won't let us,' Karen bitched back.

'I don't have to put up with this – Brent, say something,' she ordered her silent husband to speak.

'He can't get a word in edgeways, poor bloke.'

'You leave my husband alone!'

'Ha! I think you should listen to yourself and maybe you should leave him alone,' Karen was beginning to enjoy this. It was obvious that no one had ever challenged this woman.

'I've always thought that this place was going downhill. I don't know why they've lowered their standards by allowing riff raff like you to dine here.' Valerie decided that it was time for the gloves to come off, and to direct her aim below the belt.

'Firstly, you snotty bitch, we are not riff raff, and secondly at least we know how to behave in places like this, you stuck up cow.'

One of the waiters came marching over.

'George can you please remove these people, they are upsetting my husband and I...'

'Don't even think about it,' Greg said, standing up. He had remained silent for too long, 'If you and your husband want to argue, bitch and fight, please, for the sake of the rest of us, don't do it here. We work hard so that we can eat in places like this – today is a treat for our sort, whatever sort we are,' Greg turned, glaring at the waiter, 'If you're going to kick anyone out, it's going to be her – understood?'

Another man walked over, 'I'm the manager, what seems to be the problem?'

'There is not a problem here, just a misunderstanding, that's all. My wife and I are leaving. May we have our bill please Frederick and I would like to buy these two fine people a drink, by way of an apology,' the woman's husband said, giving Greg and Karen an apologetic smile – immediately switching it to a glare at his wife. The look sent shivers down her spine. 'I am very sorry if my wife offended you, will you accept a bottle of champagne with our complements?' he continued.

'Yes, that'd be a great place to start – I want to hear it from her,' Karen smiled, still wanting more.

'I am not apologizing and that champagne is not from me, it's from him. Come on let's go,' Valerie barked her disapproval.

'If you were a bloke...' Greg laughed.

'Well, she's not a lady,' Karen interrupted. Roars of laughter bellowed from the surrounding tables.

Completely humiliated, Valerie stormed out the restaurant to a standing ovation. Brent walked over to Karen and took her hand, raising it to his lips and kissing the back of it.

'Bravo, bravo,' was all he said, through his controlled laughter. 'Please enjoy the champagne,' he added as he shook Greg's hand and left.

'The house has decided that the bill for your lunch is with our complements. Please order anything from the menu, you are guests of the house today,' Frederick smiled, bowing his head politely.

'Thank you Frederick, we will. That's very kind of you,' Karen replied, holding her head high.

Greg glanced through the window and noticed the couple getting into a very expensive-looking car, he also noticed that the number plate on the vehicle was a private number, a number he could easily memorise – a quick phone call would get him what he wanted to know. He had become a very well-connected man, with contacts in all kinds of places. Val was not going to get away with treating people the way she did. Valerie Hope had just been self-selected.

'The world was going to be a better place without her in it,' Greg mumbled to himself.

'What did you say?' Karen enquired, knocking the champagne back.

Greg did not realise he had spoken aloud, 'Nothing… I just can't understand people like that.' He winked. 'Not bad this champagne.'

'Chilled perfectly,' Karen giggled. 'To the unhappy couple,' she announced. The pair touched glasses – finely cut crystal flutes pinged with an enigmatic sound.

'Quality,' Greg winked.

Karen and Greg ate until they could not eat anymore. The pair had also consumed nearly four bottles of champagne between them. Noticing the couple's drunken state, Frederick had decided to order the pair a cab, asking Greg where they would like to be taken.

Once their cab arrived, Fredrick informed the driver of their chosen destination and paid him. When he was sure they were both safely inside the cab, he slapped the roof with the flat of his hand, signalling to the driver it was safe to move off.

Once the happy couple fell in to Greg's flat, they went to bed to sleep off the champagne – neither of them in a fit state to do anything else.

Almost four hours had past when Greg woke, his bladder acting as his alarm clock. On his return, Greg noticed the time.

'Wake up Karen, it's almost eight o'clock and we've both got work in the morning.' Greg never allowed Karen to stay on a work night.

'OK, OK – give me a minute,' a croaky-voiced Karen replied.

Greg went into the kitchen and put the kettle on. He needed to get rid of Karen. He had other urgent matters to attend to…

Chapter Twenty-Three

As Greg quietly exited the stairwell, he could hear voices and he knew who they belonged to.

'Do you think he's going to leave you here to starve?'

'Why make me swallow that key, and why bring you here?'

'I haven't got a fucking clue! But…' Martin paused, he noticed Greg's movements, 'he's here.' Both men fell silent. Their anticipation made them nervous.

'Martin, glad you could join us,' Greg said as he approached, using his alter ego's middle class tone. 'How are you both?'

'What sort of fucking question is that?' Martin growled, 'I'm fuck all to do with this so just let me go and I won't tell a dicky-bird.'

'A polite one,' Greg replied, 'but if you would rather, we can simply speed things along – unless you have any questions, that is? Because once the ball starts rolling, there's no stopping it!' Greg continued with his approach.

'Who the fuck are you?' Martin asked. 'You sound too posh to be doing this.'

'How stereotypical of you Martin,' Greg laughed. 'Does one have to belong to a lower class to do what I'm doing?'

As he got closer, and both men were able to draw him into their separate focuses, Martin understood what Hector had been trying to tell him – this guy really did exist. From the descriptions on the various news channels and tabloids, this was their guy.

'Holy shit!' Martin involuntarily mumbled, 'it's you.'

'Do I look that bad?' Greg chuckled.

'You're that guy… fucking hell,' Martin's slow, astonished voice made him seem illiterate. 'You're that guy on the news.'

'What guy?' Greg knew where Martin had identified him from, but enjoyed the game play.

'From the Swiss Cottage murder – you're all over the news.'

'I doubt that very much – no one knows I actually exist... until now, that is.'

'If you kill us both they won't!' Hector added.

'But if you let me go...' Martin interrupted.

'I'm not going to kill either of you – but all that will become clear once we wipe away the fog,' Greg said. 'Only you will be able to let you go Martin...'

Greg had completed his approach, and stood in full splendour in front of Martin.

'Fuck me, you're not that big, are you?' Martin growled, trying to test Greg.

'Size is of no significance – it's the size of your arsenal that equips each and every one of us.'

'Fuck off!' Martin spat, 'and let me go. I'm nothing to do with this.'

Greg took a large step forward and slammed the sole of his foot into Martin's chest. The impact stole the air from in Martin's lungs.

'That's where I beg to differ,' Greg growled.

'Nooo...' Hector pleaded, 'please, it's me you want. Leave him alone.'

'I just think that a lesson in control is what is needed here. I'm the one in control; your fate lies in my hands.'

Martin laid on the floor, gasping for air to replenish his empty lungs. His eyes stung as the salty tears streamed and phlegm raced up his windpipe. Martin coughed uncontrollably.

'You can stand, if you think you can offer me a respectable challenge?' Greg giggled. 'Your hands are free and you have a free kicking leg – I'll handicap myself, and I promise not to use my legs. What do you think, Martin? Are you up for the challenge?'

Martin sat up, still trying to regain his composure his mind was in overdrive without being in gear.

'You look bigger than me Martin... but Hector is bigger than both of us. I took him without any effort – what are your thoughts on the matter, Hector?'

'Martin, stay down. Please stay down, don't make things any worse than they already are.' Martin lifted his head – the fire in his eyes announced his aggression.

'Lose your temper, and you've already lost the fight!' Greg said. 'Your brother-in-law is right, stay down. Hector is the target, not you – but all that can be subject to change – your choice.'

'I've got you sussed,' Martin smiled.

'No, Martin, you foolishly think you have. I don't have time for this, save it!' Greg walked away, heading for the table.

'If you don't kill me, I'll find you, you mother fucker!' Martin barked, his anger getting the better of him. 'I'll tie you in knots and feed you to the fish.'

Greg retrieved an object from the table and returned holding Martin's mobile phone.

'I'll leave this on here,' Greg laughed, 'and to show you an act of good faith, I've switched it off in order to preserve the battery life. Your mobile phone, Martin, is your second prize. Once you have freed yourself, you can use it to summon help. Guess where your first prize is?'

Hector's face filled with horror, 'Martin's first prize is the key?' he stammered.

'Correct – sorry, no prize though. Martin, do I still have your attention?'

Martin nodded his head slowly.

'Good. Now, Hector is not a very nice man and, worst of all, he just so happens to be married to your sister. I think before we continue our talk regarding potential prizes, I should give you a bit of background information on Mr and Mrs Hector Hylie's sex life.'

Greg glared at Hector.

'There's no need… Martin hates me enough as it is.'

'How do you know all this?' Martin asked in shock.

'I know everything, Hector!' Greg snarled. 'There are certain blanks that need filling…' Greg paused. 'Your brother-in-law, in times of need, will force himself on your sister, his wife. A common word for this kind of sexual activity is rape! Your sister, his wife, gives in only to save any commotion disturbing the children. Hector would not dare deny any of this. What those on the outside don't know, they have no need to grieve.'

'Why has she lied to me?' Martin begged to know.

'Martin, remember this – your sister loves this piece of shit. We will never understand why. Secondly, lies hurt and harm but it's the truth that destroys and kills.'

Hector remained silent. His secret was out; the shame crushed him.

'OK, moving on,' Greg said, now holding a scalpel, 'as you may have noticed, Hector is not in a position to defend himself and, on the other hand, you, Martin, are only restrained by one ankle. The chain attached is long enough for you to reach Hector. The key that you need to free yourself is now swimming away in Hector's digestive system. You may need this,' Greg said, sliding the scalpel he was holding across the floor. The surgical implement stopped as it came in contact with Martin's leg.

'You want me to cut him open?' Martin gasped. 'Fucking hell! Who do you think I am?'

'How else are you going to get the key? If you don't, you'll die in here with him. Hector is going to die here. You need to choose whether you are going to die in here with him. Everything begins with choice; your next choice will shape the rest of your life Martin. Save yourself. No one will blame you. Hector's going to die anyway, why should you die with him?'

'Why don't you kill him?'

'It's not my place… you have wanted this day to arrive.'

'You fucking coward!' Martin blurted through hot tears.

'All these years you've wanted to teach him a lesson – the lesson is to be taught today, or are you not man enough?'

'Why's Hector got to die? You've taught him his lesson – you said he was going to die here.'

'Because it's Hector's time.'

'If I don't kill him… who will?' Martin interrupted.

'The bulldozers. They are going to demolish this place tomorrow with or without you in it,' Greg bluffed.

'You mother fucker!'

'Anyway, it's been a blast but I've got to be off. Things to do, people to see – you know how it is. Time is ticking away Martin. Goodbye Hector.' Greg walked away.

'Wait!' Martin begged, 'I've got money, about thirty grand, it's yours. Just let me go!'

Greg did not look back.

'Martin…'

'What?' Martin barked.

'You have to save yourself.'

'Fuck me, Hector,' Martin gave Hector a disgusted glare. 'How the fuck could you treat my sister like that? I'm not going to die here. I just don't know how to do it quick, so you don't suffer.'

Hector's eyes welled with tears – tears of horror, not pity.

'Listen, you dirty bastard, if I had of known about this before, I would have beaten the fuck out of you, and then beat the shit out of you, and then kicked you into a fucking coma!' Martin's aggression grew. 'You always knew what would happen if I ever found out, that's why Mandy has been so careful to hide it from me. What did you think I would do? You fucking mug!'

'I never realised… I love Mandy, she's my wife.'

'She's your wife, but she ain't your life. She's your whore, that's how you treat her. She's my sister.' Martin stood and made his way over to Hector.

'Hold on a minute… Please Martin,' Hector begged, 'for pity's sake.'

'I only pity my sister. If you've touched any of those kids...'

'Fuck off – not my own flesh and blood!'

'Other kids?' Martin growled, slashing Hector across the top of his head.

Hector screamed, 'No! No kids. Stop, you bastard!'

Martin started to kick Hector randomly. Then one of his kicks landed square across Hector's throat, causing Hector's windpipe to collapse. Hector choked; blood from the ruptured internal vessels spilled from his mouth. Martin, blinded by rage, stabbed Hector in the face.

Hector tried to curse, his words wheezed; blood bubbled from his lips.

'Die! Die! Die!' Martin barked, repeatedly.

Then Hector froze – his eyes fixated, though empty. A sorrowful look donned his blood covered face.

'Tell Mandy that I'm sorry. Do that for me. Kiss my kids...' Hector wheezed.

'Fuck off!' Martin replied and sliced Hector across the throat twice. Hector's body convulsed – shaking as if it had been struck by a bolt of lightning. The blood slowed with Hector's heart rate. The synchronisation of his life, soul and spirit divorced and departed from the shell that was now his corpse. Hector flopped, his whole body limp and lifeless.

Martin panted. Sweat poured from his entire body, he felt exhausted, drained.

'Fucking hell,' Martin gasped, 'you took some killing you fat fucker.' Adrenalin not allowing reality to set in. 'Where's that key?' Martin shouted, as he sliced into Hector's abdomen.

Chapter Twenty-Four

The telephone rang continuously, interrupting Terry's sleep.

'What?' he bellowed, not bothering to open his eyes.

'There's been another one, mate – another killing.'

'McFarland? What do you mean?' he said, as he sat bolt upright, opening his eyes.

'Another murder, same pattern.'

'Shit, shit, shit! Pick me up now.'

'I'm outside. Are you going to let me in? I'll make us some coffee to take with us.'

'Hold on, I'm on my way down.'

'Who is it?' a sleepy Natalie enquired.

'There's been another murder – you go back to sleep darling, I've gotta go.'

'OK – be careful.'

Terry kissed Natalie on her forehead. She had already returned to her deep slumber.

Terry dressed as he descended the stairs and unlocked the front door.

'You know where the kitchen is,' he told McFarland.

'Don't bother putting your make-up on, we don't have time,' the Scotsman joked.

'Nat's asleep upstairs, mate,' Terry said. 'Keep it down please.'

'Hurry up, and get the rest of your fucking clothes on, you're making me feel sick.'

Terry did not bother responding. He was dressed and back in the kitchen just as McFarland was pouring the milk into the cups.

'Tell me what you know,' he demanded.

'We'll go to the scene – a multi-storey car park, of all places.'

The two men got in McFarland's waiting car.

'OK this is what I know: a man phoned the three nines and was put through to a police station in Borehamwood. The caller told the duty sergeant that a man in a black rubber suit had kidnapped him, Mr Martin Pringle, and his brother-in-law, Mr Hector Hylie, and had taken them to a disused car park in Arkley. Now this is the sick bit, the guy in the black rubber suit chained Hector Hylie to the wall, hands and feet, and handcuffed Martin Pringle to the wall by his ankle. He then forced Hector Hylie to swallow the key to the handcuffs around Martin Pringle's ankle and gave him some sort of knife, telling him to choose what he was going to do. Save himself or die with his brother-in-law.'

'Which nick is he in now? Terry asked.

'He's being moved to The Yard as we speak.'

'OK, we'll go there later. Is the brother-in-law still at the scene?'

'Yes.'

'Good.'

McFarland knew that Terry would want to visit the scene of the crime first – while it was still fresh.

As they arrived at the multi-storey car park, Terry had already removed his seatbelt and was ready to get out the car. Both men took the stairs three at a time, stopping at the floor where they could hear activity. A uniformed police officer stood on the other side of the exit door.

'Oh sorry sir, please go in,' the police officer said apologetically, feeling a little embarrassed after Terry had accidentally hit him with the door.

'Keep up the good work,' McFarland said, reassuringly patting the officer's shoulder.

The two men walked in to where the crime had taken place. There was blood everywhere. The chains that imprisoned both men were still there hanging from the safety railings. McFarland and Terry paced slowly around the area, being careful not to disturb anything. The forensic team were already hard at work.

'What's the story, Dan?' McFarland asked.

'Two men found at the scene – one dead and the other in custody and no trace of anyone else being here. It's a mystery,' the short stubby man answered.

'What was the murder weapon?' Terry asked.

'Early implications suggest a scalpel as that's the only thing that's been recovered. Once we clean him up and get a closer look, I'll be able to give you a more accurate cause of death.'

'Was the weapon left here, close to the body?' Terry continued.

'Yes, indeed it was.'

'Dan, can you give us your gut feeling on the cause of death? A serious answer would be welcome,' McFarland demanded, rejoining the conversation.

'Severe lacerations to throat and abdomen causing haemorrhaging. Death inevitable, due to massive blood loss,' the short stubby man answered with a hardened sadness.

'Was the deceased tortured?' Terry asked.

'I don't know, I'll be able to tell you more when I get him on the slab. All I can tell you is this – he meant to kill him.'

'Thanks Dan. We'll talk later.'

'Nice to see you Terry.' The forensic scientist smiled – pleased that Terry was back – though he was puzzled as to what the capacity of Terry's return was.

'What is your gut telling you now?' McFarland enquired.

'No fucking idea, though, at the moment, I think there is a link. We need to go and talk to him… now!' Terry told McFarland, already making his way out towards the car.

'Hold on, hold on. I've got to make a phone call first. You can't just go walking in there,' McFarland told Terry.

'Phone away. Let's go! Thanks again Dan,' Terry replied, waving his gratitude in gesture. 'And while you're on the phone, talk to whoever it is you need to talk to and tell them to arrange for this leash to be removed.'

'Leash?' McFarland replied blankly.

'I don't need to be walked. I'm going to need more independence and freedom – freedom to roam.'

'I'll see what I can do.'

'Just do it. Please, mate.'

Both men remained silent for the whole journey, their minds in overdrive.

McFarland parked around the rear of the building – the press had camped outside the front and Terry needed to remain off their radar. Both men entered the building using an entrance only the well-informed knew about.

'How are you, Ted?' McFarland said to the sixty-something-year-old desk sergeant.

'I'm OK, and you?' Was the half-hearted response from the grey-haired man, clock-watching until his retirement alarm bell rang.

'Over-worked, under-loved.' Both men chuckled. 'Well, you know why we're here, don't you?'

'Yes, you'll have to wait whilst I get someone to take you to an interview room.'

Both men nodded. Whoever it was that McFarland had phoned was extremely powerful within The Met. Terry had not needed to introduce himself. He thought that his past may have helped, or maybe the desk sergeant thought that he was there on behalf of Thames Television.

A young WPC escorted them down to the long narrow corridor; then she directed them into an interview room.

'Good luck!' was all she said.

As both men walked into the interview room, they noticed that Martin was sitting at the table, his head resting in his hands. He did not bother to look up to see who had entered the room.

'Hello Martin. Are you waiting for legal representation?' McFarland said, opening the conversation.

'No!' Was all he got in return, Martin was not in the mood for talking. He looked exhausted.

'Would you like someone to represent you?' McFarland tried again.

'No thanks.'

'Would you like something to eat or drink? How about a cigarette?'

'I don't need anything,' he said with his head still placed in his hands, his emotions the same.

'You know why we're here, don't you?'

'Yeah I've got a good idea. But I haven't been charged yet… why?'

'We need to clarify a few things first,' Terry said, joining the conversation.

'You're that reporter off the telly aren't you?'

'That's right, but I'm also here trying to help the police piece this jigsaw together.'

'Terry Bane, from the news?' Martin said.

'We're here to talk to you about your dead brother-in-law, Martin.'

'Yeah, I did it, though only to save myself,' Martin replied.

'I need you to tell me what happened,' Terry said. 'Tell me what you know.' Both men sat down, Terry chose to sit directly in front of Martin.

'I woke up chained to a railing in a fucking car park. Hector… Hector… my dead brother-in-law, who was still alive at the time, was chained to another railing.'

'Take your time,' Terry said, reassuringly.

'Hector was already there, like I said. We waited and this guy appeared dressed in a black suit, the suit was stuck to his skin. He wore a mask, but the kind I've never seen before. It was like his face, but it wasn't his face. Anyway, he had made Hector swallow a key, the key to the chain around my ankle.'

'Do you know how you got there? Were you snatched in your sleep?'

'Yeah, I must've been. I'd been out on the lash, so I don't even remember going to bed.'

'Do you live alone, Martin?'

'No, I live with my bird,' Martin paused, 'but I'd been out with my mate, Greg, and I'd planned on crashing at his place, but I honestly don't remember leaving the pub.' Martin sobbed gently.

'Did you see Hector swallow the key?' Terry asked.

'No.'

'OK, please continue,' Terry smiled.

'He then started telling me all kinds of fucked up shit... about Hector and my sister.'

'What kind of things, Martin?'

'I don't wanna go into that now.'

'Are you OK to continue, or would you like a break?' McFarland interrupted.

'I'm OK. Can I have a cup of tea, two sugars, and a fag? I'll go outside and smoke it if you like?' Martin asked, smiling, raising his hand to his face and wiping a tear that was trickling down his cheek. His hand trembled.

'You can smoke in here. Nice try though, can't let you go outside just yet.' McFarland used the phone on the wall to order the prisoners request, which arrived within moments.

'You can keep the packet, but I'll need the lighter,' McFarland said, trying to wear a pleasant smile. He found it difficult to smile whilst he was at work, the seriousness of his job did not allow him that luxury.

'Thanks,' Martin quietly replied as the prisoner lit up a cigarette, savouring the nicotine that entered his body. The comfort of the hot sweet tea lifted him although the reality of the situation quickly returned.

'Do you know why you were taken there?' Terry wanted to keep the questioning going.

'Yeah, to kill Hector.'

'What did this man say to you?'

'He made Hector swallow the key to the handcuffs around my ankle and said if I wanted to live I had to cut him open to get the key.' Martin blatantly ignored the question.

'What were you supposed to cut Hector open with?'

'He gave me a blade.'

'Hector is in a right old state. Who did that to him?'

'I did.'

'A bit erratic, the guy looks like he's been mutilated, when the key would have obviously been in his stomach, Martin.'

'I lost it... my temper I mean – I kicked the fuck out of him before I cut him, OK?'

'Was he abusing your sister?'

'Yeah, you could say that.'

'So this guy told you that Hector was abusing your sister and you believed him. Why?'

'Cos Hector didn't deny it. That bastard had it coming.'

'But you would have had to kill him to get the key – so why mutilate him?'

'I told you, I lost it… I freaked out!' Martin snapped.

Terry looked at Martin, allowing for silence to cool the air. He wanted to test Martin.

'Tell me more about this man. What he looked like, what he was wearing, how he spoke, anything you think might help us with our enquiries.'

'OK, he wore a black rubber suit, black boots, like boxing boots, and a mask. The mask looked like it was his real face, but it wasn't. He was fucking strong and fit. He spoke sort of posh at times. He seemed polite, well-spoken, with a funny twang, and then at other times he was a right bastard. He didn't fuck about, he meant business.'

'What makes you say he was fit?' That comment had intrigued Terry.

'His build was very muscular, shaped… you know, defined, cut, well-cut, not an ounce of fat. The sort that lifted a lot of weights.'

'I hope you don't mind me saying this Martin, but you look like the sort of fella that can handle yourself.'

'I'm no mug, if that's what you mean.'

'I've seen Hector, listen I don't think you're a mug.'

'He was slick and skilful.'

'So you woke up there. How did he get you there? Did he abduct you from your bed while you slept?' Terry asked, wanting to test Martin's previous answer.

'I think I stayed at a mate's place. We'd been out on the lash, I've already told you this.'

'What's your mate called?'

'Greg O'Hara. We used to work together on the bins, before he went on the sweep.'

'Where does this Greg O'Hara live?'

'On Empire Way, Wembley.'

'Get me an address please,' Terry asked McFarland.

McFarland used his mobile phone, and whispered into the mouth piece.

'Got it,' he replied seconds later.

'So you went out with Greg O'Hara and had a skinfull. At the end of the night, you went back to his and crashed out – woke up in the multi-storey and you can't remember anything in-between?'

'I've told you all I know…'

'I don't believe you have, Martin. Did he say anything else to you?' Terry asked, leaning forward in his chair.

'He fucking didn't shut up! I can't remember everything, he went on about choices and how fucking choices change everything.' Martin was starting to feel pressured.

'Who killed Hector?' Terry decided to throw the question back at Martin once more.

'I did,' Martin answered swiftly, shaking his head in disbelief on hearing his answer.

'Did this man make you kill Hector?'

'No!'

'What made you kill Hector?'

'If I hadn't, I'd still be there with him and I would've died with him. No one would have found us there, would they? That car park was gonna be demolished, with us in it!' Martin was trying to justify his actions as he fought back the tears.

'So you…' Terry tried to gather his thoughts, 'had to kill Hector in order to save your own life?'

'That's about it. Listen, Hector raped my sister. He raped men too. He was a nasty piece of shit. If I'd found all this out on a different day, fuck knows what I would've done to him… I might have killed him. But, in that car park, I didn't have a choice, I had to save myself. You would've done the same thing.'

'Let's hope I never have to find out, Martin.'

'So I am going to be banged up for this then?'

'If we can find the man in the rubber suit, your sentence may be reduced to involuntary manslaughter.'

'Without him we have nothing,' McFarland confirmed.

'If there is anything else you think of please let someone know and we'll come back and listen,' Terry said, standing up. McFarland used the phone on the wall to alert the officer outside the room that they had finished talking to the prisoner.

'Do me a favour and catch that bastard before he does someone else,' Martin called to the two men and he was led out of the room.

'He already has done someone else,' McFarland said quietly to himself.

Terry overheard the comment and thought the same as his Scottish partner.

'We are going to have to warn the public – make a statement to the press,' McFarland said.

'That's what the bastard wants. You need to tell the gaffer and then it's his call. I'd advise him against it.'

'Listen, Terry, we've got ourselves a serial killer running around,' McFarland said with a bemused look.

'That's where you're wrong McFarland. He hasn't killed anybody yet!'

McFarland took his mobile phone from his pocket and began to dial a number from the listed memory.

'Hello, sir,' he said into the phone's receiver, 'I need a meet with you.'

'OK, how urgent is it?' was the response.

'There's been another killing. It's all pointing in the direction of the same guy who wears the black suit.'

'OK, meet me in the coffee shop outside Regent Street tube station in about an hour… bring Terry with you.' The voice on the other end did not wait for confirmation, he simply ended the call there.

McFarland looked at Terry and spoke. 'Regent Street Coffee Shop, in an hour…'

'Nothing changes, does it?' Terry replied, with a smirk on his face.

'He wants you there too.'

'In for a penny, as they say?'

***

The two detectives sat with the tall, hard-looking man drinking coffee. The tall man, McFarland's boss, and the sole point of contact in this case, had agreed with Terry in the first instance, though he had now decided that a press release was the natural course of action.

'I'll arrange a press release for this afternoon. McFarland, I want you there. You can answer whatever I don't.'

McFarland nodded.

'Terry you can't be there for obvious reasons. Though we may soon have to allow you to surface.'

'I'll watch it from home, with respect, sir.'

'Cutting to the chase, Terry, this is my call and I'm calling it. If we don't warn the public and this does leak, they'll be all over us like a pack of rats. People will start asking questions, the first of which will be about you. I am not willing to put my career on the line because you may have a gut feeling, Terry. You both know the procedure here. I have to follow protocol. There have been two murders; all we're doing is confirming that they are linked.'

'You'll do what you think is right – avoidance is better than cure,' Terry said, privately gritting his teeth.

'Has someone informed the next of kin?'

'Yes, sir,' McFarland replied, 'hopefully this press release will prompt the guy in the rubber suit to make contact,' he added.

'He won't. He's not doing this for the glory, he's doing this for personal reasons. He doesn't want to get caught, that's why he's being so careful, that's the reason for wearing black –concealment – a black rubber suit, think about it. He's not left any trace of himself at either of the two crime scenes, has he? We are totally blind with this one and he knows it. He's playing with us and he's good at it. The way he's doing it tells us that he's in charge; he's not randomly selecting these people, his victims – or, if the truth be told – the victims of others. They've been carefully researched. The first was a drunk who beat his girlfriend, the second was a man who led a double a life and let's not forget he also abused his wife. There might be a link there. If we catch him before he orchestrates another murder, what could we charge him with? From what we've been told, he hasn't told either of the two to kill. He hasn't directly threatened anyone, he does it indirectly.' Terry was only trying to point out the obvious, his frustration building.

'Do you respect this guy?' McFarland's boss enquired.

'I think he's very clever and calculating, but to answer your question, no I don't respect him in what he's doing, but I respect his planning... I'm only trying to say that he's going to be hard to catch.'

'So that's your psychological profile of this man, Terry?'

'That's just how I see him and what he's done. Try to think about the planning that must have been involved. These weren't random.'

'Terry, hold on a minute, you're saying that he wants the press coverage and then you're saying he doesn't. Make your mind up, what is it?' McFarland seemed puzzled by Terry's last statement.

'I didn't say that. You're not listening,' Terry said scratching his head.

'We're going to have to follow procedure here,' the boss said.

'OK, please humour me. What are you going to tell them? We've got two murders that are linked, and the man who orchestrated these horrendous crimes actually did what? Orchestrated?'

'You are not going to change my mind, Terry. We follow procedure. That matter is closed. Am I clear on that?'

Terry nodded. 'We tell them the facts.'

McFarland looked at him giving him a sideways glance. Terry returned the look shaking his head with frustration and confusion.

'I wish you luck, mate.'

'Piece of cake,' McFarland said, not reassuringly.

Chapter Twenty-Five

Sitting slightly out of sight, amongst a few homeless people, Greg viewed the comings and goings of his latest crime scene.

'Do you want some?' a homeless man enquired, offering Greg a bottle.

'No thanks – too early for me.'

'It's never too early or never too late, too late to go back home and patch things up.'

'I know,' Greg replied, 'I just need time.'

'Just don't let the grass grow under your feet,' the homeless man smiled; his toothless smile seemed friendly.

Greg returned to his surveillance.

'I know you,' Greg said, spotting Terry exit McFarland's car.

'What?' the homeless man asked.

Greg simply ignored the question, choosing to stand and walk away from the stench of stale body odour and infested filth.

Removing his mobile phone from his pocket, he quickly accessed the internet, searching for a phone number for Thames Television. Within moments, a number appeared. He selected the direct dial option and waited for an answer – all he got was an out-of-office robotic answer machine.

Three hours later, Greg tried the phone number again.

'Thames Television, how can I direct your call?' a female telephonist answered.

'Terry Bane, please,' Greg replied, using his alter ego's accent; already putting a name to the face he had seen earlier that morning.

'Putting you through.'

Greg waited.

'Hi, this is the voicemail of Terry Bane. Please leave a message, or if it's urgent you can contact me on my mobile – 07777 555 444. Thanks for calling.'

'Thank you,' Greg smiled.

***

McFarland could feel his legs trembling as the press filled the room. Knowing that Terry was at home watching did not make it any easier.

'Good afternoon ladies and gentlemen. I'm Chief Inspector Jasper Ward and, to my left, is Detective Inspector James McFarland of New Scotland Yard. I will invite questions after I have read out a brief statement, please do not interrupt me and please be patient, we will try to answer all your questions.' The tall man paused taking a sip of water from the glass in front of him. 'The reason we have called you all here today is to inform you and the public that during the last two months, two members of the public have been murdered. We, at New Scotland Yard, believe these murders are linked and therefore would believe that it is in the public interest to share the information that we have already attained though, at this moment, this is minimal. The first murder was at fifty-four Tinckerton Street, Swiss Cottage, about eight weeks ago. A white male named Brian James was brutally murdered by his partner, Sharon Buckle. The other was in Borehamwood in a disused car park last night. A South African man named Hector Hylie was brutally murdered by his brother-in-law, Martin Pringle. Please can we urge you not to contact the families of the deceased, or the families of the two other people involved. Simply as a mark of respect, let them mourn their loss privately.' He paused again for a slurp of water, the coolness rehydrated his throat. 'Both of the people that we are questioning claim that another person was involved; they simply describe this person as a man wearing a mask and a black, shiny all-in-one suit. He talks using a well-spoken accent and he forced them to commit these awful acts. Now, if you have a question, raise your hand and I promise I will get to you all. One question each though,' Jasper pointed to a man at the back of the room. 'Yes.'

'Bill Davis, the *Sun*. Can you tell us how you know these murders are linked?'

'This is one for you, James,' Jasper said.

'At the moment, both of the people involved have mentioned the man in the shiny suit. Therefore we have to consider that both these crimes are linked.'

'Gill Morgan, *The Times*. Have any of these people been formally charged, and if so can you tell us what they have been charged with?'

'Me again,' McFarland said, 'I can confirm that we have formally charged both people we have in custody with murder, whilst we are still conducting our enquiries.'

'Reginald Morris, the *Mirror*. Do you think that this third person will strike again?'

'Yes, is the short answer, we are looking for a third person who we believe to be linked with this case, it is our belief that this person is doing this for reasons we are yet to understand. We believe that this man in the shiny suit is very skilful and extremely dangerous. We would urge the general public not to approach this man, but to contact us if they have any information.'

***

'You're playing into his hands, you fucking idiots!' Terry shouted at his television, almost choking on his coffee.

***

'Fulton Myers, the *Daily Telegraph*. What exactly can you tell us about the person you seek?' he enquired calmly.

'Not a lot really, we don't know too much about him at the moment. We know that the person is a man of athletic build, very confident and he chooses his victims well. Let's be clear about one thing, these two murders have not been random, a lot of planning has gone in to them. I'm not able to go into too much detail, with the case being ongoing, but we do know that this person is extremely dangerous. Any more questions?' McFarland felt awkward.

'Gareth Charles, the *Standard*. Do you have any idea why he chose these two victims, and have you any idea who is going to be next?'

'We don't know, is the truthful answer to your question Gareth. We do know that he will continue until he is stopped. These murders were extremely violent and orchestrated without any hesitation. I must stress that this is one very dangerous individual we are looking for.'

'May I ask another question?' Fulton Myers asked, breaking the silence that had filled the room.

'Of course,' McFarland replied.

'You say that he orchestrated these murders. From that are you saying that he did not actually carry out these killings?'

'That's correct, from the information we have managed to collate, he was there as an instigator.'

'So, in the case of the second murder,' Fulton enquired, 'did this person actually abduct the two men?'

'Yes, he did abduct both men and held them against their will. As I said, this is a complicated case,' McFarland looked at his boss, seeking support.

'I'm sorry that's all we have time for. Please be very selective in what you write and show respect and some decorum. Think of the victims' families before you submit your stories to press. I must make you aware that this investigation is live and ongoing. Thank you all for your time and your questions,' Jasper announced as he and McFarland left the room quickly.

'I felt like a right prat in there,' McFarland told his boss.

'Yes, I know what you mean. They were ready to rip us to shreds weren't they? We gave them enough I think.'

'I'm not looking forward to reading tomorrow's papers.'

'Don't worry about it and don't dwell. What's done is done. We've followed the letter and kept to procedure. Let's hope they consider what they're writing about before they put it in their newspapers tomorrow,' Jasper knew that the tabloid press would crucify him and The Met, along with all those involved in the case. 'Keep me regularly updated, James.'

'Yes, sir.'

'Catch this bastard for me.'

'We will, sir, you can count on it.'

'I know I can, that's why I've got two of the best. Up your efforts, bend the rules, if you have to, crack a few heads. Just get a result,' he smiled.

'Thank you, sir. Terry needs...' McFarland felt slightly embarrassed.

'Whatever it takes James, give Terry whatever he wants. The clock is ticking.'

The men shook hands and parted.

Chapter Twenty-Six

Greg picked up Hector's mobile phone and switched it on. He waited a few moments while the device powered up. He dialled Terry Bane's mobile number and waited for him to answer.

'Terry Bane,' the voice on the other end answered.

'Good afternoon, Terry,' Greg said, adopting his alter ego's well-spoken tone.

'Yeah, good afternoon – who's this?'

'I'm the one you are looking for.'

'And why would I be looking for you?'

'Because I'm making this call on Hector's phone.'

Terry's eyes blinked wide, 'So are you going to hand yourself in? Is that it?'

'That would take the fun out of the hunt, out of the game, Terry. It's all part of the game.'

'What do I call you? You know my name.'

'Do I need a name? Let me think…' Greg smirked.

'Why are you contacting me, shouldn't you be talking to the police?' Terry interrupted.

'Terry, I think you already know that I'm well informed – enough to know that you are working with the police. Though I must say, you are an excellent reporter. I enjoyed your coverage of the Swiss Cottage story.'

'OK,' Terry seemed confused.

'I understand that this must be a bit of a shock. Well, after all I have been involved in a couple of grizzly crimes. That said, I have not killed. The killing, the blood of those whom have perished is on the hands of those in your custody. Murder, well that is the ultimate crime. Wouldn't you agree?'

'Only if you get away with it. What do you want me to call you?'

'You can call me "The Ultimate". How are Sharon and Martin? I hope that you are looking after them both.'

'Let's just say that they've both had better days. Why them?'

'Why not them. Brian and Hector selected themselves – I did not select them,' Greg laughed, 'as will others. I'm cleansing the streets of London, a job that our finest have failed in.'

'You will be caught, you know that?'

'Not if I continue to play the game, using my rules. You won't catch me, Terry,' Greg laughed.

'So, why have you contacted me?'

'Terry, we are both educated men. I think that, thus far, you know how well I like to plan. I am a slave to detail. I will never leave any trace of my true identity, so I will continue to lead you into a cul-de-sac every time.'

'How long do you think you can carry on with this… with your reign?'

'My reign?' Greg paused, wanting to lead the conversation elsewhere. 'I would wager good money that the press conference that took place earlier was not something that you wanted? How can these people expect to catch the likes of me, when it is me who is leading the way? Amateurs – don't you agree Terry?' Greg snapped.

'I told them it was a mistake – but it made you want to contact me, break the ice.'

'Contacting you was something I had planned before the press conference. I watched you at the car park. I saw you with James McFarland – I am everywhere, Terry. I got your number from your voicemail. Just in case you were wondering. Information is easy to attain. If people leave it so readily available,' Greg giggled, 'I'll always be too far ahead of the game Terry.'

'This is a game to you. Who's next?'

'Do you think that the great Hercule Poirot would ask me that question Terry?'

'I'm not him,' Terry gritted his teeth. 'So when do you plan to strike again?'

'I'm not the detective, you are.' Greg paused. 'Pass a message on to James McFarland – what you sow, you shall reap. Thanks for the chat,' with that Greg ended the conversation.

'Don't go…' Terry cried, but all in vain. Terry quickly dialled McFarland.

Chapter Twenty-Seven

Sitting quietly, pondering his conversation with The Ultimate, Terry waited for McFarland to arrive.

'He contacted me,' Terry announced, the second McFarland was through the door.

'Who contacted you?'

'The monster that we're looking for. He called himself "The Ultimate"... he knows far too much, he...'

'Slow down, mate.'

'We need to get the number he used checked out. And please don't tell me to slow down. This fucker isn't going to stop – it's all a game, his game!' Terry grabbed McFarland's arm. 'He watched us at the second scene and he left a message for you. He told me to tell you what you reap, you shall sow. I've no idea.'

'Did he say why he contacted you?' McFarland decided to ignore the message.

'I think it was just so that we know that he's in control. Not to warn us off. But, I don't understand what he was trying to say to you.'

'That's not the issue here, Terry. He contacted you.'

'I'm worried about this one. He's too confident, far too... Fuck knows!'

'We've gotta go and see the pathologist, he has something to tell us.'

'I want us to go and see this Greg O'Hara first. I wanna talk to him.'

***

Greg jumped off the settee and turned on his laptop. Whilst he waited for it to boot up, he made himself another cup of tea. Once he returned to his laptop, he used Google to find the phone number for the DVLA so that he could try to find out where Val lived. He then picked up the telephone and dialled the number.

'Hello, DVLA registrations, Swansea, Heather speaking, how may I help?'

'Hello Heather. I'm in a bit of a jam. I'm after a number plate for my mum's 50th birthday. I've not been able to track this particular plate, though I do know that it is unavailable at the moment. I thought that if I could contact the owner, I could try to persuade them to sell it to me,' he said, firmly crossing his fingers.

'Well, sir, I'm not sure if I'm supposed to offer that kind of information.'

'What harm could it do? Listen, Heather, you are my last hope,' he pleaded. 'If I wasn't in such a jam, honestly, I would not have needed to call you… please, please, please.'

'This would cost me my job.'

'Well, I won't tell anyone if you won't. I promise.'

'OK, but don't tell the owner where you got their details from!'

'Listen, you have my word,' he crossed his fingers.

'What's the number?'

'VAL 111H.'

'OK, one second… that registration belongs to Mrs Valerie Hope, telephone number 0207 555 5555.'

'Do you have an address?'

'You'll get me hung for this: 1895, Bishops Avenue, Golders Green.'

'Yeah, I know where that is,' Greg rudely interrupted. 'May all the angels smile on you, and God bless and watch over you. You have secured your place in heaven.' Before Heather could reply he hung up the phone.

'Too easy,' Greg said to himself.

Greg had no intention of approaching Valerie, he was doing his research. Research, was something that he did remarkably well.

Greg decided that he was going to have to get to know Brent and he wanted to know more about that heated exchange in the restaurant. Greg still had some holiday owing, so decided that he would book about a week off in order for him to carry out a bit of surveillance work. A loud bang on his front door interrupted his thinking.

'Hang on,' Greg shouted. Greg opened the door, holding his breath, preparing himself for the worst.

'Mr Gregory O'Hara?'

'That's me,' Greg replied through the gap between the door and the door frame. 'Who wants to know?'

'James McFarland and Terry Bane from New Scotland Yard. Can we come in, sir? We have some questions.'

'Yeah come in – what's going on?' Greg needed to remain as his own character, leaving his alter ego hidden, allowing his double-bluff to commence. The two men entered Greg's flat and were ushered into the living room.

'Do you know Martin Pringle?'

'Yeah, I know Martin.'

'When was the last time you saw Martin?' Terry enquired.

'We went out for a drink and he crashed here – a couple of weeks ago I think… maybe.'

'We're going to need you to be more precise Mr O'Hara,' Terry smiled.

'How precise? We went out on the piss; got a taxi back here. Oh, we picked up a curry on the way. We got back here, ate the curry, sank a few beers and watched a porno. Then we crashed.'

'In the same bed?' McFarland smirked.

'No, dickhead. Martin slept in here and I slept in my bed,' Greg snapped. 'Old Bill or not, watch your mouth please mate,' Greg smiled.

'What time did Mr Pringle leave… the following morning?' Terry enquired.

'I've got no idea. When I got up, he'd left.'

'What, without as much as a goodbye?' McFarland asked, wanting to niggle at Greg. It was his way.

'If he did say his goodbyes, I was asleep so I missed them.'

'Have you heard from or seen him since your night out?' Terry continued.

'No, not a word.'

'Is that normal?'

'Yeah, we're mates – we're not married,' Greg replied, looking at McFarland. Terry looked around the room, everything seemed immaculately tidy, pristine.

'Is Martin in some kind of trouble? When we were out on the piss, he told me about his brother-in-law going missing, or not going home.'

'Do you know Mr Pringle's brother-in-law?' McFarland enquired.

'I used to work with both of them, so yeah, I know them both. What's this all about?' Greg replied, choosing his words carefully.

'Mr Pringle's brother-in-law is dead and Mr Pringle is a witness. This all transpired after his night out with you Mr O'Hara.' McFarland was unable to control his tongue.

'So Martin topped Hector? Fuck me, I never thought he'd actually do it.'

Greg was lapping this up. Feeding these two idiots fool-food was more fun than Greg thought it would be.

'Mr Pringle is a witness at this moment… I didn't say anything about him killing Mr Hylie…'

'What do you mean by "actually do it"?' Terry asked, sitting forward.

'Listen, it's not for me to say, but Hector wasn't the most popular guy you'd ever meet. Not very nice if you catch my drift?' Greg was back in game play mode. 'He was a bully and he and Martin never got on. After all, Martin never liked the idea of his sister marrying Hector. Martin would always threaten to kick Hector's head in, but he never did, only because his sister protected Hector. Everyone knows about the bad feeling between them and, let's be honest, if you're looking for people that had a gripe with Hector, you'll have a fucking long list. Talk to HR at the council where he worked.'

'That's a nice television you have Mr O'Hara,' McFarland commented.

'Yeah, I think so.'

'Do you watch the news on it?'

'No, I watch the news on the one in the bedroom,' Greg laughed. 'What sort of question is that?'

'So, have you not seen the press conference surrounding this?' McFarland continued.

'No. When was it?' Greg was playing shrewd.

'It was earlier today.'

'I've been at work – early finish.'

'What time did you get home?'

'About an hour ago,' Greg lied easily.

'So you never watch the news on this television?' Greg did not answer the question, he simply smirked.

'What do you watch?'

'None of your business,' Greg barked. 'Where's this going. My telly and what I watch on it ain't that interesting is it? And it ain't none of your business,' Greg smiled. 'Are you deliberately trying to piss me off?'

'No, my colleague is not trying to piss you off,' Terry said. 'We're just trying to piece together the missing parts. Tell us more about Mr Pringle please.'

'What do you wanna know?'

'A bit of background... I dunno... What type of person is he?'

'Martin's a diamond, he's my mate, what do you want me to say about him?' Greg needed to play his game. 'Put it this way, he's no mug.'

'Handy with his fists, is he?'

'Like I said, Martin's not a mug.'

'OK Mr O'Hara, I think we've taken up enough of your time. Thank you for talking to us,' Terry smiled, as he stood.

'We'll find our own way out!' McFarland grunted. Greg just looked at the two men, deciding not to say anything.

'One more thing,' Terry said, pausing his exit. 'Do you have any travel plans?'

'Not that I know of... but then, you never know, with all these last minute bargains that pop up, do you?'

Both detectives left...

Chapter Twenty-Eight

Terry sat looking at the telephone. He did not know who to ring first but someone made the decision for him. He picked up the receiver.

'Hello,' his voice sounded exhausted.

'Hiya darling, I saw it, how are you?' It was Natalie, her timing was excellent, Terry needed to hear her voice, it was the closest he could get to her right now and it made him feel a bit better.

'I'm OK. I told them not to.'

'I know darling. I've had to tell mummy. Hold on, she won't tell anyone. She thought we'd had a bust up, what else could I have said?'

'Fine, that's the least of my worries at the moment. Darling, please explain the importance of me remaining anonymous during the investigation. I'm happier knowing that you are with your mother and that you are both safe. We haven't got a clue how this guy selects his victims, that's if you can call them that.'

'I'll stay here until he is caught if that makes you happy. I know it's only a matter of time before he's behind bars. I miss you Terry.' A single tear drop fell as she announced her feelings.

'I miss you too darling. It's for the better that you're out of the way. He contacted me today. I'll pop up and spend the weekend with you in a couple of weeks, hey?' he said, trying to soften the blow of them being apart.

'You spoke to him? Bloody hell Terry, he's a cocky git. I won't pry darling. Sounds good about you coming up in a couple of weeks – catch him quickly. Put that monster behind bars,' Natalie said angrily.

'We will. I'll phone you soon.'

'I love you darling,' Natalie said, thinking about how long the next two weeks would feel.

'I love you too darling. It won't be too long,' he said, unconvincingly. Natalie blew him a few kisses down the phone before hanging up.

The phone rang immediately.

'Hello.'

'Alright, mate? Was it as bad as it felt? You were ghostly silent when I dropped you off earlier.' It was McFarland.

'No, it was fucking bad, mate. You need to keep that bad cop image under control. O'Hara went all defensive as soon as you opened your mouth.'

'Good cop/bad cop. You know how it works, Terry.'

'Only when they're banged to rights. Not just answering a few questions,' Terry snarled.

'OK, what did you think about the press conference? We didn't get time earlier.'

'No, that was fucking worse. McFarland, you know how to kick a man when he's down.' Terry laughed loudly, seeing the irony. 'The press were laughing their socks off. Jasper made himself look a right fool. He knew sod all about the case and made The Yard look like a bunch of amateurs.' Terry had every right to feel embarrassed.

'He had to be there, a senior ranking officer and all that.'

'Pencil-necks,' Terry paused. 'It's all complete bollocks if you ask me. That bloke will now set out to send us a message, a message to explain what he's doing and why,' Terry stopped. 'Wait a minute.'

'He's bound to try to contact us again,' McFarland said.

'No he won't, not yet, he's far too clever to do anything like that. He'll leave us a message.'

'He'll leave us a clue,' McFarland said, trying to turn the negative in to a positive.

'I wouldn't count on it. Where are you now?' Terry asked.

'Not far,' McFarland quickly mapped his location, 'about ten minutes away, why?' he replied.

'Fancy helping me demolish a bottle of malt, mate?'

'Aye, I fancy getting pissed tonight. It'd be rude not to accept your invitation,' the Scotsman replied.

'Don't be too long I'm pouring two glasses now,' Terry said, teasing his long-time friend.

Once McFarland had arrived, the two men talked. Their conversation flowed, as did the ten year old bottle of malt whiskey. As the alcohol worked its way through their bloodstreams, their barriers lowered. Feeling the pressure of the case, they both needed a release; most officers drank heavily when working on demanding cases like this one.

'What do you think about this nutter, The Ultimate?' Terry said, struggling with his pronunciation.

'I think that he's going to fuck up and lead us to him, they always do, Terry.'

'We've got nothing on him so far. We've not even got a clue what he looks like.'

'Let's try… I mean…' McFarland laughed. Both men laughed.

'Tomorrow's another day. For all we know, he's out there now, and… well, it doesn't bear thinking about.'

'What do you think, from what he said to you Terry?'

'I think he's educated, calculated and very much a thinker… and that, my friend, makes him different and very fucking dangerous,' Terry sighed.

'Terry, he will fuck up. Listen, mate, they always do.'

'But how many other victims? We don't…we can't afford that time. We can't allow him time McFarland.' The full bottle of malt was now empty.

'I don't have any answers at the moment…' McFarland was far too drunk to finish his sentence. It did not matter as Terry had passed out.

***

Terry woke in the chair that he had passed out in, feeling a sharp pain in the back of his neck. McFarland was still asleep. Deciding to allow his friend to wake in his own time, Terry climbed the stairs and emptied his bladder before undressing and stepping under the shower's hot jets of water.

McFarland woke on hearing Terry's attempt at *Singing in the Rain* and put the kettle to boil.

'What's the plan for today then?' McFarland asked, as he heard footsteps coming down the stairs.

'I want to talk to Sharon again. Can you arrange it for this morning?'

'Aye, no probs.'

'I think I'm going to need to talk to Martin again at some point too.'

'Today?'

'Yeah, try and do that this afternoon.' His mind was preoccupied.

'No probs,' the Scotsman replied in a relaxed manner. 'We can see Sharon at any time this morning as Mr Barnford is with her all morning.'

'Oh that prat,' Terry commented. 'She's lucky that the death penalty has been outlawed. I wouldn't wanna put my fate in his hands.'

Both men laughed.

'Let me use your shower and we'll be on our way,' McFarland smiled.

'OK, mate. I'll get you some clean towels.'

During the drive to see Sharon, neither man spoke. Once they arrived at Colindale police station, both men were escorted to the interview room where Sharon and her solicitor were eagerly waiting.

'Good morning Sharon, Mr Barnford,' Terry smiled, slowly sucking on a mint.

'Hello,' Sharon replied. Her solicitor decided to nod while he scribbled something on his note pad.

'There's been another murder, Sharon,' Terry said.

'Yeah I know, Mr Barnford told me – now do you believe me?'

'I never doubted you, it's the jury I doubted,' Terry smiled.

'Sharon, what I'm about to ask you may seem a little odd, even a tad unconventional, but please hear me out – you too Mr Barnford,' Terry smiled. 'We are going to need to interview you with our other suspect present. What are your thoughts on that?'

'What?' Was Barnford's automated reply, 'What do you mean? You can't do that! My client won't do that. That is an insane suggestion...' he flustered, still outraged by Terry's request.

'Hold on for one moment and listen to what we are suggesting. Both crimes, we believe, are linked. The second suspect or, witness if you'd prefer, well, he's mirroring your story about the guy in the rubber suit.'

'I've seen it on the news,' Sharon said quietly.

'And...' Terry paused, 'a man has contacted me, claiming to be the man in the shiny suit.'

'How did he contact you?' Barnford was intrigued.

'That's not important, it could be a prank,' Terry knew it was not. 'What's imperative to our investigation is that we get you both together in the same room, with your respective legal representation. Just to see if you would be able to bring something to light that may have been overlooked.'

'This is outrageous,' Barnford exclaimed, 'a man has contacted you confessing and you want to interrogate my client.'

'Mr Barnford, please calm down... firstly, this man did not confess to anything, and secondly, as I stated, this could have been a prank. We get them all the time,' Terry said, trying to bring the tempo down. 'This is the black and white of where we are. Your client is going to be spending some time behind bars; all we want to do is catch the orchestrator of these hideous crimes and ensure the safety of the public. Now, if we don't catch him, firstly, there'll be more blood spilt, and secondly, your client will be charged with murder. With the orchestrator in custody, we could get the charge lowered to involuntary manslaughter. You'll be out before your baby reaches double figures. We are here to work together, as a team. Without your help we are blind.'

'Can we have some time to discuss this?' Barnford asked.

'Of course,' Terry replied. Barnford indicated that Terry and McFarland should leave the room. Both men waited in the corridor.

'It's the old rock and a hard place, and they both know it,' Terry confided to McFarland.

'Aye, that we know… but Barnford's a fucking prick and he can't see the bigger picture here.'

'But Sharon will, my friend… Sharon will.'

Barnford poked his head out from behind the door and said, 'You can come back in now.'

They both went back in to the room and sat down.

'My client has decided that she would be happy to co-operate. But she needs some reassurances from you.'

'I'm listening,' Terry said leaning forward.

'That, at the most, she is only charged with involuntary manslaughter on the grounds of diminished responsibility. Now my client wants to see this man behind bars as much as you do. That said, my client does not want to miss her daughter growing and maturing so a minimal custodial sentence would be what we are aiming for.'

'I can pull a few strings with the CPS but let's concentrate on the matter in-hand.'

'Who's the CPS?' Sharon interrupted.

'The CPS is also known as the Crown Prosecution Service, Sharon. All the evidence surrounding any legal case or investigation has to be put to them. They decide whether you have to face criminal proceedings. Now, we tell them what we intend to charge you with, under certain sections of the Criminal Code of Justice, they impartially look at what evidence we provide them, and they make a decision,' Terry replied. 'Now, we can apply for a lesser charge, in your case and we can suggest a minimal sentence on the grounds of your co-operation. In other words…' Terry paused. 'Put it this way, we can do our best to see that you don't spend too many years behind bars…' Terry paused again, this time to clear his throat. 'What we are suggesting you do to help us is, let's say, very unconventional, so please understand that what we are asking you to do can never be revealed. If it is, the whole case will be thrown out leaving the orchestrator to continue to roam free and continue his reign of terror and the CPS will then look at you and the other person we have in custody. I must tell you now that we have not spoken to the other person about this proposal but we are sure that he will agree as he has declined his right to legal representation, which indicates that he wants to help us as much as he can.' Terry's back was against the wall.

'Though this goes against the grain,' Barnford began, 'my client and I think that if this unorthodox style of investigation brings this case to a speedy resolution, and, of course, my client gets the minimal custodial sentence we agreed, then we would be delighted to assist you. My client fully understands the implications of any of the contents of the investigating interviews being leaked and assures me that any leaks will not come from her side of the table. To protect my client's best interest, we would need a legally binding document, signed by both parties. My client must have reassurances, you understand?'

'You watch too much television Mr Barnford?' McFarland scoffed.

'What my colleague is trying to say, Mr Barnford, is this: our word is enough. Deals made for co-operation have only ever been verbal, if anything is put on paper, then that changes from, co-operation to coercion.' Barnford felt small, like he was back in the classroom.

'Sharon, we need to know... sorry I'll start again. We need to hear what you think, and what you know about the second murder,' Terry spoke softly.

'I don't want to go to prison and be away from my baby. I want to help you find that bloke. I don't know how, cos I don't know what you want me to tell you, I don't know fuck all. I only know what I saw on the telly. What that Scottish copper said, and what that bloke on the news said, that's all I know.'

'Are you sure that you understand what we are asking of you, and that you are comfortable with what we are suggesting?'

'If Mr Barnford says it's alright, then it's alright.'

'The other thing we would like to do, is to show you a model of the first crime scene and have you talk us through it.'

Sharon turned her head and looked at Barnford, the fear evident in her eyes. 'I don't want to relive that fucking nightmare again, do I Mr Barnford. Do I have to?'

'My client…' Barnford began.

'That's fine. If at any time there is anything that you are not happy with, please just let us know,' Terry interrupted, cutting Barnford off in his stride. Terry just needed to see Sharon's reaction. She had been far too quiet.

A knock on the door interrupted them. McFarland left the room in order to find out why. As soon as he returned, he looked at Terry. 'It seems there have been some developments. Can we pick this up another time, or have we finished here? I'm sure Sharon could do with a break?' McFarland said, nodding at Terry.

'Yes, I agree, that would be fine. Please keep me abreast of the proposed joint interviews,' Barnford said, as he helped Sharon to her feet.

'But of course,' Terry replied. The two detectives stayed in the room, waiting for Sharon and her solicitor to leave.

'What's happened?' Terry asked eagerly.

'A young male has walked in to West Hendon police station and wants to talk to us about Hector.'

'Who is this guy?'

'Only one way to find out.'

'I'm going to need to see the pathologist's report on Hector… Oh, and I'm going to need to know what Hector's mobile number is, or was.'

'We can pick that up later. I'll phone a mate of mine now but I think we should go and see this bloke at West Hendon nick first, mate.'

'Yeah, I agree. Knowing our luck he's the local nutter!' Terry laughed.

***

As the two men walked in to the reception area of West Hendon police station they were met by another detective.

'He's in interview room three,' the detective told them, pointing to his left, 'I'll buzz you through.'

The young male was waiting patiently, in silence when the two detectives entered the room.

'Detective McFarland, I saw you on the television, I have so much to tell you.'

'OK, what's this all about?' McFarland asked the scrawny camp man.

'What's your name?' Terry thought that it would be better if they knew a little about this guy.

'My name is Julian Jones… you can call me Jules if you like. I'm twenty-two, and I live on my own on Chalkhill Estate, Wembley Park. One hundred and nineteen Gold Walk.'

'What do you want to tell us, Julian?' Terry enquired. Both detectives leant forward indicating that Julian had their full attention.

'I witnessed Hector's kidnap. I was there.'

'I hope you are not wasting our time Julian?' McFarland said impatiently.

'Honest… I was there…' Julian began to panic.

'Go on, tell us more,' Terry smiled, his interest in what story he was about to hear grew.

'OK… Hector and I had met in the Penny Farthing and he bought me a few drinks. We got talking, and he told me that he was married with two children. He enjoyed a bit of both worlds, if you know what I mean?' Julian giggled awkwardly.

'Get on with it, we haven't got all day,' McFarland barked, wanting Julian to cut to the chase.

'OK, OK… Hector was known to a few of the more regular clientele in the Penny for picking up someone and getting some action in the alley round the back of the pub. Apparently, he was well hung. Well, on Friday…'

'Is that this Friday just gone?' Terry wanted Julian to be precise.

'No, about two weeks last Friday. Well, Hector and I went round the back and started doing what we do and when we finished, Hector started hitting me, telling me how disgusting I was. I begged him to stop, well we'd just made love for fuck's sake… when all of a sudden this hunk appeared knocking Hector to the ground.' Julian paused, his manner seemed a little uneasy, even scared.

'Please go on,' Terry instructed.

'Well, Hector fell to the ground with a crash and this man wearing a skintight rubber suit stood there. I told him not to hurt me. He was a mean hunk of a bastard.'

'Did he say anything?' Terry asked.

'Yeah, he told me to fuck off before he changed his mind.'

'Changed his mind? About what?'

'I don't know, about letting me go without giving me a good hiding?'

'What did he look like, this man?'

'He wore a mask and it was dark. I couldn't see any of his features really. He was very athletic; he seemed powerful, strong, a body to die for… oops, sorry,' Julian chuckled. His nerves were not helping.

'Have you ever been in trouble with the police?' McFarland asked.

'No never,' Julian snapped. 'What's this? I came here under my own volition.' There was a nervous edge to his voice.

'What made you come in here under your own volition and decide to tell us all this?' Terry continued.

'I just think that it's my duty. Hector was a bastard; everyone who knew him knew that. But he didn't deserve to die.' That was when all his emotions came flooding out, crying and sobbing. 'He was bisexual. So fucking what? He liked a bit of rough after. Every one of us knew that he was a bastard, but he didn't deserve to die.'

'McFarland, get him a cup of sweet tea would you?'

'Aye, I will.'

'Was that particular Friday your first time with Hector, Julian?'

'No,' Julian lifted his head, 'but you already knew that, didn't you?'

'You were in love with Hector, but you had always known he would never be yours, yours alone, and that's why you're so upset, heartbroken.'

'Hector was only mine when Hector said so. He was a bastard, but that's who he was. Detective, I slept with other men as well and Hector slept with others. I don't know why that guy killed him and let me live.'

'You did the right thing Julian, coming here and telling us this. You've been a massive help.'

McFarland came back in the room.

'Get a WPC to come and sit with him until he's ready to go. Take your time drinking your tea Julian and, once again, thanks for coming in to see us. What you've told us may help us with our investigations. May we contact you if we need to talk to you about anything that we think you could help us with?'

Julian sharply nodded.

'And please feel free to contact us,' Terry said as he stood up once the female officer entered the room. 'Look after him won't you?'

'Yes, sir,' the young inexperienced uniformed officer replied. McFarland placed his card on the table in front of Julian.

'McFarland, let's go talk to Martin.'

The two men left the police station and got into McFarland's car.

'There's a pattern emerging,' Terry said.

'Aye,' McFarland replied, not knowing what his partner was on about, 'and what's that?'

'Both murdered victims treated their women like shit. And this guy, The Ultimate, knew this. How did he know this? He told me that he knew everything, that he watched us, specifically you. We need to find out if Hector's wife knew about his double life. I'll go and talk to Martin, and you go and talk to Mandy Hylie. We need to know how she's coping with her husband's death.'

'Right. How are you going to get home from Borehamwood nick, have you thought about that?'

'Good question.' Terry paused. 'Plan B we'll both go and see Mandy Hylie, Martin can wait,' his thoughts had raced away with him.

Placing his right foot on the brake pedal and his left on the clutch pedal with a swift down selection of gear, McFarland swung the car around so that it faced the opposite direction. Terry braced himself.

'Fucking hell, mate!' Terry cried.

The smell of rubber from the screeching tyres filled the cabin of their vehicle.

'Yeee-haarrrrrr!' the Scotsman yelped.

Chapter Twenty-Nine

Both men stood outside the front door waiting for someone to open it. This time McFarland banged on the door using the side of his clenched fist.

'Hold on, hold on I'm coming for Christ's sake,' the voice behind the closed door said.

As the door opened, a petite woman emerged.

'If you're from the papers you can sling your hook, go on piss off!'

'Hello, I'm Detective Inspector James McFarland, and this is...'

'I know who you are, I saw you on the telly. I'm so sorry for being so rude – I'm sick of journalists,' Mandy interrupted. 'Please come in...'

'Thank you,' Terry replied. Following Mandy, Terry could not help but notice how quiet the house was. 'Where are your children?' Terry asked.

'At my mother's, I want them out of the way until all this mess is sorted. Would anyone like some tea? I'm sure I could find a couple of digestives.'

Both detectives were directed to the living room.

'Find a seat and I'll be with you in a moment.'

Almost fifteen minutes later, Mandy emerged from the kitchen carrying a tray which she set down in the middle of the coffee table in the living room.

'You seem to be handling this whole situation very well Mrs Hylie,' Terry commented, and then continued, 'How are you holding up?'

'You have to carry on. Life goes on. OK, I did love him and, yes, I will be the first to admit, he wasn't a brilliant husband... but, all said and done, he was my husband and, yes, I have been freed from him. Sorry if that sounds terrible but that's the terrible reality of life, and life is with my children now.' She was being very open. 'If I had my time again, I wouldn't have married Hector, but then I wouldn't have my two beautiful children. He wasn't always that way, the way people say he is. Once upon a time he used to be a gentle, kind man. I think it was when he decided that he wanted to bat for both sides, that was when he started to punish others.'

'How long has, or sorry, did Hector embark on these bisexual conquests?' Terry asked, sipping his tea.

'I don't know and I suppose I never will know exactly how long it was.' Mandy paused for thought, 'I found out about four years ago, but I know that it had been going on for a lot longer.' She shook her head, 'What I don't know, won't hurt me – that is what he always told me. But it tore me apart. You can understand that can't you?'

'Yes, we do understand. Have you been to see Martin?'

'No, not yet, I'm not ready for that. Anyway, I'm the last person Martin would want to see. My God, his poor girlfriend and their baby.' Her emotions seemed rock solid.

'Do you know why Martin did it?'

'He had no choice. Anyone faced with what he was faced with would have done the same. Tell him that I forgive him and that I love him. He will always be my brother and before you ask, I'm well aware of Martin's hatred for Hector and that the only reason Martin never laid a finger on him was me.'

'So you knew about Hector's double life?'

'Oh come on. It was hardly a double life. He would go out to a gay bar and find a man to have sex with... I knew, oh I knew.' Mandy took a sip of hot tea.

'Did it bother you that he had unprotected sex with these men?'

'Of course it fucking bothered me! What could I do? If I said anything, Hector would give me a right-hander. He used to threaten to bugger me if I didn't shut up. Yeah, give it to me up the arse.'

Mandy reached over and picked up a biscuit, 'Want one?' she asked.

Both detectives declined.

'I'm a woman who married in to hard knocks. I'm simply hardened to it all. Hector was a nasty bastard and now he's dead. But I'll tell you one other thing, he never got near my arse!' She automatically burst in to tears. Maybe she wasn't so tough after all.

'We will catch this man for you.'

'Don't catch him for me, catch him for Martin, catch him for my kids. He freed me by imprisoning my brother. Ying and yang, pleasure and pain, there's a lot to be said for those Chinese people. All that karma they rant on about – there's something in it, I think.'

'Well, thank you for the tea, and thank you for sparing us your time. I think you are a very remarkable and honest woman.' Terry held Mandy's hand in both of his, 'Have a great life Mrs Hylie. Now you can truly begin to live your life with complete freedom.'

'Thank you, I will. Once this is all over, I'm going to take my kids to Spain. I've got a friend who lives there. We'll stay with her for a while,' she smiled. 'What is your name?'

'Terry, Terry Bane.'

'Thank you Mr Terry Bane.' Mandy closed the front door behind the two men.

'I want someone to go and check on her, and also that her children are alright. She gave me the creeps,' Terry said.

'Yeah me too, good God, if talking was an Olympic sport.'

'That's just her way of dealing with it.'

'Maybe...' To McFarland, everyone was a suspect.

Chapter Thirty

Martin was escorted to an interview room. He had been told why he had been summoned there, though he did not understand why the two detectives wanted to talk to him again.

'Hello Martin,' Terry said walking into the room.

'Hello.'

'We've just been to see your sister, and that's why we're a little late. Sorry for that.'

'How is she? How's Mandy?'

'She is remarkably well and handling the whole thing very smoothly if you ask me. She wants us to tell you that she forgives you, and that she still loves you.'

'At least she's free, free from that fat bastard.'

'How you've changed your tune. May I ask what has brought this on?'

'I'm fucked aren't I? I'm gonna get life for this, but at least I can serve my time knowing that my sister hasn't got to put up with that bastard any longer.'

'OK, calm down and listen please Martin. The real reason for our visit is to ask you if you'd be interested in an idea that we've had. As you know, you are the second person this guy has forced to kill. We have been talking with the first this morning. I must inform you at this time that she does have legal representation and if you'd like us to appoint you with a duty solicitor please let us know. If you're in agreement, we would like to interview you both together at the same time. What do you think?'

'What has her brief said?'

'Mr Barnford is in agreement with our suggestion. I must also inform you that if you do agree, you must also agree that this remains strictly confidential. If this was to become public knowledge then the whole case would be thrown out and the orchestrator would walk free.'

'What's in it for me?'

'OK, at the moment you are looking at a charge of murder. If we can catch this guy, there is a chance of your charge being reduced to involuntary manslaughter.'

'About ten years, pal, but you'll get out after about four if you behave yourself; keep your nose clean and your mouth shut,' McFarland summarized.

'Why would talking to us together help?'

'There are definitely some similarities with both crimes. By sharing your information and feeding off each other, there is a chance that you might unearth something.'

'I know how you lot operate, you'll twist our stories and land us in the frame. The Old Bill have never helped me in the past, why should they now?' Martin slouched back in his chair folding his arms and oozing arrogance.

'OK Martin. Let's put it another way, if you won't help us, how can we help you? We're doing the best we can here, but we need your co-operation,' Terry said standing up, 'without it, we're snookered in this part of the investigation. I'm only trying to help you. Unless we catch this man, he will continue.'

'I'll take my chances thanks.' Martin looked away.

'OK Martin you've had your chance, fifteen to life it is then. Oh and I'll make sure that the CPS knows how much you wanted to co-operate and help us during the investigation. Listen, the offer stands until midnight tonight; if you want to talk to us, you know where we are.'

'Hold on a minute, if the girl's willing to do this, I'll do it for her. I'm not doing this to help you, I'm only doing it to help her and so you can catch this geezer.'

'That's the only way we think.'

'OK, set it up,' Martin growled begrudgingly.

'Come on, McFarland, you owe me a pint,' Terry announced.

Chapter Thirty-One

Greg had already managed to obtain the details of where Brent and Valerie lived and he had also managed to follow Brent to his office a few times, timing the journey. He had been on Valerie's tail and had unearthed the secret that she was having an affair with one of the fitness coaches at her gym. Though he was unsure how long this torrid affair had elapsed, Greg wanted Valerie's husband to be confronted with her filthy betrayal.

Brent, on the other hand, was a hardworking, loyal husband who had only ever put his wife's needs before his own. The lifestyle that he provided for her was that of dreams. Greg decided that it was time for the dream to become a reality... no, no, no... a nightmare.

Greg noticed that, as part of Brent's daily routine, he always lunched in a wine bar called Jollies just outside Old Street Station. Greg was going to accidentally bump into Brent during one of his routine lunches. Today was that day. The timeline was now dragging on, though he wanted to be sure that he had everything in place. Five weeks had passed in a flash. He didn't want to rush and get sloppy. He knew that if he did, gaps may appear and the police would knit those gaps together and be onto him.

As Greg walked in to the wine bar, he noticed Brent sitting at a table on his own, eating his tuna salad, the same tuna salad that he had every day for who knows how long, quietly reading his copy of *The Financial Times*, oblivious to Greg's presence.

'Hello, fancy meeting you here,' Greg said, hijacking the businessman's precious tranquillity.

'Sorry, old chap, but I can't place where we know each other from.'

'A couple of weeks ago, you and your misses were eating in the Punch & Judy at Covent Garden. You were having a barney when my bird told you to keep it down.'

'Oh yes... ha, ha, ha... how embarrassing, please except my apology. My memory is like a colander these days. May I buy you a drink? I'm sorry, please allow me to introduce myself, I'm Brent.'

'Greg, Yeah, I'd love a cold beer please.'

Brent walked over to the bar and ordered Greg's beer – Greg had prepared himself for this.

'Cheers,' Brent said as he handed Greg the beer.

'Cheers,' Greg replied, 'just the job.'

'What brings you to these parts? I don't think I've seen you in here before. Do you work around here?'

'Nah, I've never been in here before. I was in the neighbourhood visiting someone in the hope of drumming up some business.'

'Any luck?'

'Dunno, but he said he'd call me and let me know.'

'I wish you good luck. What is it you do Greg?'

'I'm in IT, I'm an IT analyst. It's tough out there at the moment.'

'Yes, I know what you mean, I'm in the software business myself.'

'Are you?' Greg said, disguising the fact that he already knew exactly what Brent did for a living. 'What are you, a designer?'

'How did you know that?' Brent asked excitedly.

'A lucky guess. Well, that suit you're wearing is a big give away. You can tell that you're successful Brent by the way you dress.' Greg deliberately wanted to boost Brent's ego. He knew how these guys worked.

'I run a web design software business. Have you ever done any kind of design?'

'Nah, wouldn't know where to begin. There's a lot more to that than people realise.' Greg was trying to sound as though he knew what Brent was on about.

'Listen, Greg, if anything comes up I'll give you a shot if you'd like?'

'Yeah, thanks that'd be great. Tell you what, have you got a card or something with your number on that I could have? It'd be easier for me to contact you.'

'Of course,' Brent said handing Greg his business card, not giving proper thought to what Greg had just said. 'My email address is on there too, so please feel free to drop me an email and we can touch base that way,' Brent smiled politely.

'So what were you and your wife arguing about then?' Greg needed to change the subject. IT was not his subject.

'Valerie… she's a difficult woman at the best of times. I am so very sorry for upsetting you and your wife.'

'Me and Karen aren't married. But that don't matter, we enjoyed that champers that you gave us and the manager gave us everything on the house,' Greg said sounding as they'd had a fair result all round.

'Oh good, I am pleased. Right, I have to dash back to the office. You have my card, please give me a call or drop me an email and I'll see if there's anything I can throw your way.'

Greg felt awkward shaking Brent's hand, though he offered a smile as camouflage.

Greg stayed in the wine bar and had two more beers whilst he went over the plans for the next stage. There were a few potential obstacles to be considered. Greg worried that the guy Valerie was having an affair with would be too strong for him, so how could he up his own ante? Greg sat back and looked at the painting on the wall. A man sitting in a field surrounded by countryside. He studied the painting and then, all of a sudden, he thought about all the open space the man had in the painting – room to move, all that freedom of movement.

He had already decided that he was going to wait for Valerie to go to the fitness instructor's flat. Greg was then going to give them a little time to settle down to business, then he was going to let himself in using another of his internet purchases, a pick gun. Pop it in the lock, squeeze the trigger, and bingo, you're in. It was that simple. Then Greg thought about it for a few more moments. Maybe he could get himself some kind of gun that fired electricity.

He knew that he would be able to get hold of one of those taser guns fairly easily, as he had seen them before on one of the private websites he had visited.

Chapter Thirty-Two

McFarland had not expected the reception that he and Terry had received from Martin, and had grown suspicious about his reaction. All they were trying to do was to help the man. Though once he had done a bit of digging in to Martin's past, he then began to understand.

Martin was no stranger to the police. He had even served a little time behind bars – three months for non-payment of a fine for criminal damage. Nevertheless, he had brushed the wrong side of the law, and now the shoe was on the other foot. Martin could not bring himself to admit he was at the mercy of the people he hated so much. McFarland knew that there was nothing anybody could do to change the past and it was only Martin that needed to find some clarity, move on, and put his past experience behind him. It was his future he needed to focus on.

Martin had given up on himself, he had accepted whatever punishment was going to be dealt. Sharon, on the other hand, was begging for help and it seemed as though Martin was her key to the help she craved.

'Terry,' McFarland said, 'what are we going to do?'

'I haven't got a clue at the moment, mate. We're completely snookered.'

'He's going to kill again isn't he?'

'He hasn't killed anyone.'

'Terry, you know what I mean.'

'Yeah I do. I would bet my mortgage that he's already chosen who's going to be next, he's just choosing the right time. He's a thorough bastard.'

'He made contact, identifying his stance, Terry.'

'His contact was more about stating his authority. But he's methodical and enjoys leaving nothing of himself behind.'

'But he wanted you to know of his existence, Terry.'

'Yeah, and he wanted to give us something to call him.' Terry paused. 'I don't think he's going to rush things though.'

'A keen eye for detail; making sure not to leave any loose ends.'

'He only let Julian go because of two reasons: firstly, he knew that Julian could not tell us anything that we don't already know, and secondly, Julian was never part of his plan. Julian was a victim. He will only do what he feels is necessary to make sure his warped form of justice is served.' Terry began rubbing his head. 'My head is pounding.'

'It's as though he disappears into thin air,' McFarland said, placing his empty beer glass on the table. 'I wonder what he does for a living because, now tell me if you think I'm wrong, but he seems the kind of guy that would have a professional job, a normal working class man, the guy next door. Sharon and Martin both told us that his accent stood out as being posh.'

'That's what scares the shit out of me. Are you going to get those glasses filled up or do I have to die of thirst here?' Terry slid his glass across the wet table.

'OK, OK. We should go and talk to some of the people we have already questioned.'

'That's an idea, but a shit one, and I'll tell you why when you come back from the bar.'

McFarland enjoyed the buzz, he loved it when they bounced off each other like this and they were able to look at all possibilities, all the things that one person may miss. 'Here you go,' McFarland said, teasing Terry.

'Just give it to me.' The cold lager cleared his head.

McFarland obliged and sat down. 'Right then, the reason I said that was a shit idea is that we can't waste time going over old ground. We're under the cosh here, with all eyes looking and the clock keeps ticking. We need something new to go on but I'll be fucked if I can think what it is.'

'OK if that's a shit idea, why don't you think of something? At the moment, pal, we have fuck all to go on. That means we are no closer to catching this arsehole than we are to winning the lotto,' McFarland was feeling frustrated, and wanted Terry to feel the same.

'I know,' Terry looked at the Scotsman and smiled, 'a public appeal! You and the adorable Jasper call another press conference and ask for the public's help. Someone has got to know something. It's seen as a bit of a last resort, we risk looking desperate, but we're up against it here.'

'Hey, that's not a bad idea!'

'Not bad… it has worked in the past, why shouldn't it work now? He contacted us, The Ultimate, he'll contact us again.'

'I'll run it by Jasper in the morning.'

'Tell Jasper about the contact he made, and tell him the real reason for this press conference…'

'I will, mate, and I'm sure that Jasper will be happy to oblige.'

The conversation continued. Both men only focused on the case, they did their best lateral thinking whilst under the influence of alcohol. It was in drunken moments like this, when any thoughts or ideas could be shared and it did not matter how stupid or diverse, all were welcomed as part of a productive process. The only thing was that the more they drunk, the less they would remember in the morning.

Chapter Thirty-Three

Karen had decided that she would invite herself round to Greg's. She got her mobile out of her handbag and used the speed dial and waited for him to answer.

'Hello, I wasn't expecting to hear from you,' Greg answered.

'I know, I went to see my mate and she's not in, so I thought that I would see if you were.'

'Well I am. Are you coming round?' Greg did not like this, but tried to keep his irritation out of his voice.

'I am, if that's alright, just a flying visit. I wouldn't like to intrude,' Karen said jokingly.

'Yeah, of course you can. The flat's a bit of a tip though.'

'I'll be there in two minutes.'

'Fuck me, that's quick,' Greg panicked.

'Not tonight, and yeah, I think that sometimes, ha ha!'

Greg did not find any of this funny, he was in a panic. There was packaging lying around from the mail order stuff that he had ordered off the internet. Greg had not cleared all the mess away. He had not planned on seeing Karen until next weekend and she was here on the door step. He quickly shoved all the paper under the cushions on the settee. All the stuff that he had printed off from the internet was shoved in the magazine rack under the coffee table and anything else went in to the draws under the television cabinet along with the purchases.

He was out of time. There was a knock on the door. He shouted in frustration before gaining control and calmly greeting Karen.

'OK, I'm on my way,' he responded, 'for fuck's sake!' he added as he dashed to open the door.

'Hi.'

'Hey, you're sweating. Are you OK?'

Karen felt the moisture on her skin as Greg leant forward and kissed her.

'I'm fine, I've been dashing around trying to tidy up before you got here.' Well it was the truth, he thought.

'I'm not royalty, you know.'

'I know, but I wasn't expecting anyone round. I don't bother so much when I'm here on my own.' He took in some much needed air. 'Drink?' he asked.

'I'll tell you what, as I have interrupted whatever you were doing, I'll make the drinks. What'll it be?'

'Right then, I'll have a beer, there should be some in the fridge,' Greg replied, thinking that with Karen out of the way in the kitchen, it would give him a few extra minutes to give the living room the once over.

'OK,' Karen replied as she entered the kitchen. 'Think I'll join you, do you want yours in a glass babe?'

'I don't want a glass, I'll drink mine straight from the bottle.'

'You may be a commoner, but I'm not drinking from the bottle – last time it left a funny aftertaste in my mouth.'

'They are in the cupboard next to the cooker hood.'

'I know where they are,' Karen replied. Greg darted across the room to remove the offending paperwork. 'Shit! Where do you keep your cleaning cloths? I spilt some,' Karen said, as the first bottle she opened slipped on the work surface. The lager inside frothed and bubbled out of the open top of the bottle.

'In the cupboard under the sink,' he replied, only thinking of where to hide the papers. As Karen opened the door she noticed a funny-looking bottle that was directly in front of the J-cloths and decided to see what it was. 'Embalming Fluid' the label read. 'Why would Greg want embalming fluid?' she thought. Then she remembered the sleeping tablets that she had stumbled across in the medicine cabinet and felt a little uneasy.

'Are you OK in there?' Greg asked. 'You've been ages.'

'Yeah, just cleaning up the beer I spilt.'

'That's sacrilege that is, spilling beer. The beer police should lock you up for that,' Greg said, laughing.

'What have you been up to then?' Karen called from the kitchen whilst she closed the cupboard door.

'Not a lot really. This and that, you know?' Greg gulped a mouthful of his beer.

Karen came back in to the room and tried to act normal but she could not help but notice a leaflet that had fallen under the coffee table, she only spotted it because of the bright yellow lightning-like twin lines that went across the paper. She decided that she would have to wait to see what it was.

'That beer has gone right through me, back in a second,' Greg said leaving the room, eager to remove some of the packaging he had hidden in the bathroom.

Karen shot forward and picked up the leaflet and slid it in her handbag in a brief single movement. She'd read it later.

'Fancy another?' Greg asked, returning from the toilet.

'OK then,' she replied, not wanting Greg to feel her anxiousness, 'but it'll have to be a quick one, I'm going to see if Mum wants to go to the bingo… I'll just text her while you go and get them,' she smiled.

Greg slipped into the kitchen.

'You don't have to rush off babe,' Greg smiled, giving a suggestive wink.

'Too late,' she smiled, 'I've told Mum I'll meet her at the bingo.'

'I hope it's not summit I said?'

'Nah, I said it was just a flying visit didn't I?'

'Yeah, you did, but…'

'But nothing, I've interrupted you enough. See you next weekend, hey?'

'Yeah,' Greg was stunned by the way Karen was leaving so suddenly. 'We'll go out for a drink somewhere if you'd like?'

'Cool, see you later. Give me a bell,' she said, planting a kiss on his lips.

Greg had no time to respond, he was still stunned by her sudden departure. Leaving like that was not normal for Karen. In the past, she had always taken her time to say Goodbye…

***

Karen waited until she was sitting on the train before she looked at the leaflet. She unfolded it and saw a picture of a taser gun. In the bottom right hand corner of the page it said 'Thank you for your purchase.' Did this mean that Greg had purchased this item, and if so why?

Karen thought about going to the police. Was her boyfriend involved in something untoward? She could not think of Greg ever being like that, though the people you least expect are the ones to watch. Karen went home thinking about nothing else. These things: the embalming fluid, the taser gun, potent sleeping tablets – why? All kinds of questions where racing through her head and tears streaming down her cheeks. Her heart ached with sadness, pulling her insides, like a tug-o-war. 'Greg.' She unknowingly murmured his name…she would wait.

***

Greg had not noticed that the leaflet was missing as he finished tidying away anything that should not be left lying around. The evening was spent planning his next strike. Valerie was due to go for her weekly sleazy session with her fitness coach on Thursday evening, as she did every week. During his surveillance of the Hopes, Greg had timed Valerie's movements, she was like clockwork and had never let her punctuality fluctuate. 'We are all creatures of habit,' he reminded himself. 'Timing is key… timing is everything.'

Chapter Thirty-Four

As soon as he was showered and dressed, McFarland looked at the clock which sat on his dressing table. It was time. He picked up his phone and dialled. 'Morning, sir...'

'Good morning, James. What's on your mind?' Jasper knew that he was only ever contacted by McFarland this early in the day when he was after something.

'Well, sir, we think that we should call another press conference and appeal to the public for help,' McFarland cringed.

'Not a bad idea. Though haven't we already done that recently, James?'

'But, sir, this time we want Terry in front of the camera.'

'Terry Bane can't be seen and you know that.'

'Sir, with respect, he's part of this investigation,' McFarland interrupted.

'I'd like to remind you who is the superior officer here.'

'Sir...' McFarland took a deep breath, 'Terry has been contacted directly by the guy who has been orchestrating these recent crimes.'

'What?' Jasper interrupted.

'He calls himself "The Ultimate" and we know that he's the real deal because he phoned Terry using Hector Hylie's mobile phone.'

'He would have to come back on to the payroll James. That's the only way I would be able to wangle it.'

'No, that is not what this is about, sir. It's about catching this guy. It's about public safety, let's forget the pride of The Yard and concentrate on why you called Terry back in.' McFarland felt like he was almost clutching at straws but continued, 'To catch the person responsible for these hideous crimes. We thought that it was a one-off until he struck again, now we are helpless, waiting for him to dish up another corpse. Why shouldn't the public know that you've had to call Terry back in? Tell them that we have been contacted by this monster and that this monster has named himself as "The Ultimate". Get this on the front of every newspaper. Sir, I guarantee that you'll have their undivided attention, along with their full backing.'

'I don't know about this… I agree with you regarding the public's right to know, but we don't want people running scared… what I mean by that is we don't want vigilantes roaming our streets, James.'

'What then? What do you suggest we do, sir? Terry and I are dancing in the dark. What exactly have we got? We have two people in custody, we have an eyewitness who told us what we already know. What I'm trying to say, sir, is if we don't appeal to the public, we are no further forward than when we started this investigation. It is our opinion that we tell the public as much as we legally can. Sir, please trust us with this. We've always delivered results in the past.'

'OK, James. Meet me at The Yard, in about…' Jasper checked his watch, 'let's say, a couple of hours. We can debrief and draw up a statement for the press. James…' Jasper growled, 'don't keep me waiting,' Jasper hung up.

'Yes,' McFarland yelled, punching the air. He then dialled Terry.

'You'll have to come back full-time you know?' McFarland stated, in a quiet tone.

'Jasper agreed? Fucking hell, wonders will never cease,' Terry chuckled. 'And no I won't,' he replied calmly.

'It's the only way he'll agree for you to face the press and be in full sight of the cameras, mate.' A silence followed.

'Did you tell him about the contact with The Ultimate, McFarland?

'I had to, mate, but it was your idea, and listen, we have to keep him in the loop. He would never have agreed to it if I hadn't. We've been summoned to his office – a couple of hours. We need to go through the press release, agree on a formal statement, and blah-de-blah, mate.'

'I was just checking… If it means me putting pen to paper.'

'How do you want to play this press conference then?' McFarland interrupted.

'Let's see what Jasper says, hey?' Terry knew that he would be provided a script, which would have been edited over and over.

'I'll be with you in about thirty minutes.'

Chapter Thirty-Five

Greg decided that he should do a final scout of the area surrounding the fitness instructor's flat. Lavender Gardens was a nice residential area of London, right next door to Kensington Gardens, ideal for Greg, who could park his van on the other side of the park, slip across the park undetected, do what he had to do and slip away across the park again. 'Perfect,' he thought.

Conrad Michaels had been a fitness instructor for over ten years, he had a history of sleeping with wealthy married women, a guy getting the best of both worlds, you might say. At thirty-four, Conrad looked great but none of this was natural, he had worked very hard to achieve his physical prowess. Various cosmetic surgeons had played their parts in chiselling his looks. Women couldn't help themselves.

Greg understood, and mildly respected, that Conrad must be a man of discipline – though vanity drove his strict training schedule. Nevertheless, Conrad was behind many a divorce, though somehow he always managed to come up smiling of roses. Nothing ever stuck to him – Teflon – nonstick.

Greg had also managed to find out that Conrad had studied karate and earned his black belt, this was why Greg, who by his own omission, was and is a very accomplished martial artist, did not want to have to waste time and energy overpowering Conrad. Weapons weren't cheating – they left nothing to chance.

Chapter Thirty-Six

Both men approached the door to Jasper's office in silence – in order for them to compose themselves. This press conference could make or break the case. McFarland reached for the door handle and opened the door, leading the way.

'Good morning, sir,' McFarland said.

'Good morning again, James. Good morning, Terry,' Jasper smiled. 'I'm sure you both know Kyle?'

'Mr Secretary…' McFarland said greeting Kyle. Terry gestured, nodding his head once. Kyle Moran's official capacity was that of Secretary of New Scotland Yard. In the eyes of the Metropolitan Police, he was God and Jasper was Jesus – although unofficially it was the other way round. Kyle was a man never to be crossed.

'So, Terry… you want back in?' Kyle asked, his face stern.

'I never said I wanted back in, Kyle.'

'Terry… it's Mr Secretary,' McFarland stated, worried that this had started badly.

'No, McFarland, its Kyle, whilst I'm still a civilian.'

'It's only a matter of time Terry… before you come back,' the hardened man replied. 'It's the only way that you'll get your press conference.'

'My press conference?' Terry looked amazed, 'Jasper, you called on me for help. I only offered my help, not my soul.'

'Terry, I would never allow you to be a spokesman for The Yard, unless you rejoined the family, and you're not dim enough to have thought otherwise,' Jasper said, joining the conversation.

'Is that the offer?'

'Let's leave the past where it belongs Terry, in the past,' Kyle said taking a small step forward. 'You know how we play the game here,' he added, holding out his hand. 'Please, shake my hand Terry. We were all under the cosh back in the day and we had to get the job done. OK we won't ever exchange Christmas cards, but that doesn't mean that we can't move on. Does it?'

'Let's cut to the chase,' Terry said as he shook Kyle's hand. 'Cards on the table time.'

'You rejoin the family and it's your call, and your case.'

'McFarland?'

'My place in heaven is guaranteed, mate,' McFarland grinned.

'OK, where do I sign?'

'Jasper will make the address, then you'll read from the script and open the floor to the Q and As.'

'And after?'

'And after… what?'

'This has all been put to bed; The Ultimate has been locked up.'

'Once a result has been achieved, is that what you mean?'

'Yes, that is exactly what I mean, Mr Secretary.'

'Business as usual, as per the status quo. Your days as a reporter will be a distant memory.'

'OK, show me the script.'

***

Jasper led the way followed by McFarland and Terry. The room was very noisy. Camera lenses began to click as soon as Terry emerged from behind McFarland.

'OK, OK, please calm down,' Jasper yelled. The room fell into silence. 'You all know who I am, but for the record, I am Chief Inspector Jasper Ward. To my left, you have Detective Inspector James McFarland and to my right, Mr Terry Bane, Former Detective Inspector and the leading Detective Inspector In Charge.' Jasper looked at Terry, and gave him a small smile. Camera shutters made a frantic united click. 'I will invite questions once we have finished our announcement,' Jasper said trying to maintain order. 'To bring you all up to speed – Detective Inspector In Charge Bane was approached by New Scotland Yard to assist in the apprehension of the person who is solely responsible for two recent brutal crimes. I am going to pass you over to D.I.I.C. Bane who has a brief to give you and then questions will be welcomed. Let me please ask for your complete co-operation while the brief is given, thank you. Terry...'

'OK, as you know there have been a couple of brutal killings recently, linked by a man in a shiny black suit. We are no closer to catching this guy than we were at the beginning of the investigation.'

Some of the journalists started barking like dogs.

'Come on, please calm down!' Jasper ordered. 'If you don't let him speak, we'll have to call a halt to this press conference!'

'Thank you,' Terry said holding his hands in the air. 'As I was saying... we have been contacted by a male calling himself "The Ultimate". We know that this is a genuine claim, but as you are well aware, I am unable to divulge why we know this. We owe it to the victims, Brain James and Hector Hylie, we also owe it to the victims' families so I implore anybody who thinks they might have any information surrounding recent events to come forward. I can guarantee complete anonymity and confidentiality. Without your help, we are blind. This man is among you; he is out there walking and stalking our streets. Until we catch him and put him behind bars, where he belongs, those streets, our streets, are his. We urge you not to try to apprehend this man alone, call for assistance. He is a truly dangerous person; the details of these horrendous crimes clearly spell that out. We are going to make a freephone number available twenty-four hours a day until we catch this criminal,' Terry paused for a sip of water. 'Now ask your questions one at a time.'

'Blake Ward, the *London Echo*. Are you admitting that you haven't made any progress?'

'That's not what I said, we're just trying to use the media to gain as much coverage as we can; that is why we are asking for your help today.'

'Fulton Myers, the *Daily Telegraph*. Isn't this what The Ultimate wants... to be in the headlines? You're playing in to his hands, giving him his glory.'

'No, Mr Myers, I disagree. He dresses in black, he leaves no trace of his presence at any of the scenes. None of the victims, or witnesses, can give us any kind of a firm description. He wants to remain anonymous. That is why he fades to black.'

'Blake Ward, the *London Echo*. What's he hoping to achieve?'

'We're not sure on that; we think that there's a link, but until we are certain...'

'Fulton Myers, the *Daily Telegraph*. How long have you been working on this case?'

Terry looked at Jasper, who nodded his approval. 'The day I reported the first murder, I was approached and I had a meeting with New Scotland Yard.'

'Who approached you?' Fulton Myers fired back.

'You know that's strictly confidential, Mr Myers,' Terry smiled.

'Bill Davis, the *Sun*. Both victims have been male, does that mean that women are safe?'

'No Bill, that's not true. It would be foolish for us to assume that. The first murder victim was male, though the person who murdered him wasn't. It is too early to guess any kind of pattern and it would be foolish if we were to make any assumptions.'

'Blake Ward, the *London Echo*. Do you have any idea what his motives are? Or is that a foolish question?' Intermittent laughter followed, though only briefly.

'At the moment, we have a number of theories, but until we are sure, we would only be guessing – as you would be foolish to guess, Mr Ward. We need your help,' Terry had warmed to this reporter.

'Gill Morgan, the *Times*. Why "The Ultimate"?'

'That, Mrs Morgan, is something we don't know, we think he is some sort of vigilante who sees himself as giving the ultimate justice. All we do know is that he is going to strike again and again until he is caught.'

'Gill Morgan, *The Times*. When do you think he'll strike again?'

'The only honest answer to that is soon. He will continue until he is caught. At this time, it is too early for us to gauge any kind of time pattern. But we don't intend on giving him enough time to establish one.'

'Gareth Charles, the *Standard*. I think that my colleagues and I would be more than happy to ensure that this appeal is printed on the front page of tonight's edition of the *Standard*.'

'Thank you. I would respectfully request that you all do that. It goes without saying that we hope this is going to make the front page of all your papers. That way we can get as much coverage as possible.'

'OK, thank you ladies and gentlemen,' Jasper concluded.

'Thank you all,' Terry added.

'Do you want Mr Ward silenced, Terry?'

'No don't, we need him. He's done us a lot of good and he knows it,' Terry said calmly. 'He did that on purpose.'

'Why?' McFarland asked.

'To demonstrate that we meant what we were saying, that we weren't just trying to lay down a smokescreen; that we are not just guessing. McFarland, the press have always thought that we have always held back the truth until a case is solved. He thought that by directing his questions the way he did, my answers would demonstrate that we truly showed them, and the British public, our hand and that our cards are on the table. Now, The Ultimate, who I can guarantee would have been watching this – will be fucking pissed off and this will hopefully force him to play his next card. We have won over Mr Blake Ward, along with all his fellow journalists, but I think he didn't need winning over. You remove the smoke from their eyes and they can report with better clarity, mate,' Terry said, placing his arm on the shoulder of the Scotsman.

'Welcome back Terry,' McFarland chuckled.

'It feels like I never left,' Terry laughed.

Chapter Thirty-Seven

Greg waited, surrounded by the darkness of the foliage. His thoughts traced back to the charade that he had watched on his television. He needed to block it out and remain focused on the task at hand. Control was everything. He watched intently as Valerie parked her car; his heart began to race. He continued to watch and wait until she had gone in to the building, allowing Valerie and Conrad enough time to occupy themselves.

His body started to shake as the adrenalin started to rush its way through his bloodstream. He could hear the echo of his own heartbeat as his nerves tried to kick in. The thrill was getting bigger every time.

Greg made his way across the road and in to the building. Once outside the main entrance, he used his snap gun to pick the lock. He was standing in the main hallway within seconds. He darted up the stairs, taking them two at a time, but stopped and smiled at the front door to Conrad's flat. Carefully, he placed his ear to the door, the noise coming from inside confirmed it was time for him to make his entrance. He quickly used the snap gun and, closing the door quietly behind him, Greg walked softly to the bedroom where Valerie was facing the bottom of the bed, with her back to Conrad, jumping up and down like a rodeo rider. Valerie opened her eyes for a split second, seeing Greg's silhouette, she stopped dead.

'Let me give it to you from behind,' Conrad said, completely lost in his own pleasure, unaware of Valerie's reason for halting.

'What?' Valerie was shocked at seeing their uninvited guest.

'Please finish. I can wait,' Greg said calmly.

'Conrad!' Valerie said, too shocked to be alarmed.

Conrad pushed Valerie off, and attempted to stand up as to confront Greg. Greg stepped forward and struck Conrad with the back of his fist. Conrad fell backwards onto the bed, then, without control, he slid awkwardly on to the floor.

'Stay down,' Greg ordered.

'I'll fucking kill you!' Conrad's threat fuelled with anger.

Greg calmly raised his right arm, aimed the taser gun at Conrad and squeezed the trigger. Two electrically-charged probes fired in to Conrad's abdomen causing him to convulse violently. His eyeballs rolled around until only the whites of his eyes were visible. Greg stepped forward and took a tube of pepper spray out from a compartment concealed in his belt and sprayed Conrad directly in his eyes. He released the trigger of the taser gun, stopping any further electrical discharge, turning the taser gun in Valerie's direction.

'No, no, no! Please no!' she pleaded. Panic-stricken, she tried to hide behind one of the pillows that had been pushed up against the headboard.

'Keep your voice down and I won't hurt you.' Greg's voice was chillingly controlled.

Conrad had now entered into a state of semi-consciousness. Valerie froze. She glanced at Conrad.

'He can't help you now, Valerie.'

Greg put both items back in his suit and pulled out some zip ties. Conrad still had not recovered from the electric shock and was struggling to breathe as he passed out.

'That makes that a little easier,' Greg said, as though it was all in a day's work for him.

Greg zipped Conrad's thumbs together and then his big toes. Greg then manoeuvred Conrad, laying him back on the bed next to Valerie. 'Valerie, he's a big lad, isn't he?' Greg confirmed.

'If you want money, my handbag is in the other room!'

'Valerie Hope... Mrs Valerie Hope, please tell me how long you've been shagging Conrad behind your husband's back?'

'What? Is he behind this? Has Brent paid you to do this?'

'Mr Brent Hope has no idea. He doesn't know anything about this… yet!'

'Who are you? What do you want?' Valerie was petrified and couldn't understand how this was happening.

'Valerie, Valerie, Valerie… don't you watch the news? I'm all over the news at the moment. I'm the hot topic, the latest headline.'

'What are you on about?'

'Oh dear, Valerie. Let's wait for big boy to wake up first, I don't want to have to go through it all twice. Nice tits by the way. I bet Conrad has never thought to thank Brent for those.' Greg laughed.

'Fuck off!' Valerie replied covering up. She was silent for a few moments whilst her mind raced. 'Oh shit you're… you're…that bloke in the rubber suit aren't you? What is it they call you?' Tears began to drip off her chin.

'They call me "The Ultimate".'

'What?'

'I'm the person that will see that the scum that has been allowed to breed in our society is culled. I will make sure that the filth is cleaned and all the stains they have created are removed.'

'Are you going to kill me?' she asked fearfully.

'No, Valerie. I'm not going to kill anyone.'

Conrad began to move. His eyes were still burning. He was struggling to breathe. 'Who the fuck sent you?' he murmured, his throat burning.

'Oh good, I'm glad you could join us.'

'Cocky fucker, aren't you?' Conrad barked in reply.

Greg walked over to the bed and raised his right leg, hovering the flat plain sole of his boot in front of Conrad's face.

'You are not in a position to be speaking to me like that. Please don't make me hurt you.'

'OK, OK,' Conrad humbled.

'I am here to right all the wrong that you two have brought in to the world. I really feel for Brent, he is the victim here – so I'm victim support,' Greg laughed.

'What?' Valerie asked, astounded.

'This is a listening exercise Val, so shut the fuck up and listen. In a moment, I'm going to give Brent a call and let him know where we all are. I'm also going to let him know what you two have been up to, and for God knows how long. I will invite him to join us; he will then see the pair of you with his own eyes. Who knows what will happen once the realisation kicks in and he finds out what his wife has been up to behind his back. All this time he thought you were playing bridge or something.'

'What's going to happen to us?' Conrad asked.

'Well, that will be up to Brent to decide. I think that he's not going to be too pleased to see you both. I think he's going to hurt you Conrad. I think he's going to hurt you bad. I'm not sure what he'll do to you though... I would not want to be either of you,' Greg said, looking at Valerie. 'May I?' he continued, as he picked up the cordless telephone that was sitting on the bedside table. He dialled Brent's mobile number from memory.

'Good evening, Brent.'

'Good evening. To whom am I speaking?' Brent enquired.

'That's not important, what is important is who I am with,' Greg paused for a reaction.

'OK, enough of the games. What is it you want?' Brent had never been patient.

'Direct, straight to the point, I like that. I am standing in the bedroom of a flat that is owned by the man who is fucking your wife. He has been fucking your wife for some time now.' Greg paused. 'Please don't ask me how long this deception has been going on for, because I don't know... What might be a good idea, is if you come over here and ask her for yourself.'

'What?' Brent could not digest this information. 'What did you just say?' Brent shook, dropping the glass he was holding.

'Exactly what you thought I said. I have your wife here and I must say that she does have fantastic tits, they must have cost you.'

'What do you want... money? I have money...' Brent became worried.

'No, this isn't about money. I want you to come along and join the party to see for yourself what your slut of a wife has been up to behind your back.'

'OK, where are you?'

'Brent... be sure that you come alone, otherwise I won't be able to guarantee Val's safety if you know what I mean?'

'You have my word, the word of a Mason, please don't hurt my wife.' Oddly Brent had become fearful for his wife's safety.

'She doesn't realise how much you love her... OK we are at flat 5a, Lavender Gardens. Do you know where that is?'

'Yes,' Brent was already contemplating alerting the police.

'Remove that thought from your head, Brent. I think you know that I am not playing games here, this is the real deal. You have ten minutes,' Greg ended the conversation abruptly.

'What kind of sick game are you playing?' Valerie asked.

'I am a firm believer that ye shall reap what ye shall sow. For a long time now, you have treated your husband as a means to an end. If it wasn't for his money you would have left him a long time ago.' Greg stopped and pointed at Conrad. 'He doesn't want you. He is a habitual adulterer, responsible for many a marriage break-up, a homewrecker. Conrad, why is it that you can't find your own fruit, you have to have the forbidden type?' Greg was becoming agitated by Brent's awaited arrival.

'I don't know, but I promise that I won't look at another married woman again, how's that?' Conrad pleaded.

'Not my decision I'm afraid, it's out of my hands. We'll see what Brent thinks... speak of the devil.'

A quiet knock on the door alerted Greg to Brent's arrival. Greg opened the door, shielding himself behind it, holding a StunMaster 5000 volt stun baton aloft as he did.

'Nice and easy does it,' Greg assured Brent.

'Hey take it easy. I'm here and I'm alone. Now what's going on?' Brent acted very calm and controlled though, in truth, he was petrified. Greg was not expecting this. Brent saw the man in the shiny suit and blurted, 'You're that guy they are talking about, The Ultimate!'

'Follow me,' Greg said, ignoring the question, 'everyone's in the bedroom.'

Valerie was crouching up against the headboard of the bed, trying to hide her nakedness behind a pillow. Conrad was lying on his side; Brent noticed that his hands and feet had been fastened together.

'As you can see, they both seem to have lost their clothes, and there's no one else here for them to blame. I won't go in to the compromising position I found them in, though, put it this way, I did offer them the opportunity to finish before the real fun began.'

'This may seem like a stupid question, but what's going on Val?' Brent asked his wife.

'You were never supposed to find out like this,' she replied, pathetically.

'How was I supposed to find out?' Brent was extremely dignified in his approach.

'I don't know.'

'You weren't... it was just a bit of fun,' Conrad joined the conversation.

'Are you trying to defend my wife? How admirable.'

'No, I'm not, it's just that you deserve the truth.'

'I want the truth from my wife. I'd advise you to keep quiet,' Brent's tone sharpened. 'OK where do we go from here?' he said, turning to look at Greg.

'And I was beginning to get all emotional too, Brent. Everything begins with a choice, your next choice will shape the rest of your life: the unfaithful wife, the scorned husband and her lover. It all snowballs doesn't it? Firstly, what are you going to do now you have discovered that this guy has been fucking the arse off your wife for God knows how long? I'd wager that you've not been getting any action, if you know what I mean? So, with that in mind, you should be able to calculate how long this man has been pickling your rhubarb Brent. No man should asunder those whom God hath joined! Any man found infringing another man's consummate rights should be dealt with swiftly and punished vigorously. Any woman found to have betrayed her husband should be punished as her scorned husband wishes. Who has the right to break another's heart and soul? I know what I'd do, but then maybe you are more forgiving… more mouse than man.'

Silence filled the room. Greg went in to the kitchen, returning seconds later holding a bowl of cold water. He threw the water over Conrad completely saturating him and the bedding that surrounded him.

'Everything begins with choice, Brent, make your move,' Greg spoke softly handing him the taser gun, in the knowledge that his rubber suit kept him safe, should Brent attempt to turn the gun on him.

'Val, get off the bed,' Brent ordered.

'Please don't do it,' Conrad pleaded.

'Val, you have two seconds or you'll fucking fry with him. Now move!'

Brent could feel his pulse pounding in his neck. His penis became slightly erect and he felt a glowing feeling in the pit of his stomach. Adrenalin rushed up from the tips of his toes; when it reached his brain he automatically squeezed the trigger, sending two darts flying towards Conrad. Puncturing his flesh, the darts then began to fill Conrad's body with electricity. Valerie had placed herself in the corner of the room and wrapped the pillow around her head to soften the screams echoing through her eardrums. Conrad was shaking violently, his body convulsing and contorting. Blood started to ooze from his nose and both ears. A burning smell filled the air, the smell of burning flesh. The noises that came from Conrad were of desperate pain and suffering. The complete lack of control over his own body made him feel disconnected, as though his soul had already vacated the premises that it had lived in for so long. He had accepted his demise and that was when he lost control of his bowels. Urine and excrement left his body in rapid propulsion spraying only the immediate area around him. Only Valerie was hit by this propulsion. Conrad's body began to slow and took on more of a quiver as his violent contortions ceased. His body had given up; he was dead.

Brent turned to see what Greg was doing but Greg was gone, vanished. In all the excitement and fear he had not noticed Greg's departure. The Ultimate had slipped away and disappeared into the night. 'WHAT, what have I done? Oh fuck, oh shit, I can't believe what I have just done!' The reality of his actions shocked him. 'What are we going to do, Val?'

'Am I next?' she asked, slowly raising her head. 'Am I?' Tears streamed down her face, her gaunt look suggested that she had suffered enough. Her sobbing was interrupted by nervous hiccupping, making her speech frantic.

'No, I would never hurt you, the way you have hurt me. I love you, Val.'

'You should call the police,' Valerie suggested. 'You've just killed a man, our marriage is over.' She foolishly felt that the danger was over.

'What do you mean? I only killed him because I love you so much. He, The Ultimate, made me do it,' Brent stuttered, trying to justify his actions in the hope that his wife would change her mind and take his side.

'He never made you do anything Brent. Anyway, he was right, I am only with you for your money and I stopped loving you when I met Conrad. You have taken that away from me. How can I ever forgive you? How could I ever love you again? You're a murderer now.'

The silence was broken by the sound of sirens wailing in the background. A neighbour had heard the noise, spotted Greg leaving and decided to call the police.

'Here they come. They're coming for you Brent; you're going to prison Brent, out of my life. I'm not greedy, half of everything will do for starters while you're locked up.'

Brent felt the adrenalin return, though this time it filled him with uncontrollable rage. Pacing over to his wife, Brent took hold of the lamp that was on the bedside table and swung it in the direction of Valerie's head. She instinctively raised the pillow in front of her face. The crashing blow rocketed her head backwards, bouncing it off the wall behind. The impact spilt her skull and she felt the warm liquid ooze out and run down the back of her neck, continuing its journey down the crevice of her spine. Blackness filled her world; she knew her life had come to its end.

'Fancy going like this,' she spoke in to the pillow that shielded her face. Sadly, she was the only person to hear her final sentence. Brent stood up straight, his body shaking as his overdose of adrenalin subsided.

'STEP BACK FROM THE BODY, AND PUT YOUR HANDS WHERE I CAN SEE THEM!' a voice commanded. Brent turned, almost in slow motion, to see who it was that had shouted at him. An armed policeman stood shining a torch at Brent's face, his pistol drawn, safety off. 'ARMED POLICE, STEP AWAY FROM THE BODY SIR. I WILL ONLY ASK YOU ONE MORE TIME!' the uniformed officer ordered.

'OK, OK, I'm not going to try to resist,' Brent replied.

'LAY DOWN ON THE FLOOR, FACE DOWN, PLACING YOUR HANDS BEHIND YOUR BACK. I MUST WARN YOU THAT WE ARE ARMED AND ARE USING LIVE ROUNDS!' the officer continued as if reading from a script. Brent did as he was ordered. He was then bundled in to the back of a police van and taken to Kensington High Street Police Station.

Chapter Thirty-Eight

McFarland rang Terry from his car on his way to Terry's house.

'Mate,' he began, 'there's been another!'

'Fuck, fuck, fuck!' Terry replied. 'Where this time?'

'Lavender Gardens, Kensington.'

'Yeah, I know where that is.'

'I'm just pulling up outside your house now.'

'OK I'm on my way. Two minutes...'

Terry grabbed his jacket and house keys before closing the front door behind him. He jogged to McFarland's car, trying to save a little more time.

'Tell me what you know,' he ordered closing the car door.

'They have a man in custody. OK, the police were called to the property by a worried neighbour. The neighbour had heard screaming coming from the next door flat and, after a while, looked out of a window to see if there was anything going on outside. She noticed a black shape, that seemed to have come from the building, quickly disappear into Kensington Gardens. When our boys arrived, there were two dead bodies, one male and the other female, and another male standing over the female's corpse. All in the bedroom, the dead male was lying on the bed. It seems that the woman was the wife of the only man alive and the dead guy was her lover. He says that our man in the black suit was there.'

'It was obvious that he would strike again. How did the two die?' Terry was already thinking ahead.

'The guy was electrocuted and the woman had her head smashed in.'

'Murder weapons?'

'A taser gun and a bedside lamp!'

'Where is the prisoner being held?'

'Kensington High Street nick.'

'Name?'

'Brent Hope.'

'Let's go to the scene first, hey?'

'Good idea, we can talk to him later.'

Once at the scene of the crime, both detectives started to look for inspiration. Terry started outside the building whilst McFarland went inside. Terry looked over at the park known as Kensington Gardens; he loved the way we named things according to their location.

***

'Has a statement been taken from the neighbour?' McFarland asked one of the other detectives.

'Yes, sir, though it's basically what we already know. The man in custody is being very helpful,' the rotund man replied.

'OK, thanks,' McFarland half-heartedly replied.

McFarland's attention was drawn to the amount of water on the mattress, just enough to do the job he thought, a novice would have soaked it. As he leant forward, he took a whiff of that smell they had not been able to place at the first scene. It filled his nostrils.

'What's that smell?'

'That's pepper spray, sir,' the rotund detective replied.

'Can we get a sample of that for analysing?'

'Yes, sir, I'll get the forensic boys on it.'

'It's all over this pillow,' he pointed out, so the detective could pass on the information.

***

Terry had walked all the way across Kensington Gardens. He knew that was where the getaway vehicle had been parked. No

CCTV though. There were already officers combing the park looking for clues. Terry knew they would not find anything and decided to have a look inside the building. As he entered the flat, he looked at the door frame and noted that the lock did not seemed to have been forced. He could not understand how The Ultimate had got in. After talking to McFarland, the two detectives decided that it was time to talk to the man in custody – Brent Hope.

***

'He's in interview room four, sir,' announced the desk sergeant.

'Just through here?' McFarland asked.

'Yes, sir, on your left,' the uniformed WPC replied, pressing an electronic button that released the heavy security door.

As they entered the room, Brent was sitting next to a man in a very expensive suit.

'Hello, I'm Detective Inspector James McFarland, and this is Detective Inspector In Charge Terry Bane of New Scotland Yard,' he said, with pride.

'Hello Detectives, I'm Mr Dominic Fortroy-Holmes, Mr Hope's lawyer.'

'We would like to talk to Mr Hope with regards to the two recent murders at 5a Lavender Gardens and what his role was. What actually happened? Are you happy for us to do that?' McFarland enquired.

Brent nodded his acceptance.

'Mr Hope, we are going to need your full co-operation if we are to get to the bottom of this,' Terry interrupted.

'I have nothing to hide and I am willing to answer any of your questions – if I can,' Brent confirmed.

'Tell us what exactly happened,' Terry instructed.

'I was at home reading a book and sipping on a fine cognac, when I received a phone call. A man informed me that my wife was in a flat with another man having… sexual intercourse. He told me to come to the flat alone.'

'Who was the man who phoned you?' Terry interrupted.

'It later transpired that it was the man whom is now known as "The Ultimate", detective.'

'OK, please continue,' Terry nodded.

'He told me where to go and I heard my wife's voice in the background...' Brent began to sob, 'when I arrived I was shown into the bedroom. My wife was on the bed, and so was a man. The man's hands and feet were tied together. He then told me that my wife and this man had been having an affair for some time and that my wife was only with me for my money.'

'Were they dressed or naked at this point?' Terry asked.

'Naked. He said that when he walked in they were having sex!'

'Did you believe him?'

'Yes, I did.'

'Why?'

'Because the man still had a condom on his penis and my wife didn't even try to deny it. She told me after... about the affair.' He paused, taking a sip from the cup containing hot tea that his lawyer had bought him before the interview. 'Val told me that she loved Conrad and that she didn't love me anymore... as far as she was concerned, our marriage was over.' Brent became more upset, reliving it all.

'The man, "The Ultimate", have you ever met him before?'

'Come on... What kind of a question is that? I have no idea what this man looks like, let alone anything else about him,' Brent grimaced.

'What about Mr Michaels, had you ever met him before?'

'No, never!'

'OK, tell us what happened next,' Terry wanted Brent to continue.

'The Ultimate left the room and returned with a bowl of water. He then threw the water over Conrad and went on about choices saying that everything begins with choice and handed me that taser gun...'

'Did he tell you that you had to use the taser gun? Did he tell you to shoot Conrad with it?' McFarland interrupted.

'No, he didn't, he didn't say anything, he just gave it to me. I knew what he wanted me to do. I told Val to get off the bed because I didn't want to kill her. She got off and I shot him with the gun and when Conrad stopped moving, I looked and he was gone...' He placed his head in to his hands.

'Do you mean The Ultimate was gone?'

'Yes, who else would I mean?'

'I'm just trying to get the facts here, Mr Hope,' Terry said reassuringly.

'If he didn't tell you what to do, how did you know that was what he wanted you to do?' McFarland seemed confused.

'Think about it, he threw water over Conrad and then gave me the gun... what do you think?' Brent snapped.

'How much cognac had you had to drink, Mr Hope?'

'What? Are you going to arrest me for drink driving too?'

'Please answer the question. I'm just trying to understand what your state of mind may have been like.'

'Put it this way, I was over the limit to drive but I wasn't drunk.'

'Sometimes, when people are under the influence of alcohol, things can seem a bit blurry if you catch my drift.'

'I do. But I'm recalling the events as they happened, with crystal clarity, detective.'

'OK please continue...' Terry gave McFarland a gentle nudge.

'Val then told me to call the police...'

'Did you?'

'No, we got in to an argument. We always argued. She told me that she was going to divorce me when I was in prison. She said that she was going to take half my money and start a new life. I lost it!' He stopped and looked at the man sitting opposite him. McFarland's eyes widened. 'That's the first time in my life that I have ever lost control. I am a placid person, which was why she treated me so terribly. I always loved her, worshipped her, you know? I'll never stop loving her. She walked all over me and it was my overflowing love for her that allowed her to do it,' he said with a sincere look on his face.

'Can you tell us about your wife's murder?' Terry was genuinely sorry for Brent, but he had a job to do.

'Yes, sorry... I didn't want... I suppose if I couldn't have her I wasn't going to allow any other man to. When I saw her there with Conrad, I felt sick to my stomach, so when I heard that she was going to start a new life without me, I walked over to her and picked up the lamp and hit her with it.'

'Where did you hit her?'

'She had tried to hide behind a pillow. The pillow was over her face. I hit the pillow with the lamp and her head hit the wall behind her.'

'How many times did you hit her, or should I say, hit the pillow with the lamp?'

'I don't know... once maybe twice, but no more... No hold on, it was only once. I suppose I've blacked that out of my memory. I can remember picking the lamp up, then the rest is a little fuzzy. The next thing I remember is being told to move away from Val by a policeman pointing a gun at me.'

'Who killed Conrad Michaels?' Terry did not want Brent to diversify.

'I guess I did!'

'And who killed Valerie Brent?'

'I did!'

'Did anyone force you, either mentally or forcefully, to kill the two victims? Did The Ultimate force you in to the actions that you took?'

'No,' was his one word answer.

'That said,' Brent's lawyer decided to break his silence, 'The Ultimate lured my client to Mr Michaels' flat, premeditating the outcome. If The Ultimate had not contacted my client, then none of this would ever have happened.'

'That The Ultimate orchestrated this, Mr Fortroy-Holmes, is a fact, but The Ultimate did not kill either Mr Michaels or Mrs Hope – your client did and your client has confessed as much.'

'What's going to happen to me now?'

'Let's not think about that now Mr Hope, what we need to concentrate on is how we are going catch this person, The Ultimate, the orchestrator. We know that you committed these terrible crimes, but we know that you did not do them as in a premeditated sense. We are going to recommend that you be charged with manslaughter because these murders were not premeditated. Do you understand what I have just told you?'

'Yes… You must stop this man.' Brent reached out to Terry, as if he was pleading for him to save others from feeling the self-punishment that he was now going through.

Chapter Thirty-Nine

Karen's eyes were fixated on the television screen. She could not believe what she was hearing, so she had to concentrate solidly in order for the newsflash to register in her brain. A single tear fell, landing on her lap, and she knew what she had to do. She picked up the cordless telephone and went in to her bedroom, closing the door behind her.

'Are you OK?' Karen's mother asked. Silence was her reply. Karen dialled the freephone number that was given during the newsflash, it rang only once.

'Hello, New Scotland Yard, incident room.'

'Hello, I know who's responsible for these murders. I know who the man in the rubber suit is… I know the identity of The Ultimate.'

'OK, can I have your name please?'

'Karen, Karen Hogan.'

'Right then Miss Hogan what makes you think that you know who this guy is?'

'He's my boyfriend. I'd rather do this face to face with someone, it'd be easier.' Karen's hands were shaking like a leaf, her heart pounded.

'Fine, when could you come in to us?' the male call centre operative replied.

'I can come in now. I'm only half an hour away. I have to talk to the detective that I saw on the news.'

'OK, when you get here give reception your name and they will know why you are here. Don't tell them anything else, for security purposes, you understand?' the man on the phone softened his tone.

'Yes, I'm on my way,' Karen replied, leaving the phone on her bed and darting out of the front door before she had time to change her mind.

***

'McFarland,' the Scotsman said in to the microphone of his hands-free set.

'Hello James. We've got a young lady, Miss Karen Hogan, coming in to see us. She claims to know who the guy is in the rubber suit. She says that The Ultimate is her boyfriend!'

'It's Wardy,' he told Terry, who was sitting next to him in the car. 'So Miss Hogan's on her way in now?'

'Yes, that's what I just told you. Where are you?'

'We're just leaving Kensington High Street nick, we've been interviewing the latest…'

'I need you both to get back here as fast as you can.' Jasper rudely interrupted.

'Yes, we're on our way,' McFarland ended the call.

Terry leant forward, flicking the siren and lights on. McFarland selected a lower gear and pushed the pedal under his right foot to the floor, the engine roared.

'Are you going to tell me what that was all about?' Terry asked impatiently.

'A woman has phoned the incident line claiming to know who The Ultimate is. She's on her way in to see us now,' he replied driving his car like a maniac.

On arrival, the two men headed directly for Jasper's office.

'Where have you put her, sir?' Terry asked hurriedly.

'She's in interview room one, drinking a cup of coffee and eating a bar of chocolate. Gentlemen I think that she is the real deal.'

'What makes you think that? Have you talked to her, sir?' McFarland asked, his excitement evident.

'Yes, I have spoken with her. You'll see what I mean when you talk to her.' He gestured them to leave his office. 'Go on then, don't keep the poor girl waiting any longer and remember…' He paused. 'It's taken a lot of courage for her to come in here today, she is a little upset and very fragile. Kid gloves fellas, treat her gently – that's an order.'

'No worries,' Terry answered.

'That was directed at you James,' Jasper confirmed.

'Aye I know… no worries from me too, sir.'

As the two detectives entered the interview room, Karen sat quietly sipping her coffee. She automatically looked to see who was entering the room. A female officer kept her company. The opening door broke the stale air of silence.

'Hello Miss Hogan. I am Detective Inspector James McFarland and my colleague is…' the Scotsman began his introduction.

'I know who you are, and you know why I'm here,' she said bluntly. 'Call me Karen,' she instructed.

'OK, that's that out of the way. Tell us why you are here,' the Scotsman had been agitated by her previous outburst.

'Gregory O'Hara is the man you want, he's The Ultimate,' she said quickly.

'And why do you think that?' McFarland replied sarcastically.

'Right then, here we go,' Karen replied, as to pace herself. 'When the first one happened, I was at his flat with him, he had cooked. Once I had eaten I began to feel very weird, very tired, and I mean to an extent where I could not keep my eyes open. Greg had to undress me and put me to bed. I hadn't had loads to drink and I slept straight through. Greg had to wake me the next morning, so I think I was drugged by him. When the second murder happened, Greg and I had planned on a night out, but he cried off at the last minute, saying that something had popped up, and offered to take me out for lunch on the Sunday to make up for it.'

'I can't see where you're going with this,' McFarland said slowly.

'Give her a chance,' Terry was fixated. 'Please continue Karen.'

'Thank you,' she replied, shooting McFarland a sharp glare. 'Sunday being the very next day, he took me to a restaurant in New Covent Garden, as we were seated we overheard a couple having a heated conversation, so I asked them to keep it down, and the woman was extremely rude to us, her husband was the perfect gentleman, apologising and he even bought us champagne. The manager of the restaurant gave us our meal on the house. We got very, very drunk. We went back to Greg's to sleep it off. When we woke up our heads were banging. I asked Greg if he had any pain killers. "In the medicine cabinet" he told me. When I looked, there were these tablets with a hand written label on, the label said "Knock Out Drops", that was what he'd used to drug me. Another time, I went to his flat unexpected and he was all a flap when I arrived, something wasn't right. I went to the fridge to get a couple of beers. When I opened one of the bottles, I spilt some on the floor. I asked Greg for a cloth to clean up, "under the sink" he told me. When I removed the cloth, underneath was a half-empty bottle of embalming fluid. When I went back in to the living room, I noticed a leaflet on the floor under the coffee table. I picked it up and slipped it in my handbag. The leaflet was for an electronic taser gun, thanking Greg for his recent purchase! The couple in the restaurant were Brent and Valerie Hope. Greg worked with Hector on the bins before Greg got his road sweeping job and Martin's his so-called mate... I don't know the first man, though.' Tears were running down her face.

'Would you like some time?' Terry asked. Both detectives and the female officer were taken back by Karen's revelation.

'No, I'm OK.'

'Something to drink, maybe?'

'No thanks, I've still got this,' Karen replied, holding her half-full cup of coffee.

'Do you still have the leaflet you mentioned?'

'Yes, it's here,' she reached in to her handbag and gave Terry the leaflet.

'Yes, you are right, this does confirm that Greg had purchased this from them. I wonder what other purchases he made.'

'Have you confronted him about all this?' McFarland enquired. He felt a little out of order with the way he had spoken to Karen previously. 'I apologise for my tone earlier.'

'That's OK,' she replied. 'No, I haven't tackled him about this. You must understand that when you meet Greg, you will think that this is all a bit crazy, he's not like this. On the surface at least.

He's a kind, gentle person. OK he can be a bit of a lad at times, but that's what I loved about him. It's not that I'm trying to defend him it's just…' she had begun talking herself in circles.

'We are going to need his address and work details as well as a signed statement from you. I am truly sorry for your heartache. We will have to name you when, or if it gets to court. You do understand that we will be unable to offer you any anonymity. As you are here on your own volition, we are unable to offer you any legal representation. You may want to have a solicitor present when you give your statement. We can supply you with a number for legal representation if you'd like.' McFarland tried his best to be sympathetic, but it was very difficult for him.

'Karen, I know that what you have told us must have been very difficult for you. Thank you so much for coming here today and telling us what you know. I do believe that there may be a strong possibility that this is our man. We now will see what Greg has to say. We will keep your name out of it for as long as we can.' The genuineness of Terry's voice made Karen believe that she was doing the right thing.

'I have written everything down – that's how I do things, to make sense of things, to get them straight in my own mind first. I did that whilst I waited for you to get here. Would it be OK if I went away for a couple of days to distance myself from Greg to try to give my head a chance to take it all in?' her tears appeared again.

'Of course, but please don't leave the country, we may need to talk to you again. Be sure to leave a number that we can contact you on. If we have any news, you are going to be the first to know. Let's remember though, innocent until proven guilty. Just because things don't make sense sometimes, it doesn't mean that they always have to.'

'It doesn't look good for him though, does it?' she confirmed.

'My gut tells me, no… but let us talk to him first, hey?' Terry answered, with another question. The two men stood up and took turns to shake Karen's hand before leaving her in the company of the female officer.

'Let's talk to Mr O'Hara,' Terry said.

'Aye let's… I bet he won't be so cocky this time?' McFarland agreed.

'We can pick up a warrant to search his flat. Check if he has a car, or some kind of transport, with the DVLA, please mate. If he does, we'll have to get a warrant to impound it. If O'Hara is our man, I want this done by the numbers McFarland. Nothing left to chance.'

'I'm on it.'

They travelled directly to Greg's flat. Terry drove as McFarland had to make a couple of calls en route. One of the calls was to arrange for a search warrant, another was to the DVLA, and the last was to arrange for some uniformed officers to meet them there. They would need as much help as they were able to muster. They pulled up outside Greg's flat the uniformed officers were waiting.

'Alright guys?' McFarland greeted. 'Do you have the necessary paperwork?'

'Yes, sir,' replied the most senior of the uniformed officers.

'Thanks Sergeant,' McFarland said, acknowledging the stripes on the sleeve of the man's jacket.

'Are you all we have?' Terry asked.

'Yes, sir, we…' one of the other uniformed officers answered.

'OK let's get on with it,' Terry replied pressing the button for the intercom to Greg's flat. They waited; McFarland pressed the button, holding it in longer than Terry had.

'Hold your horses,' a voice warned. 'Who is it?'

'It's the police. We would like to ask you a few questions, just routine follow up. May we come in?'

'Yeah, come on up,' Greg gestured casually.

The buzzing of the lock alerted them that he had released the security lock.

'OK,' Terry said. 'You two come with us. I want the others to watch all possible exits. I am not risking losing him if he decides to bolt.'

'If he does, you must stop him,' McFarland added.

'Hold on,' Terry said, turning in his tracks, 'be prepared, this guy has used a taser gun and pepper spray. He is very dangerous. If there's a chance that he might get physical, then the fucking Queensbury rules go out the window.'

Greg was waiting for them as they reached his flat. He thought about Sharon, and how she had been a useful tool. Martin had shown courage, something he had not expected. He felt disappointed that he had been found so early in his crusade, though he always would have the comfort of knowing that he had served his purpose. He stretched his neck sideways in both directions, before he cleared his throat and readied himself.

'What's this all about then? Fuck me, you seem a bit mob handed this time.'

'Mr Gregory Jason O'Hara?' McFarland asked.

'Yeah… is someone going to tell me what this is all about?' Greg replied, a little uneasy by the way the officers had swarmed up the stairs.

'Mr O'Hara, we would like you to assist us with our enquiries, and we would prefer to do that at the local police station. You are under arrest on suspicion of kidnap, though we are not formally charging you with anything at this time. You do have a right to legal representation, though I must inform you that anything you say will be taken as evidence. Anything you do not say, cannot be used or relied upon at a later date. Do you understand?'

'I think so,' Greg looked confused.

'OK Mr O'Hara, we have a car waiting,' McFarland looked at Terry and nodded. 'We must also alert you to the fact that we have obtained a warrant from the local magistrate that permits us to legally search these premises. Do you understand?' McFarland looked at Greg for a reaction.

'You can fuck off. I want my brief here!' Greg had fire in his eyes.

'Please don't make us use any unnecessary force on you Mr O'Hara,' McFarland smirked.

'You fucking knob!' Greg said, panic-stricken.

Terry reached out to grab Greg, managing to obtain a firm grip of Greg's left arm, he tried to force Greg's arm around his back by twisting it. Greg turned and head-butted McFarland square on the nose. The detective's nose collapsed with the force of the blow; blood oozed from both nostrils. The bridge of McFarland's nose had split and as the skin tore, a gaping wound appeared.

'You dirty bastard,' McFarland cursed.

During the ensuing struggle, uniformed officers pounced on Greg. The sheer barrage, forced Greg to the ground. 'I'm gonna fucking nail you for this, you bastard,' McFarland cursed again, his once white shirt, now completely claret in colour.

'Bring it on you wankers,' Greg barked, as his blood pumped, fuelling his muscles.

'Assault on a police officer, interfering with an ongoing police investigation, swearing at a police officer... they're gonna throw the fucking key away once I'm finished,' McFarland growled.

'I want my brief to meet us at whatever nick you're taking me to. I'm saying fuck all without him there!'

'Please come with us, sir,' Terry smiled, leading Greg to his car.

'Wait for two of our guys to get here before you enter the premises. They'll be here any moment. We cannot risk contamination of anything that may be considered as evidence. If we get a result out of this, I promise that you will receive your silver cloud,' McFarland told the uniformed officers.

'Thank you, sir...'

'Thanks for your help,' McFarland replied.

Chapter Forty

Silence filled the car during their journey to Wembley Central police station. Greg's mind raced as he struggled to find a way to regain control of the situation. He considered his options, wondering what the best approach would be. He did not feel any remorse over what he had done but he was angry with the fact that he had been caught so early. Hopefully, he would have made society think differently, after all, he was now big news – the media would be buzzing to get the next scoop on this, his story. He hoped that the vigilante side of London's public would understand and empathise with what he had done. He had helped people. Hopefully he would be the topic of many debates; he could just imagine *News Night* .The Ultimate would not just fade to grey, being kept in the forefront of what made this city buzz. It was important for Greg that people did not remember him, he wanted people to remember his alter ego, as well as the people his alter ego had been in direct contact with. The deaths, along with those that had been punished, would have not been in vain.

A smile etched its way on his face as he thought about Sharon's baby. He had given her baby a second chance, a better start in life. Sharon had simply been a casualty, as had the others. Martin had shown a remarkable amount of courage, though his threats had not passed, unnoticed. His thoughts then took a turn, Karen entered his mind…

The two detectives gripped the prisoner, taking an arm each as they entered the police station via the rear entrance. McFarland gripped Greg's left arm and dug his fingertips into the prisoner's flesh as they walked.

'I owe you, you bastard,' McFarland told the prisoner. Greg remained focussed, eyes front.

'Sir, interview room one is available,' the Duty Sergeant announced.

'Has Mr O'Hara's lawyer arrived yet?' the Scotsman replied.

'Two minutes ago. He's already in there waiting for you.'

'Great,' the Scotsman said sarcastically.

On entering the room a tall slim man stood, wearing a very well-tailored suit spoke abruptly. 'I would like some time with my client please.'

'All in good time...' Terry replied. 'Mr O'Hara is officially under arrest though, at the moment, Mr O'Hara has not been formally charged and has been bought here for questioning.' By this time all four men had sat down.

'Please forgive me, I'm Mr Jarvis Davis-Smythe; I am Mr O'Hara's lawyer and I will be representing Mr O'Hara during all following proceedings.'

'I am DI James McFarland, and this is D.I.I.C. Terry Bane,' The Scotsman announced. 'We are the investigating officers in charge of the case of recent murders that have plagued our capital – the murders of Brian James, Hector Hylie, Conrad Michaels and Valerie Brent. We would like to ask Mr O'Hara if he knew anything about these murders.'

'I thought you had nicked some people who had confessed – that's what you said on the news.' Greg was acting dumb, still playing his game and still thinking about Karen.

'And where did you watch that particular news story?' McFarland said pedantically.

'Yes, you are right,' Terry joined the conversation. 'We want The Ultimate.'

'Where were you on the night of Brian James's murder?' McFarland asked.

'With my bird, all night... Karen Hogan,' he grinned.

'What about on the night of Hector Hylie's murder?'

'In the boozer with Lisa – you have her bloke, Martin, banged up for that anyway... You know, Martin Pringle!'

'What about the night of Conrad Michael and Valerie Hope's murder?'

'At home, on my own,' Greg smiled.

'Do you use the internet, Greg?' Terry asked.

'Yeah, who doesn't?' he casually replied.

'What do you use the internet for, Greg?'

'My client does not have to answer that question,' Greg's lawyer smelled trouble.

'I don't mind answering that,' Greg said, undermining his legal representative. 'I look at all kinds of stuff on the information highway, I use it for email, and sometimes I use it to catch up on sport, now that's not illegal, is it?'

'We are carrying out a comprehensive search of your flat at this very moment. Our team have software technicians that can take a very detailed look at the hard drive on your PC and that will tell us exactly what you have been doing on the internet,' Terry snapped back.

'You knew Hector Hylie, didn't you?' McFarland said allowing his colleague time.

'Yes, I did.' A cocky note in his tone echoed. 'We used to work together.'

'What was your relationship with Hector?'

'He drove the bin wagon. I never really spoke to him. We had nothing in common, it was a working relationship. Why?'

'You had also met Mr and Mrs Brent.'

'Fucking hell that was in a restaurant, they were having a barney and my bird told them to shut up. The geezer bought us a bottle of bubbly. His wife was a right bitch. Does that mean I killed her?'

'That's not what I asked you. I only stated that you had already met them.'

'Where's the hammer, Greg?' Terry asked.

'What hammer?'

'The hammer that Sharon used on Brian.'

'I don't know what the fuck you two are on about.' Greg looked at his lawyer. 'Can I go now?'

'No, you can't go Greg, or maybe I should address you as "The Ultimate."'

'What? I'm not The Ultimate!'

'Oh yes you are. Tell me, Greg, why did you phone me on Hector's Mobile?'

Just then there was a knock on the door. An unwelcome distraction; Terry indicated to McFarland that he should find out who it was. The Scotsman opened the door and left the room.

'I would like to carry on until my colleague returns, if that's OK?' Terry asked politely.

'Why do you think it was me?' Greg enquired, slouching back in his chair.

'We've had a tip off. We have a receipt... a receipt that proves you made a purchase over the internet of a weapon used during your reign as The Ultimate.'

'Prove it... you can say whatever you like. You've got nothing on me. OK, where did you get this, so called receipt from?'

'Miss Karen Hogan... I believe you know this woman.'

Just then, the door flew open, and McFarland came marching in, taking large military like strides as he did.

'I must insist...' Greg's lawyer announced.

'We've got you, you little cocky sod!' he said looking Greg straight in the face. 'We've got you banged to rights; nailed to the wall!'

'I must insist that you...' Jarvis Davis-Smythe tried to intervene once again.

'We have found some very interesting things on the hard drive of your PC, Greg,' McFarland said, this time in a calmer tone. 'We have also found some interesting things in your flat,' He paused again, this time a smile formed on his face. 'Oh nice van, didn't know if the floor panel came as standard though, fantastic job, but not good enough!' McFarland looked at Greg as if he was trying to taunt him.

'You don't have fuck all on me,' Greg snarled.

'Mr Gregory Jason O'Hara. I am arresting you for committing the crimes of kidnap – two counts, for holding people hostage –

four counts, for threats of violence – twelve counts, for the purchase and supply of deadly weapons for the use of crimes against human life – seven counts, of the orchestration of four brutal murders and for one count of assault on a police officer. Anything you may say will be taken down and used in evidence against you, if you neglect to mention something that you later rely on as evidence, this will become omissible in a court of law. Do you understand the charges brought against you?'

'Can my client and I have some time please? I think I need to talk to Mr O'Hara.'

'Yes, I think you have a lot of talking to do with your client. We will allow you half an hour, then we'll return. Is that enough time for you?' McFarland was telling rather than asking – he knew that they had got their man. As both men left the room, a cheer could be heard from the corridor.

Chapter Forty-One

'OK, what do we have?' Chief Inspector Jasper Ward enquired.

'Let's have a look,' McFarland answered.

'He has looked at and printed off aerial maps of each of the crime scenes. The planning was fantastic,' Terry smiled, looking at both men.

'Moving on…' Jasper Ward insisted.

'He purchased the rubber suit from an online auction site. The mask was ordered from a specialist site based in the States, *secondskin.com*. The boots could have come from anywhere. OK, the hammer that we still haven't been able to recover doesn't really matter too much. We need to trace where those tablets came from, they're used to knock horses out, he was lucky not to have killed Karen. The embalming fluid was bought from a taxidermy wholesaler, *taxidermydiy.com*. We have recovered some of the packaging from the taser gun, though all the information for this item and another, a mechanical lock pick, which I must add was recovered from his van, are on his hard drive.'

'OK, you two had better go and see what he has to say for himself. Try to play it cool. We have the bastard and he's not going anywhere without our say so. Great job guys, I'll be watching from behind the glass.'

The two men walked back in to the interview room where Greg and his solicitor were still deep in conversation. Placing a number of bags on a separate table the two detectives sat down.

'Before we begin, I'd like to point out that Mr O'Hara has decided that he no longer wishes to employ my services, so therefore I'd like to remove myself from this room.'

'Mr O'Hara is there anybody else you'd like us to call in regards to your legal representation?' Terry asked.

'No, I'll be OK.'

The four became three.

'We would like to be upfront and open with you, Greg.' Terry spoke with sincerity in his tone. 'We have a mountain of evidence; there really is no use in denying your involvement with these crimes for which you have been arrested for and formally charged.'

Greg looked at Terry, was trying to weigh him up.

'You are The Ultimate!' Terry stated.

'Tell me why you decided to stop reporting the news and go back to being a detective.'

'They needed someone to catch you and they thought I was the man for the job, and look what we have here... success. I have The Ultimate,' Terry said, pointing at Greg.

'Is the money better?' Greg continued. 'It can't be the hours, Natalie has gone to her mother's, which I bet that didn't go down too well.' This was said purely for effect.

'You seem to know a lot about other people, why's that?' McFarland asked.

'Are you proud to be Scottish, James?'

'Why are you so interested in us?' Terry asked.

'I want to understand how the minds of two great men work, the two great men that brought me in to custody. Hector liked men too,' Greg said, looking at McFarland. 'There's no shame really... is there James?' Greg wanted to taunt the Scotsman.

'Why did you select Brian as the first?' Terry was trying to get Greg to start from the beginning.

'Have I hit a nerve with Hector, James?' Choosing to ignore the question, Greg was controlling the route of the interview, continuously interrupting their line of enquiry.

'OK, let's talk about Hector.' McFarland thought that they had to start somewhere.

'Brian selected himself, Terry. I was only helping those free themselves from the hell that they were trapped in, ridding society of the scum and shit that we allow to breed!' He looked at Terry, 'You've been there Terry, when your marriage broke down you were thrown into the gutter and it was only this man that helped you, everyone else cast you aside. They thought you belonged in the gutter, like scum, they thought of you as scum. But, it was James who helped you, stood by you.'

'I need to understand what exactly happened, Greg, and why.' Terry had begun to find Greg fascinating.

'You know a hell of a lot for a road sweeper,' McFarland was getting impatient.

'It's called research, James. That is how you catch criminals, or hasn't anyone told you that?' he sarcastically told the detective. 'You got lucky...'

'You worried so much about the detail, that you lost focus of the bigger picture. You led us to you Greg, so for that, I thank you. Your research led us to you,' McFarland said, trying to get even.

'Tell me, detective, how did you catch me?' Greg leant forward in his chair, placing the palms of his hands on the table, the coolness of the table top was welcomed.

'First, you must tell us how you selected these people and why they had to die in such adverse ways?'

'They all selected themselves. James, Brian and Valerie didn't die in adverse ways. Brent was the person who decided how Valerie and Conrad would meet their demise. I didn't order any of the killings; I didn't threaten anyone... well, not directly.'

'What about Julian Jones?' McFarland asked.

'Who's Julian Jones?'

'The man present when you abducted Hector.'

'The queer I caught Hector shagging? I didn't threaten him, I didn't even touch him!'

'You told him to, "fuck off before I change my mind". Do you remember saying that?'

'Yeah, though that's not a threat, it's a statement. It was free advice, I gave him a choice; stay or leave. He chose to leave.'

'What's the speech you give about choice?' Terry asked.

'It's only for those that have decided they are for selection, Terry. It's only the chosen that get to hear that. You never know, you might get your turn one day, James.'

'That will be a long way away Greg. You're going to be locked up for years,' McFarland giggled.

'Let's see what will be. How did you catch me?'

'Where did you get the idea for Hector's death?' McFarland asked.

'I didn't order Martin to kill Hector, I offered him a number of choices and he made his own choice,' Greg smiled, 'I didn't threaten either man.'

'You forced Hector to swallow the key to the handcuff around Martin's ankle and then filled him with embalming fluid and glued a bottle to his anus!' McFarland said in disgust.

'I still never ordered the murder of any of these people!' he calmly replied, 'I simply provided them with the ability to make a life-changing choice.'

'You are sick!' McFarland said, unable to control his emotions.

'Take a look at the real world, James. I'm the sane one, it's the majority who are sick. We allow the perverted to breed, we allow the sick-minded to quench their perverted hunger, their lust, their desires… we allow them to do this without question. Brian would go to the pub, night after night and then go home and beat the shit out of Sharon and then, if she was lucky, he'd rape her for good measure! That's fucking sick!' He Looked at McFarland. 'Hector, this one's even better. Hector would go out on a Friday night, pick up a queer man, take him around the back of the pub for some unprotected buggery and, once he'd finished, he would give them a couple of slaps, then he would go home and force his wife to have unprotected sex with him. He wouldn't wash himself between sexual acts. Hector also used to beat his wife!' He looked at Terry and begun nodding his head. 'I've done society a fucking favour. I orchestrated the freedom of these people… the self-selected, were only looking for a way out, an escape.'

'If you didn't, then who did?' Terry snapped.

'They did, they put themselves forward for selection. They chose me, I didn't choose them. I could see it in their eyes, looking in to the windows of their souls. They all had an evil foundation which they needed to be removed. I couldn't allow them to continue. Brian wanted to be cleansed. Hector wanted to be freed and Valerie needed a way out,' Greg paused, giving a sympathetic look. 'There are more people in our capital who need my help, who need the help of people like me to give them the power to change their lives. No, I'm not insane, just on a crusade to clean and rid our streets of this scum.'

The two detectives were stunned by Greg's outburst. McFarland looked at the mirror on the wall for guidance, or some kind of inspiration, knowing that his boss was watching and listening to everything from behind it.

Terry sat forward, 'What about Conrad and Valerie?' he asked.

'I thought that was obvious,' the prisoner replied.

'Help us out here,' Terry smiled.

'She was having an affair. Conrad had been responsible for the break up of a number of marriages before this one. Valerie was just one in a long line for Conrad. She was only gold-digging her husband, and Conrad was gold-digging her. If you'll pardon the pun. Let no man put asunder the love that another man has found. Conrad was an evil catalyst; he had to be held accountable… Brent had to be his judge and jury…'

'How did you decide the way these people would murder their victims?'

'I didn't. I simply supplied them with the option to choose.'

'Greg you are so young. You had your whole life ahead of you… Why?'

'I've already told you why. How did you catch me?' Greg insisted on knowing.

'You made two massive mistakes,' Terry answered, 'the chinks in your armour were your girlfriend and your PC.'

'What's Karen got to do with this?'

'She was the one person who linked you to The Ultimate. She found a receipt you had left lying about.' He paused. 'You could have killed her when you drugged her with those sleeping tablets. Do you know what those tablets are used for?'

'I knew what I was doing,' Greg smiled, 'I knew what amount would be safe to prescribe.'

'Those tablets you used to drug Karen with are used for knocking horses out, for putting horses to sleep, not humans.'

'I knew exactly what I was doing. Karen, fucking what?'

'It was Karen who came to us, it was Karen who was suspicious of you, it was Karen who told us about the embalming fluid she found under your kitchen sink, the leaflet thanking you for your recent purchases, one of those being the taser gun used to electrocute Conrad. Did you honestly think that we wouldn't have caught you eventually?' the Scottish detective asked.

'No, I didn't think you would have, not this quick anyway, I thought that I was being that careful, you wouldn't believe the planning.'

'The hard drive on your PC will tell us everything we need to know,' Terry said smugly.

A knock on the door interrupted the cosy conversation that the three men had begun to enjoy. As the door opened, the tall figure of Jasper Ward emerged.

'Men...' he began, 'thought I'd share this with all of you, Mr Brent Hope was found hanging in his cell less than an hour ago, and all attempts to resuscitate failed. Mr Brent Hope was pronounced dead ten minutes ago. Mr O'Hara. I hope you are pleased with your accomplishments.'

'He made his choice; he was never forced to do anything that he didn't want to do.' Greg smiled at the tall man, 'Just another casualty.'

'You have chosen to force others to take lives,' the tall man barked.

'It is wrong of you to assume that. I offered them all choice, and they chose. Haven't you been listening from behind that mirror?' He pointed to a large mirror on the wall. 'They chose their own destiny, I made it available and that is my only crime. My only crime is offering people the opportunity to free themselves from their shitty lives. Setting people free that is all I've done,' he told the three detectives.

The three men looked at each other in disbelief, Greg was actually right, well, in a manner of speaking. He was very calculated with the choice of his words. During all the murders he had not instructed any killing. He had only offered choice.

'Time for you to go to your cell, Greg,' Terry told him.

The three men sat in the office drinking brandy from coffee cups. Not knowing what to say to each other. They were shocked by the way Greg had described his motivation for what he had orchestrated. It was clear that he showed no remorse, he described himself as doing the public a favour. They also remembered Hector's widow had quickly forgiven her brother because all he had done was to free her from the hell of a life she shared with Hector. She knew her children would now be spared from the beatings that she had endured. She no longer dreaded Friday nights.

Chapter Forty-Two

Greg was disturbed by the noise of a key turning in the lock of his cell door. As the door swung open a custody officer spoke.

'You have a visitor, there's someone here to see you,' he announced.

'Who is it?' Greg asked.

'A Miss Karen Hogan... Do you want to see her?' the custody officer asked. His sarcasm showing that he did not have time for this as his Cup-a-Soup was now getting cold.

'Yeah, why not...' Greg replied, standing up.

'I'm going to have to put these on,' the officer said, holding a pair of handcuffs. Greg simply offered his hands. 'Behind your back, O'Hara,' the officer smiled.

Once Greg had been cuffed, he was told to follow the officer. As Greg followed the officer, he noticed that two other custody officers had been waiting outside his cell. They were simply back-up. Was he regarded as a dangerous prisoner?

'Nah. It's standard procedure,' he thought.

Greg walked with the three uniformed officers being directed where they wanted him to sit. Once they had reached their destination, Greg was directed to a chair.

'OK, take a seat,' the officer stated.

Karen was already sitting on the opposite side of the table.

'There is to be no contact, no kissing, voices are to be kept at an acceptable level. If you feel that your safety is being jeopardised, Miss Hogan, please let us know. There is to be no spitting or other vulgarity...' he placed his hand on Greg's right shoulder, his grip tight. 'Please behave sonny!' he said in an undermining tone.

Greg looked up at him and smiled, 'Be seeing you!' he said. Karen had not seen this side of Greg before – it frightened her, making her feel uneasy. 'Good to see you,' Greg said.

'Why, Greg?' Karen asked, her eyes filled with sadness. Half of her didn't want to come here and do this, but she needed to know.

'You wouldn't understand!'

'I loved you, I gave you…' Karen started to cry.

'Everything all right, Miss Hogan?' one of the uniformed officers asked.

'Yes. I'm fine!'

'Why did you grass me up?' Greg enquired softly, he needed to know.

'I had to… what would you have done if I had confronted you about it? You wouldn't have stopped,' her crying abated, her sadness transformed to anger. 'When would you have stopped?'

'Not until I was caught. I would never have hurt you Karen,' tenderness echoed through his words.

'That won't work anymore Greg! I saw what you had those people do… We sat next to each other in bed watching the news flash. You drugged me. You fucking bastard, you evil fucking bastard!' Karen swung her left hand, slapping Greg across his face. The noise sounded like the clap of hands, 'you evil piece of shit,' her anger even more evident.

'Miss Hogan, no physical contact, please,' a uniformed officer shouted as he ran to Greg's aid.

'Don't worry about it, mate. I deserve it. I'll get worse once I'm inside,' Greg said calmly.

'That's not the point. You're safety is our responsibility. Would you like us to remove Miss Hogan?' the officer asked.

'No,' Greg replied shaking his head.

'Would you like to see a doctor?' the officer continued.

'No, mate, I'm perfectly all right.'

'OK… I won't warn you again Miss Hogan, and O'Hara, I'm not your mate,' the officer grunted.

'I'm not sorry for slapping you,' Karen said remorseless.

'Don't you ever lose that fire.' Greg looked at Karen, he had always admired her, 'Don't wait for me, find happiness and forget about me...' he spoke softly.

'You must be fucking mad if you think that I'd be waiting for you. For fuck's sake Greg! You're a fucking nutter. Do you think I wanna be associated with a fucking nutter?'

'You said you loved me!'

'Yeah, loved, in the past tense, time gone by, not now, and never in the future! Have they checked that you aren't fucking mental?'

'You didn't come here for an argument. If that's what you want, then you're wasting your time. I have no remorse for what has been done and I never killed anyone, nor did I order or force anyone to take the lives of others. So, if you came here today thinking that you would see me crying and whimpering, sorry you've had a wasted journey. If you came here to say good bye then I can accept that and we can both move on, draw a line finally. Well then, what have you come here for?'

'To say good bye, I needed to know that you understood why I told the police. If you hate me, then fair enough, I really couldn't give a fuck what you think of me. I don't hate you Greg, I loathe you, and it makes me sick to the pit of my stomach that we made love. I made love to a fucking homicidal maniac! That'd make a great story, hey I could make some money out of this,' Karen was on a roll, 'a film even.'

'Karen, I have forgiven you for this, but only for this...' Greg removed the pleasant look he had been wearing on his face. 'Please don't make me regret it. Don't force me to change my mind Karen.'

'Don't threaten me, you mug. You don't frighten me. Soon you'll be locked up and I'm going to watch them throw away the key.'

'Remember, Karen, everything begins with choice... your next choice will shape the rest of your life.'

'Goodbye Greg,' Karen said as she stood up and walked away, without looking back.

'So long Karen.'

Chapter Forty-Three

Silence echoed in the courtroom as the judge made his way to his seat. The bailiff instructed everyone to stand. Gregory O'Hara sat in the middle of two heavily-built police officers, handcuffed to each of the men.

The twelve members of the jury had digested the verbal diarrhoea that they had been force-fed throughout the trial. Some of them had begun to look as if they were ready to throw it all back to the sender.

The official people had developed a language of their own, how the ordinary people of the jury were supposed to understand it was beyond Greg. His request for a translator had been viciously denied. The judge had spat his disapproval, Greg had only made things worse when he explained that he did not know why the Moscow State Circus had been permitted to present the case for the prosecution. His removal from the courtroom, and the beatings that followed, all seemed a small price for the entertainment he had supplied the galleries.

The time that Greg had spent both in the courtroom and in custody, all seemed clouded by a mist, a foggy haze. All he could concentrate on was his last conversation with Karen. He had lost himself to her, though without knowing, he had loved that woman and now she had tossed him and their love aside.

The longer Greg thought about it, the more he could understand why she had acted in the way she had. The slap he had received showed passion. It warmed him to think that he had lit her flame though, sadly, now, there were no embers. Greg's mind wandered, as though in slow motion. Gazing around the large courtroom, he felt like a film star. They had all come to see him. Artists were busying themselves sketching away; the scraping of the lead on the dry paper amused the accused.

'Mr O'Hara,' the voice interrupted Greg's daydream.

'What?'

'Stand up,' the police officer to Greg's right said.

'Take the prisoner back to his cell please... sentencing will take place at 2 p.m. this afternoon,' the black cloaked wig-wearing judge announced.

'HANG THE BASTARD!' a voice yelled from the gallery.

Greg smiled, he knew the voice. It belonged to Karen.

'What time is it?' Greg asked.

'There's a clock on the wall, Mr O'Hara,' the same police officer replied. The two officers lead Greg down a flight of stairs and along a passageway until they reached the cell that Greg had been held in since the trial began – seven months had passed.

'Is there anything I can get you?' the female duty sergeant asked.

'Yes... I could really use a get out of jail card about now,' Greg smiled.

'Sorry,' the officer replied.

'He won't be laughing for too long,' one of the police officers said as he slammed the door, forcing the automatic locking mechanism to engage.

'You'd better get used to that sound, convict.' All three officers laughed.

Greg settled down, stretching out on the hard bed, placing his hands behind his head, interlocking his fingers, in order to cradle his head. He soon found himself drifting off again...

Chapter Forty-Four

As Greg was led back into the dock, he looked around. He noticed Karen was trying to look away. To catch her eye, he coughed loudly.

'Hang the bastard!' a muffled voice from the gallery said. Others echoed the same sentiment. Greg smiled and continued walking.

'Keep your mouth shut!' one of the officers he was handcuffed to barked.

***

'What do you think they'll do with you?'

'I'm not sure, though I know that I'm going to be stuck behind bars for a long time.'

'What are you going to do Greg?' the woman who had given him life, now sat opposite him, powerless.

'Stay strong, Ma,' he said, trying to comfort her.

'I love you son. The lord will provide me with all the strength I need. Don't worry about me,' she said, as she dabbed the tears from the corners of his eyes.

'Whatever happens, I need you to make me a promise.'

'What is it?' her soft Irish accent comforted him.

'I don't want any visitors. Can you tell Dad?'

'Of course I can. People back home are shocked.' Greg's mother never stopped worrying about what other people thought. It was not an Irish thing, just simply a mother thing.

'Ma, I stopped worrying about what other people thought years ago. This whole thing is about what I think, what I thought. Please try to understand!' his frustration built.

'Your father has refused to come to see you,' his mother said, choosing to ignore what her son had just told her.

'I'm glad. After today, you'll never see me again. I've done what I believed was right. Others choose to see it differently.'

'They're right, Greg. You don't know your own mind. You don't know what you're saying anymore.'

'Ma, I know exactly what I'm saying and I have no regrets. No regrets,' he needed her to understand.

'Those doctors didn't study you Greg. You need help son,' her voice still remained soft.

'This is our goodbye, Ma. Tell dad Goodbye for me. I love you both.'

'Goodbye Gregory. I'll pray for you son. Make your peace with God and remember to serve your penance,' she told her son, 'bury those demons!' her softness had disappeared. Greg smiled politely and then looked away. The woman who had given him life left, and was now gone.

***

Once the twelve members of the jury were seated, the judge looked at Greg.

'Would the prisoner please rise?' the judge said, more of an order, than a request.

Greg stood.

'Have you reached a verdict?' the judge enquired.

'We have, my Lord,' replied the spokesperson from the jury.

'How do you find the accused?' he asked.

'We find the defendant guilty.'

A roar echoed from the galleries. Some of the members of the public cheered. Newspaper reporters leapt from their seats, rushing out of the courtroom, to make those all-important, headline making, phone calls.

'Silence in court,' the judge ordered, slamming his hammer down hard on to the top of the mammoth desk that separated him from the rest of the court. 'And how was this in favour? Please inform the court of the ayes,' he continued. The formality of the judge's questions seemed to glide off his tongue.

'Unanimous, my Lord, we have twelve ayes, my Lord,' the spokesperson replied.

'The Crown would like to thank you all for your loyal service. Bailiff, you may dismiss the jury.'

The courtroom echoed into silence once more. Everyone, including Greg, waited in anticipation for the sentencing.

'The Crown has decided that we should not postpone sentencing so therefore I will be passing sentence on you today. Is there anything you would like to say to the court, before I pass sentence?' the judge addressed Greg.

Greg quickly cleared his throat.

'Yes there is,' he replied, taking time to look around the courtroom, up at the gallery area. In the brief silence, his mother could be heard sobbing. 'My day job was to clean the streets of London: sweep the gutters; clean the streets. I simply took that literally, and stepped it up another level. I believe that is all that I'm guilty of.' Greg shrugged his shoulders. 'I took the law in to my own hands, but what else was there for me to do? Most people will only ever talk; wish to do what I've done. How many times have you heard, or moaned, about the decay that is rotting our country's capital? You pick up a newspaper, turn on the television, some poor child, an old age pensioner… all this saddened me greatly; made me want to do something about it. Nobody else was bothered; I was forced to act. All I did was offer people a way out, a way to clear out their own rubbish, a way to set them free, to find their own freedom. Your honour, my only regret, is getting caught so early. I'm not going to tell you how sorry I am for what happened, but what I am going to remind you of is this: I never forced anyone to kill; I was simply preventing more suffering. There was never anyone's blood on my hands.'

The courtroom erupted. People from the galleries hurled abusive language and continuous cries of 'Hang the bastard!'

The judge smashed his hammer on the desktop at least a dozen times before the courtroom returned to order. 'That's quite enough!' he ordered. 'Silence in court!'

A haze of hush slowly filled the courtroom once more. Some of the legal team members from both sides shuffled pieces of paper, trying to hide their feelings of discomfort. Their eyes lowered in order to separate themselves from the frenzied commotion that had just taken place. The silence that followed was brief, though the tension was palpable.

'Stay on your feet,' one of the officers told Greg.

'I'm not as stupid as you look,' Greg grimaced feeling the handcuffs dig into the flesh on his right wrist. 'Go fucking easy,' he told the officer.

'That was easy. Just remain standing convict!' the officer growled.

'Just do your job, and I'll do mine,' Greg scoffed.

'I'm glad you think this is funny!' the other officer said.

'I think the circus is a funny place, don't you?' Greg laughed. His laughter was controlled, and only slight.

At that moment the judge looked up, and spoke. 'Are you Mr Gregory Jason O'Hara?' he asked.

'I am.'

'You have stood trial in this courtroom and have been found guilty of terrible crimes. You have never shown any remorse, you have shown contempt and complete lack of respect to the crown.' The honourable judge paused, in order to eye-up the man he was going to pass sentence on. 'Therefore, I think that I have a responsibility, and that responsibility should be to protect the public from those that you potentially pose a danger to. Gregory Jason O'Hara, I sentence you to be detained in a maximum-security facility for a minimum of twelve years, though for no more than twenty years. This time should be spent on your rehabilitation so that, one day, the public can feel safe and no longer threatened by you and your evil, criminal thoughts that have somehow managed to gestate inside you. You have become the devil's host. I only wish that I had more power. Let me inform you, Mr O'Hara, if the death penalty was still available...' the judge paused, in order to calm his trembling anger. 'Take him down!' he ordered, looking away, breaking his sharp eye contact.

The two officers bundled the convicted criminal from the dock. Greg looked back over his shoulder. He saw his mother, inconsolable; his father simply shook his head, partly in shame, though mainly in disgust. Ashamed of what his only son had become, the monster that he once called his first born.

Greg caught a short glimpse of Karen; hatred filled her eyes, eyes which were once filled with unconditional love for him. Others snarled, calling for the death sentence. Once Greg had been dragged down the narrow stairway from the dock, he clambered to his feet.

'Do you need to go to the toilet?' an officer enquired, 'you have a long journey ahead.'

The end... for now...

What did you think of
The Ultimate Selection?

Let us know. Please leave a review on Amazon and follow S J Wardell on Twitter to find out more about his next title coming out in summer 2012:

@sj_wardell